Johann August Starck

The banquet of Theodulus

The re-union of the different Christian communions

Johann August Starck

The banquet of Theodulus
The re-union of the different Christian communions

ISBN/EAN: 9783741185175

Manufactured in Europe, USA, Canada, Australia, Japa

Cover: Foto ©Andreas Hilbeck / pixelio.de

Manufactured and distributed by brebook publishing software
(www.brebook.com)

Johann August Starck

The banquet of Theodulus

The Banquet of Theodulus,

OR

THE RE·UNION

OF THE DIFFERENT

CHRISTIAN COMMUNIONS.

THE

BANQUET OF THEODULUS,

OR

THE RE-UNION

OF THE DIFFERENT

CHRISTIAN COMMUNIONS.

BY THE LATE

BARON DE STARCK,

PROTESTANT MINISTER, AND FIRST PREACHER TO THE COURT
OF HESSE-DARMSTADT.

One Lord, one faith, one baptism, One God and Father of all, who is above all,
and through all, and in us all.

PAUL, EPIST. TO THE EPHES. IV. 5, 6.

BALTIMORE:

PUBLISHED BY KELLY & PIET,

No. 174 BALTIMORE STREET,

1868.

PREFACE

TO THE AMERICAN EDITION.

WE offer the present work of the late Baron de Starck to the American reader, with a view to promote, as much as lies in our power, the re-union of the different Christian Communions.

It was the author's most ardent wish to see all Christians, believing the one faith revealed from heaven, and belonging to the one church established by the Son of God. Great, it is true, are the obstacles against such a re-union, desirable as it may be; however greater yet is the power of grace.—Can we not hope that fervent prayers and constant efforts to make the truth known, will at last bring all under the *one Lord, one faith, one baptism, one God and Father of all, who is above all, and through all, and in us all?*

When this work appeared in Germany, it

produced the greatest sensation, and passed rapidly through several editions. It was afterwards translated into English, and published in London with the title of *Philosophical Dialogues* on the re-union of the different Christian Communions. It is this translation that we now republish under the original title of the work, and with a few slight corrections. May the Almighty give his blessing to our undertaking, and may we see the day when all the children of God will form but one fold under one shepherd.

THE RE-UNION

OF THE DIFFERENT

CHRISTIAN COMMUNIONS.

It was on one of the finest evenings of the autumn of 1809, a year so fruitful in unforeseen events, and which were the precursors of still greater events, that I was walking along the banks of the Rhine, with my friend Edward, the faithful companion of my youth, and the depository of all the sentiments of my heart. It was natural that what was at the time the object of our dearest interests, should also have become the principal subject of our conversation. Every thing brought us back, and often, notwithstanding all our efforts, to the distresses of the moment, to the extraordinary revolutions we had witnessed, and to the causes which had produced them. We concluded by being of opinion, that it was nearly demonstrated, that none of those who had contributed to the construction of this formidable edifice, had suspected that it would become what it was. "How has it happened," exclaimed Edward, "that the contrary, absolutely the contrary of all which it was intended to produce, has taken place? We know perfectly well what was intended; the numberless works which appeared during the last sixteen years of the 18th century, sufficiently proved it. We also know what has really happened, and the result contains this great lesson, that we should not be in a hurry to realize every dream and every project of the imagination, because man, ignorant of the future, has not in his power *contingent futurities*, which often depend on mere trifles."

The emotion of my friend, on thus comparing the projects of the cosmopolites and philosophers with the results of those projects, was visible; not that he had ever approved the latter, but because all the new events and all the new order of things were not to his taste; and this observation induced me to give another turn to the conversation. We began to talk politics at random, and to make a review of prophecies, from the apocalypse, down to the predictions of modern times: we examined what John Müller said of the wonderful year 1788, three centuries before that epoch; what John Greulich wrote on the overthrow of the *kingdom* of France; what Herman de Lechnin announced concerning the destinies of the house ef Brandenburgh, and in short what Bartholomew Hobzhauser had foretold of the misfortunes of the German empire, and of the consequences of those misfortunes. We even ventured to dip into the astonishing commentaries of Benzel, on the 17th chapter of the Apocalypse, as they appeared some years ago in the *Seer's Views;*[*] for, when the present has no longer any attraction, we retrogade into the past, or dart into the future, in order to find enjoyment in recollection, or consolation in hope.

Conversing in this way, we came up insensibly to a spreading oak, the branches of which, extending across the road, seemed to invite the passenger to repose under its shade; we both sat down, and passed some minutes in contemplating the setting sun, whose last rays were playing among the ruins of an old castle, which crowned the summit of a neighbouring mountain. "Such," said I at length, "such, my dear Edward, is the image of our existence! nothing is lasting here below. The sun rises and sets, night succeeds to day, and gives place, in its turn, to a new dawn. What is become of the masters of this ancient domain? Where are their knights, their squires, their chaplains, and their troubadours? All has passed away. Of this formidable citadel, which seemed destined to last till the end of the world, nothing remains but shapeless ruins, while foul and voracious animals occupy the habitation of its ancient heroes. It is thus that every thing changes; and, consequently, what right have we to complain of the events of our times? No, there is nothing new, but what has even often happened before we lived; nothing, in short, but what is conformable to the nature of every thing in this world. The only excusable motive, strictly speaking, for our discontent is, that this catastrophe should have happened precisely during our life-time. God alone, and his religion, are not subject to these vicissitudes. They will be found as immoveable as at present, when, of all the kingdoms now existing, there are fewer vestiges than even those of this ruined castle." At these last

* Die Seher blicken.

words, Edward interrupted me with a tone of surprise. "What, is religion exempt from the fate of human things? Abandoned to the management of men, it is also connected with the destinies of nations; it rises and falls with them; perhaps, even in a few years, no trace will remain of what formerly cost our countrymen so much blood." "This is not what I fear; truth is *one*, and is immoveable. Given to man, its external forms may from the circumstances of the moment, undergo different changes; but it cannot itself be degraded or fall with men. A sacred property of the human mind, no force can reach it." "Yes, so it is to those who possess it and preserve it; or, to speak more correctly, who wish to preserve it: for it seems to me that the explanations and the philosophy of our sages have already contrived to deprive many of us of it. We are on the brink of a new epoch; we are about to be frustrated of the most valuable of our possessions by other means, and by different ways, and are on the point of being thrown three centuries back." "Have you then forgotten the project of the re-union of all religions, which has been the subject of so many discussions and so many writings, and for the success of which an appeal was even made to the powerful arm of Buonaparte? (1809)" "Is that the only subject of your fears? Be comforted, the conclusion of that great affair is very far off, and even should it succeed, its success would only serve to prove what I have just said." "I confess I do not understand this at all."

I was going to attempt to dispel the solicitudes of my friend, when we observed Theodulus coming towards us, whom we had already perceived at a distance. "Here is a man," said Edward, "who can prove to you better than any one, how well my alarms are founded."

Theodulus had been to our house after us, and having been told what direction we had taken, had followed us to invite us to pass the evening under his roof. We accepted his invitation, and on entering his house, found several of our common friends already assembled, who were waiting for us. Soon after arrived Odilon, formerly abbot of St. Appollinaris, who was lately come from France, and whom Theodulus was very anxious to make us acquainted with. We soon perceived that he was a man of a sound and penetrating judgment; and as his mildness and cordiality appeared as great as his zeal for religion was pure, we had all reason to congratulate ourselves on having made such an interesting acquaintance.

of the Reformation, though at the same time it is well

Our conversation soon fell on the great changes which had just taken place in the states of Europe; and as we were all full of the subject, it soon became the exclusive topic, each expressing his fears and hopes, according to his character and his way of considering things. From the spirit of indifference which distinguishes modern times, we seldom see religion take a part in conversation; and as great potentates have ceased, in their treaties of peace, to stipulate, as formerly, for the security of religion; so individuals, on their side, occupy themselves very little with the fate of religion, in great political revolutions. Notwithstanding, it insensibly became the subject of a very animated discussion among us; which was naturally brought on by the negociations, now in hand, concerning the Concordat (1809); nor could we omit saying a word on the numerous writings which then appeared in France, some of which made pressing entreaties to Buonaparte, to induce him to exert his influence towards the re-union of all Christian communions, in the same external worship, and under the same ecclesiastical head.

Upon this, Ulric of Stettin turned towards Odilon, and said, "Well, abbot, what is your opinion? Do you not think, that even in a political point of view, it would be well if all parties could be re-united *under one cap?*" "It must be one, Sir, of very large dimensions; and, moreover, I must inform you, that as an ecclesiastic, and especially a monk, politics are very little in my way." "That may be; but you will agree, at least, that religion and the state have a reciprocal influence on each other. 'The re-union of the churches,' says Mr. Beaufort, 'is necessary to give strength and stability to the government, and to ensure its prosperity. The natural result would be a national religion, which alone would be sufficient to produce every virtue, and to form the manners of the nation.' You will allow that this would be a very great advantage." "Yes, provided the unity of faith was the foundation of this unity of religion. It seems to me, according to my weak judgment, that in that case, such an event would be of great importance to religion, morals, and government. The solidity of a government depends on the principles of its subjects; while they, on their side, have a guarantee in the principles of their rulers. This truth did not escape a celebrated modern writer." "And this is what Beaufort requires, and what brought him to say, one religion, or no religion.'" "This I think rather hard.

Jesus Christ said, 'Let both grow till the harvest.'* More-over, it remains to be known, whether Mr. Beaufort, in forming his project, thought of a conformity in the points of doctrine; for, without that, a real re-union of the separated churches appears to me impossible, and would never produce the advantages he expects from it." "According to this, you do not appear to me to be favorable to the system of the proposed re-union." "But why shouldn't he?" said Edward, all of a sudden, (who before, while we were walking, seemed to be very much taken up with this subject already); how is it possible to find fault with writings, which have excited a great sensation in Germany, and have already given rise to several reflections and salutary observations on this important subject?"

Odilon. I think that the authors of those writings were not acquainted either with Catholicism or Protestantism; how, therefore, could they make propositions analogous to the object in view?

Edward. You astonish me! I should wish to think they were perfectly acquainted at least with their own doctrine, since they not only came forward as pacificators, but even declared that the re-union in question was very easy.

Odilon. I cannot better prove to you, how little primitive Protestantism and Catholicism are exhibited in these writings, than by citing several passages drawn up expressly to show that all the obstacles against a re-union would be levelled, as soon as it was agreed to allow priests to marry, to abolish auricular confession, and destroy the influence of the Pope.

Edward. And you will allow that the suppression of those three great obstacles would infinitely facilitate the success of the matter; and it is a fact, particularly of late, that several Catholic priests, tired of celibacy, have ventured to disapprove of it publicly.

Odilon. You are quite right in using the expression, *tired of celibacy;* and did I not listen to Christian charity, I might add severer epithets. But it is not necessary to inform you, that in the beginning of the Reformation there was no question whatever of those three articles.

Edward. I was rather of a contrary opinion; granting, however, that those objects were not the immediate cause

* Sinite utraque crescere usque ad messem.

known, that almost all the priests, who then adopted it, took wives.

Odilon. You are right; and it was this made the that satirical Erasmus say, that this great tragedy ended like a comedy; that is, by the marriage of all the principal characters.*

Edward. As to auricular confession, it is certain that the Lutherans soon abolished it, though they preserved at the same time a particular confession. But with respect to the Pope, all Luther's writings are full of violent invectives against him.

Odilon. You may possibly be mistaken on all these points; they were not so hasty, as you imagine, in suppressing auricular confession. Luther himself, if I do not forget, was extremely favorable to it. In a passage of his writings, he says with his usual warmth; " I would rather endure the tyranny of the Pope, than consent to the abolition of confession;" and this was saying a great deal for a man of his character.

At these words, Ulric of Stetten took up the conversation, and said : " That is not possible ; for, in the *Confession of Augsburg*, and in Luther's small Catechism, it is expressly said that it is not necessary to confess to the priest all sins and crimes." Is not this formally disapproving and suppressing auricular confession?

Odilon. If we had before us the passages you have just quoted, you would see that you have omitted something essential.

" We can easily remedy that," said Theodulus, who immediately produced the *Confession of Augsburg*, Luther's works, and some others, which he thought might be necessary from the turn the conversation had taken.

Odilon. Read, gentlmen, what is written in the eleventh article of the *Confession of Augsburg*. " On confession, we are taught, that in the church, *particular absolution* must be obtained, and not be neglected, though it is not necessary to enumerate all sins and crimes, as that is impossible." The 18th Psalm says : " *Who knows sin?*" Whence it follows very clearly, that though it be not obligatory to accuse oneself of sins, all of which we do not know, or have forgotten, it is absolutely necessary to confess all those *we remember.* Lu-

---

* Erasm. Epist. lib. xix, ep. 7 & 41.

ther, on this point, conducts himself like a true Catholic; for no priest ever required of his penitent to confess sins he did not know of.

Ulric of Stetten. I must allow what you say; but, perhaps, this opinion of Luther belongs to those ancient maxims which he had derived from Catholicity, and which he abjured afterwards.

Odilon. I very much doubt it; you know he lived in 1546; and here is what he wrote that same year in his small Catechism : " We must confess ourselves guilty of all our sins, before God, even of those we do not know; but, to our confessor, we need only declare those we know, and which we feel in our hearts. What are those sins? Examine your condition and state, according to the ten commandments; that is, whether you are a father, mother, son, daughter, master, mistress, servant: see whether you have been disobedient, unfaithful, slothful; whether you have offended any one by words or works; whether you have stolen, neglected, damaged any thing." Follow him in what he says immediately after in the formulary of confession, drawn up by him, and remark the scrupulous method he requires; if they are servants, he requires them to confess, " whether they have served unfaithfully; whether they have sworn, excited their masters to anger," &c. if, on the contrary, they are masters, they must confess " whether they have not brought up their children in the fear of God; whether they have given bad example, caused damage to their neighbors, spoken ill of them, sold bad merchandize, or substracted any part of it."

Ulric of Stetten. You are perfectly right; after these passages it cannot be denied, but that auricular confession subsisted in protestantism, as it came from the hands of Luther, and that according to his intentions, it ought to have been preserved.

Odilon. I could easily produce other very remarkable passages from his works, which would prove what esteem he had for such an exact confession of all one's sins; how much he insists on this subject, and even places penance among the sacraments; but I confess, that your preceding observation on the primitive opinions of Luther, which he afterwards disavowed, has made me scrupulous in this respect, and forces me, if I may say so, only to select those opinions of his, which he delivered in the last years of his life.

Ulric of Stetten. Did not you just say, that Luther had even placed penance in the number of the sacraments?

Odilon. Undoubtedly! see on this subject what is contained in the Apology of the *Confession of Augsburg,* printed in 1531, and which was classed among the symbolic books in 1580. "Now Baptism and the Lord's Supper, and *absolution,* are real sacraments; for they have the command of God, and the promise of grace." What is still further, in the last years of his life, Luther wrote against the theologians of Louvain: "We willingly allow that penance, with the power of absolution, or the key that unties, is a sacrament; for it has the promise, and it guarantees pardon by the love of Jesus Christ."

Edward. This is, really, very strange!

Odilon. Luther could never agree with himself on the number of sacraments. In the passages quoted, he admits three; but in other places he only acknowledges two, namely, baptism and the eucharist. On another occasion, he joined with them confirmation and extreme unction. We even find that he sometimes allowed this character to matrimony, and maintained its indissolubility.*

Ulric of Stetten. I admit that it is impossible to make any reasonable objection to what you have told us respecting confession; but you will not find it so easy to get clear of the question concerning the Pope.

Odilon. I grant it, and the writings of Luther's last years afford no passage in favor of the Pope; but in the beginning, the veneration and obedience of this reformer for the Holy See was without bounds. Read the end of the letter which he wrote to Leo X, in 1518; examine his protestation against cardinal Cajetan; his work against Prierias, and you will see that notwithstanding his natural impetuosity, he never departs from his profound respect for the judgments of the Church and the Apostolic See, and protests that he wishes to live and die in those sentiments. But when the Pope had declared against him, Luther gave himself up to all the violence of his passions, to such a degree, as not only to throw out invectives and insults against the head of the church, which were condemned by all decent persons at that time, but even went so far as to call him Antichrist, and the whore of Babylon.

* Op. Lat. Wittenb. tom. viii, f. 373; ibid. fol. 34, tom. v. fol. 17, tom. iv, fol. 562.

Edward. All modern protestants, who respect each other, are equally indignant at these indecent expressions; and every man, who believes in the Holy Scriptures, knows very well that the Pope cannot be Antichrist; for St. John says: "He is Antichrist who denies the Father and the Son; he who does not acknowledge that Jesus Christ came into the flesh, is not of God; and that is the spirit of Antichrist." We may therefore let alone what Luther himself thought on this article.

Odilon. Very well, since you wish it, I shall confine myself to one of the other chiefs of the Reformation, a confidential friend of Luther's, and whose opinions were more moderate than those of the latter.

Ulric of Stetten. And who may this personage be?

Odilon. No other than Melanchton himself. You know undoubtedly how Luther behaved on the occasion of the articles of Schmalkalden, calling the Pope antichrist, &c. Melanchton, indeed, signed those same articles; but he took care to add: "As to the Pope, my opinion is, that for the peace and general tranquillity of those who are subject to him, or who will be hereafter, we may grant him, provided he will admit the Gospel, the superiority over bishops which he already possesses by human right."

Ulric of Stetten. A singular condition indeed! Should we not be tempted to think, that by this expression, " provided he will admit the Gospel," Melanchton granted the superiority to the Pope, only on condition that he became a Lutheran.

Odilon. No, Melanchton was too well informed to conceive such an idea.

Ulric of Stetten. It is true, Camerarius and he shine the foremost among the most learned authors of the Reformation.

Odilon. Hear what he says in one of his letters, when he was not hindered, of course, by Luther from expressing freely his way of thinking: "There is no dispute on the superiority of the Pope and of the authority of bishops; the Pope, as well as they, may keep this authority; for the church must have superintendants to maintain order, to look after those who are called to the service of the church, to examine the doctrine of the priests, and carry Ecclesiastical sentences into execution; and, therefore, if there were no bishops, it would be necessary to make them. The monarchy of the Pope would also contribute much to preserve the unity of doctrine among different nations; if other points could be settled, we should soon agree respecting the supremacy of the Pope."*

Ulric of Stetten. May not this be one of those expressions without any meaning, that escape in the familiarity of the epistolary style?

Odilon. I beg your pardon, I can quote several others. Here, for example, is what he wrote to Theopulus: "We consider the authority of the Pope of Rome, and the whole Ecclesiastical establishment with a sentiment of respect." He delivered the same opinion in his letter to the bishop of Augsburg: "I desire, as far as I and several others are concerned, that you may be convinced, that we sincerely wish the inviolability of the authority of the bishops to be maintained, for we consider it as very salutary to the church." We see also by one of his letters to Carlowiz, *that he wished the preservation of the whole Ecclesiastical constitution then existing, and to which he gave the name of Ecclesiastical police,* annexing to it all that he called *the degrees of government;* that is, *a supreme head of the church, bishops, priests, and deacons, because without that the church would run great risks.* But, what is more, several judicious Protestants even now begin to perceive the great advantages of the hierarchy of the Catholic church, and feel that the re-establishment of archbishops and bishops is henceforward the only means of saving Protestantism from total ruin. We may be convinced of this by reading the second number of the periodical German work, entitled, "Journal of the Protestant church and its Clergy." The learned author of the work, entitled, "The Holy Supper, a dogmatico-historical Examination," also appeals to that Journal; and, at page 102, expresses his wish, now that the consistorial constitution is almost entirely destroyed among Protestants, that the Episcopal government should be established, as it is in England, Sweden, and Denmark; and, he observes, that already in 1711, when attempts towards a re-union were made in Prussia, Leibnitz had proposed the same measure. But I forget that I was speaking to you only about Melancthon, and his opinion concerning the Pope and the hierarchy.

Ulric of Stetten. I confess that I am much surprised at

* Melanch. resp. ad. Bel.

this from Melanchton ; and it is clear that in his eyes the Pope was not antichrist, as in those of his friend Luther ; for it would be ridiculous to confide the government of the church of Jesus Christ to antichrist.

Odilon. Most certainly. Moreover, as judicious Protestants have acknowledged the advantages of our hierarchy, by desiring the return of archbishops and bishops, so several Calvinists also have done full justice to our church.

Ulric of Stetten. What, Calvinists! I declare you will not easily persuade me that a single one ever appeared favorable to the Papacy.

Odilon. Nothing, however, is more true. The estimable and pious Tobler of Zurich, in his *Discourse to Sorrowful Souls at the present Time*, 1808, thus expresses himself, page 22 :—" The Papacy itself, was, in those ages of affliction, the best religion of that period ; without it, no decent or common religion would have remained in the world ; what do I say? this indispensable religion would itself have disappeared ; and we ourselves, as a church, should have died in our fathers, or rather, should have never seen the light." It is clear therefore, that this good man also did not consider the Pope as antichrist, since he had so fair an opinion of the church of which the Pope is the head.

Ulric of Stetten. All this gives me the greatest surprise.

Odilon. It does not surprise me at all ; for people at last get rid of their prejudices. I could easily show you some other important testimonies of Calvinists, as well as Protestants, which would surprise you much more than those of Tobler.

Edward. Would you have the kindness to communicate them to us?

Odilon. The great Leibnitz, in the first part of his Letters, published at Leipsig, in 1733, says :—" As God is the God of order, and as it is of divine right, that the body of one only Catholic and Apostolic church should be regulated by one only hierarchical universal government, it follows that it should also have a surpreme spiritual magistrate, restrained within due bounds, by virtue of the same right, and that he should be invested with all the dictatorial power and force necessary to the exercise of his charge, for the welfare of the church."*

Ulric of Stetten. I should not have expected such an opinion from Leibnitz; but, as to the Calvinists, I cannot believe them to be so favorable.

Odilon. The English autor Cowel, in a work which appeared in 1564, by this title: *Examination of the Doctrine against the Action of the Cause of the Innocents*, says : "It is necessary that one should be placed above the others, to avoid dissension and schisms. It was the best step that could be taken then, (in the time of the apostles) in the Primitive church, because the grace of God was given more abundantly and more frequently than in our days. The union between the apostles would certainly not have been so strong, if one of them had not been placed over the others."*

Ulric of Stetten. This, I grant, is saying a great deal, and more than I could have ventured to imagine; but, it is probable, that in Cowel's time, more than one head was still infected with the prejudices of popery.

Odilon. Well, I shall now have recourse to a quotation, to which I defy you to make that objection. You remember, no doubt, that in 1775, the French Protestants presented a Memorial for the purpose of obtaining civil rights and legitimating their marriages. Here is a passage of that Memorial: "We will not attempt to conceal, that, in the parrallel which we sometimes make between your church and ours, notwithstanding the abuses introduced among you, the great features are in your favor. You were certainly before us, since you go back to the time of the apostles; and we have not yet existed three centuries; for, in 1515, your ancestors and ours communicated at the same mass, celebrated Easter together, and lived in a perfect unanimity of sentiment. Moreover, the chain of tradition, *the first link of which was*

* Cum sit Deus ordinis, et corpus unius Ecclesiæ Catholicæ et Apostolicæ uno regimine hierarchiâque universali continendum juris divini sit, consequens est ut ejusdem sit juris supremus in eo spiritualis magistratus terminis justis se continens, directoriâ potestate, omniaque necessaria ad explendum munus pro salute Ecclesiæ agendi facultate instructus.

* Unum cœteris præponi necesse est ad evitanda schismata et ad dissensiones tollendas. Hoc tunc, tempore apostolorum, optimum fuit remedium in primitivâ Ecclesiâ, cum Dei gratia major et copiosior erat quam nunc eam conferri videmus. Imo, ipsi duodecim apostoli vix satis inter se convenissent, nisi unus cœteris præfectus fuisset.—Examinatio doctrinæ contra actionem causæ innocentium.

fixed by Peter and Paul to the church of Rome, has been so well perpetuated among you, that if the Irenæuses, the Gregories, the Cyrils, the Athanasiuses, the Chrysostomes, were to come again on the earth, it would be in the *church of Rome* only that they could find the communion of which they were members." It is not necessary for me to explain to you more fully the further sense of this most remarkable passage.

Edward, who till now had been profoundly reflecting on all that had been just said, took up the conversation, and said: "I see now perfectly well, those who wished for the suppression of such passages, because they thought them obstacles to a re-union, were not acquainted with Protestantism; or rather, with the real opinion of its first founders." But did you not add that they were no better acquainted with Catholicism?

Odilon. Yes, and it is the case; and I cannot get the better of my astonishment, when I see persons presenting themselves as mediators, while they are so completely ignorant of the state of the question.

Edward. Are these points then, which seem to me to be merely objects of pure discipline, so important, that they cannot be suppressed?

Odilon. Permit me to tell you that it would be a great error to suppose that they are merely articles of discipline.

Edward. How! when the good of religion is concerned, would it be absolutely impossible to make some changes in points which have not in their favor the proof of divine establishment; a subject, however, which I shall wave for the present.

Odilon. And so will I; for it would lead us too far, our whole life would be hardly sufficient to read what the two parties have written on the subject. I shall therefore only speak of it in the sense of well-informed Catholics.

Edward. And do not they consider auricular confession as a simple affair of discipline?

Odilon. They are, in this respect, of the same opinion as Luther, which I explained to you before. Every well-informed and sensible Catholic is persuaded that this confession is of divine origin, that it is proved by Holy Scripture, and consequently cannot be subjected to arbitrary changes. This opinion of it was also expressed by the council of Trent in the small catechism published by its order.

Edward. If this be the case, Beaufort, who proposed abolishing auricular confession, cannot have studied his catechism much.

Odilon. I think so; but, independently of the opinion of every well-informed Catholic on this point, it is certain that the effects of this institution are as salutary to morals as to religion, and I suspect that Protestants have already sufficiently learnt to their cost, that the metamorphosis of auricular confession, so much favored by Luther himself in to a particular confession, and afterwards into a simple preparation in the manner of the Calvinists, has every day relaxed, to the great detriment of religion and morals, those ties which formerly so intimately connected the pastor with his flock. Catholics are very far indeed from wishing to run the same chance. I therefore tell you frankly, if this institution in our church is an obstacle to the re-union in question, it never can take place.

Edward. I believe I may also assure you, on the part of Protestants, that this point alone, which must appear very troublesome to all of them, will meet with great difficulties.

Odilon. I do not doubt it; and those who have many shameful sins to confess will not accustom themselves easily to such a disagreeable practice.

Ulric of Stetten. It seems to me, that all that concerns confession in general, against which, the pious Schade, among the Lutherans, exerted himself with much warmth, belongs to those things which the Roman church has transported from Paganism into Christianity; for we know that certain consecrations among the Pagans were always preceded by auricular confession.

Odilon. Would it not be more simple to believe that this confession is founded in nature itself; for I recollect having read in the *History of the Apostolic Mission to Thibet,* by *Horatio della Penna,* that auricular confession is established, and greatly esteemed in that country. Whence do you suppose that people derived this practice?—From ancient Paganism also?

Ulric. That is certainly very extraordinary: nevertheless. . . . . .

Odilon. And why should it have been absolutely necessary to borrow this practice from Paganism, when the confession of sins to the priest was already known in the Old Testament? Is it not said in St. Matthew, chap. iii. v. 6, that those who came to the baptism of John, confessed their sins, which even learned Protestants have not hesitated to consider as a *special* confession of the faults of which they felt guilty? But what will you say, if I bring two modern philosophers before you, as apologists of auricular confession?

Ulric. What do you mean? that is impossible.

Odilon. The first is Raynal. Hear what he says in the third volume of his Philosophical History, p. 250: "After the example of the Incas, the Jesuits have established a theocratic goverment, but with an advantage peculiar to the religion which forms its basis: this is the practice of *confession,* exceedingly useful, as long as it is not abused. The best of all governments would be a theocracy, with the tribunal of *confession;* provided it were always conducted by virtuous men, and on reasonable principles."

Ulric. Very well; but you must allow, notwithstanding, that the opinions of a philosophical abbé may have been influenced by the prejudice of his profession. But who is the other?

Odilon. The patriarch of philosophers, Voltaire himself, whom, I conceive, you will not reproach with having any thing sacerdotal. In the *Annals of the Empire,* tom. 1, p. 41, he expresses himself thus: "The enemies of the Roman church, who have declared against so salutary an institution (auricular confession) seem to have taken from men the greatest restraint that could be put on their secret crimes. Even the sages of antiquity were sensible of its importance."

Ulric. This is very strange indeed!

Odilon. But I only wish to prove, that with Catholics, auricular confession is one of those things that cannot be arbitrarily changed. Go back to the first ages of the church, and you will find traces and proofs of it. You know with what hatred the Greek and Coptic churches are animated against that of Rome: well, notwithstanding, confession is in use among them.*

Ulric. However this may be, I am persuaded at least, that

* See New Memoirs of the Missions, tom. 2, p. 68.

your principles respecting the Pope are not so severe, and that you will allow, that according to circumstances and the necessity of the times, his power and influence may in some degree be retrenched. Ecclesiastical history, moreover, shows that it was only progressively that the Popes attained their present power.

Odilon. This history, perhaps, would not be so favorable to you as you seem to think. But, I may say to you, in my turn, what a difference between the feeble beginnings of the church and its actual extent!

Edward. Can you deny the terrible abuse the Popes some-times made of their power, and the great evils that resulted from it?

Odilon. But history will also tell you all the good they did, and certainly I think you have a great deal too much sense to maintain in general that the abuse of a thing is a reason for destroying it. You know that no human society could subsist without a head and an interpreter of its laws. *One must be ruler,* said the Greeks, and the same maxim is applicable to your own testimony, to determine how much your religious society has insensibly decayed, since it lost its head, and since each one is at liberty to think what he likes, and to interpret scripture according to his fancy.

Edward. It is possible that Protestantism may have suffered some inconvenience for want of a spiritual head; but, I think, nobody among us has as yet complained for want of a Luthe-ran Pope. The very idea would be shocking.

Odilon. Undeceive yourself: though Puffendorf was such a zealous Protestant, nevertheless, in his book on the *Monarchy of the Bishop of Rome,* he says, that the cause of the religious dissensions among Protestants, proceeds from the want of a spiritual head, and that a monarchical government alone, to the exclusion of every other scheme, is alone suited to the church. As to Leibnitz, you have already heard what he has said on the same subject.

Edward. Let us leave the opinion of these writers, and merely answer me this question: do Catholics think on this article as on that of confession.

Odilon. This institution is certainly not a sacrament, as Luther himself said of penance; but every well-informed Catholic is convinced, from the testimony of all the fathers, from the first ages of the church, that our Lord Jesus Christ meant that his church should have a monarchical government; that, for this purpose, he established St. Peter his vicar and prince of the apostles; that this primacy and power passed to all his successors in the Episcopal See of Rome, and consequently, that the bishop of Rome, as successor of St. Peter, is the head of the Catholic church, and the visible vicar of Jesus Christ upon earth, with respect to his church.

At these words, Ulric of Stetten maintained that this primacy of St. Peter, and his bishopric of Rome, were two points by no means decided, and that very serious doubts might be entertained concerning them.

"Every fact," answered Odilon, smiling, "certainly loses something by the progress of time; but what would you say, if somebody were to take it into his head to call in question the stay that Luther made at Wittenburg, or that of Zuingle and Calvin at Zurich and Geneva? Could you help laughing at such a piece of extravagance? Well, there is in favor of the primacy of St. Peter, at Rome, the testimony of all Christian antiquity, from Papias and Irenæus, who both lived in the second century, and the former of whom was a disciple of St. John the Evangelist. It is also a fact, that, the doubts on this subject, raised during the heat of discussion, have been contradicted by some very learned protestants."

Ulric. Notwithstanding your appeal to the testimonies of Papias and Irenæus, these two points of the primacy and episcopacy of Rome have certainly been contested by men of great erudition, and I am perfectly unacquainted with any Protestant author that has ever maintained your assertions on this subject.

Odilon. I shall convince you of the contrary. As to the primacy of St. Peter, it seems to me that the 19th verse of the 16th chapter of St. Matthew, speaks in an incontestable manner in favor of the supreme power, granted by Jesus Christ to this apostle, in the church, or new religious society, that was about to be formed. Keys, it is well known, were the sign of *sovereign power.* We see in Isaias, xxii, 21, that Eliacim, by the delivery of the keys into his hands, became *administrator of the empire* after Joseph. You will also find in *Dempster, on the 18th chap. of book* v. *Rosini's Antiquities,* that the keys of the house confided to the Roman women, at the time of their marriage, were taken from them when divorced. The expression, *kingdom of heaven,* must be applied here, as in other passages, to the new religious society, founded by Jesus Christ; it is over this society that he sets . Peter, by the delivery of the keys, on account of the praise and solemn testimony which he had given of his Divine Master, according to St. Matthew xvi. 16, 17, 18. Jesus Christ indeed confers, Matthew xviii. 18, on the other disciples also the power of binding and loosing; but he does not give them the keys; and, consequently, does not establish them like St. Peter, Matthew xvi. 19, as head of his church. If the *kingdom of heaven* does not mean the church, but the other world, have the goodness to tell me what these things signify? what power they confer on St. Peter? and give me, in general, a better explanation of this passage.

Ulric. Supposing even I admit yours, which I will not examine more at length, still, I should be very curious to know who were those distinguished Protestants, who, according to your assertion, have endeavored to dispel the doubts raised against the sojourning of St. Peter at Rome, and his episcopacy in that city.

Odilon. Basnage says, that no tradition has more testimonies in its favor than this, and that, unless we reject all historical motives, it is impossible to doubt of the arrival of St. Peter at Rome. Pearson, in his *First Dissertation on the Succession of the first Bishops of Rome*, chap. vi. & vii. believes that no ancient writer ever questioned the foundation of the Roman church by St. Peter, or that the Popes were his successors. The first who dared to throw any doubt on this fact, was William, the master of John Wickliff; but the agreement of all those, who call the See of Rome *the chair of St. Peter*, is so unanimous, that neither Luther, nor Calvin, nor the Centuriators of Magdburg, ever ventured to attack this truth: moreover, Basnage, whom I quoted before, is not the only learned Protestant who attests it.

Ulric. Who are the others?

Odilon. I have lately mentioned Puffendorf, and I could find some authors among the Calvinists also, who were of the same opinion; and who, in consequence of that opinion, have expressed themselves very favorably towards the Catholic Church.

Ulric. You are certainly mistaken. At least I cannot think that any *great* writers among the Calvinists held such an opinion; for what you said before of Tobler, will not serve here, as now we are speaking exclusively of the primacy of the bishops of Rome.

Odilon. I flatter myself that you will not refuse the celebrated Grotius a place among the *most learned* men of his time; the history of his life, by Burigny, is sufficient to convince one of this. Read also his letters, and you will find the most unequivocal expressions, and all founded on Christian antiquity, in favor of the primacy of the Roman Church, its hierarchy and episcopal succession, as well as on the promise of Jesus Christ, to preserve it till the end of the world. You have not forgotten, besides, the mention I have made already of Cowel's opinion, nor that maintained in the Memoir, circulated by the French Calvinists in 1775.

Edward. We will not go into this subject either, as it would lead us too far from the principal topic. I am satisfied with knowing that your opinion on the church and the Pope, is the invariable doctrine of the church; and, if so, it seems useless to think of a re-union.

Odilon. Yes, it is decidedly its invariable doctrine, and you will find it announced as such in the catechism of the Council of Trent. Thus, as we maintain firmly that this establishment was formed by Jesus Christ himself, it is impossible for us to deviate from it.

Edward. But how then could writers, calling themselves Catholics too, propose, as a step towards this re-union, to suppress the primacy and influence of the Pope?

Odilon. I have already told you, because they did not know their religion; and I confess I am not at all surprised at it.

Edward. What is there that can surprise you then?

Odilon. Charity forbids my believing, that in all this there was an intention to overturn religion, though it is evident, that no society can subsist in a state of anarchy. I only wonder that a proposition could ever have been made so senseless in itself.

Ulric. What dispositions prejudicial to religion might this proposition contain?

Odilon. Since you desire it, I will open my thoughts to you on the subject. All that had been undertaken hitherto, and in so many ways, against religion, had failed; the manœuvres of philosophism had ended in the destruction of monasteries and churches, in proscribing every sort of Divine worship, in assassinating or transporting priests; but religion itself remained standing and immoveable.

Edward. Nothing more true; she showed herself to mankind, from the midst of the ruins, with which she was surrounded.

Odilon. It was necessary, therefore, to have recourse to more prudent measures and better fitted to attain the end.

Edward. And what do you understand by these measures?

Odilon. The design of depriving the Pope of all power over the church. By this means, the centre of unity would have been destroyed, and the whole edifice of the hierarchy shaken in its foundations. When the latter was once overturned, the downfal, of religion must have soon followed, without any thing to save it.

Ulric. I cannot think this project was really conceived.

Odilon. I began by saying, that charity also forbad me from entertaining this sinister idea, and I merely believed that I could not imagine a plan so senseless in its very nature.

Edward. Pray explain yourself!

Odilon. Whether the proposers of a re-union, proved by their ignorance of the opinion of the whole Catholic church on the prerogatives of the Pope, how little they knew their own religion, or that, supposing them well-informed, we are forced to say, that for fear of shocking the whole church, they did not dare to ask for the complete suppression of the Pope, certain it is, that there is great contradiction, and a great want of judgment, in wishing the Pope to remain, indeed, the head of the church, the first of bishops; while, on the other hand, he was deprived of all influence.

Edward. You are perfectly right. It is the height of absurdity, to acknowledge the Pope as head of the church, and as supreme arbiter in matters of dogma and discipline, and refusing him, nevertheless, any influence over those two things. What would our kings and princes say, if some visionary republican came to give them a lesson, and were to say: " We are willing to acknowledge you as our head, placed by God for the maintenance of public order, but do not expect to be allowed the least influence over that order, or the administration of the State!"

Odilon. You now know what is the true maxim of the Catholic church, respecting the person and power of the Pope, and you will admit that propositions, tending to weaken his authority, not only suppose a great ignorance of the principles of that church, but are, in themselves, contrary to all reason and justice.

Edward. It is not the same, at least, with ecclesiastical celibacy, which is a matter of pure discipline, and a new institution, imagined by Gregory VII.; it is, moreover, a law quite opposite to nature, and therefore I am certain that, by abrogating it, a great obstacle would be overcome, to the infinite advantage also of religion and morals.

Odilon. Permit me to say, that you embrace too many objects at once for me to satisfy you in one answer. Let us, if you please, proceed progressively.

Edward. With all my heart; and I repeat, therefore, that it cannot be denied, that the celibacy of the clergy, is a simple affair of discipline, and a new invention; which dates chiefly from the time of Gregory VII. I remember also to have read, in the German paper, called the *General Indicator,* "That vows of chastity, and the celibacy of the clergy, were unknown in the first ages of the *pure* Church; that the idea first sprung up in Italy, especially at Milan; and that Gregory VII. gave this notion the force of a general law."*

Odilon. As to the first part of your proposition, I admit the truth of it, and every honest Catholic will allow, that this celibacy, not having been instituted by Jesus Christ, and being consequently of pure discipline, may be liable to changes; but as to the latter point, I think you are in a great error; and, however prodigal the author of this passage is of learned quotations, I take the liberty of thinking that he had not well studied ecclesiastical history. I could not help smiling, when, on reading him, I acquired a fresh proof of the assurance with which, in our days, so much base metal is thrown upon the public.

Edward. Notwithstanding, I do not think I am mistaken in this respect; for nobody can deny, that there were many married clergymen before the time of Gregory VII.

Odilon. I will grant a great deal more than this, and will even cite some who were so even in the three first ages of the Church, as Valins, priest at Philippi, whom St. Polycarp

* General Indicator, for the year 1809, No. 170, volume 1981.

mentions; Charemon, an Egyptian bishop; Cœcilius and Munidius, Carthaginian priests, and some others. But all these happened to be married before they became priests, and you will find it difficult to prove that any of them received the sacrament of marriage, after that of the priesthood. I even maintain, that so early as the second century, a project was on foot, to convert the celibacy of the clergy into a general law.

Edward. In the second century?

Odilon. Most certainly; for Denis, bishop of Corinth, opposed this project, as you may see in Eusebius's Ecclesiastical History.

Edward. I remember, also, that in the Council of Mida, in the forth century, an Egyptian bishop, named Paphnatius objected to the same law.

Odilon. This is very true; but this opposition, even from this bishop, so far from authorizing Protestants, and some Catholic priests, eager for matrimony, to shout out victory, should prove to them, on the contrary, that celibacy existed in the earliest time of the church.

Edward. This would, indeed, be very singular, and what I certainly did not expect.

Odilon. This is the account which Socrates and Sozomen give of the business. It was proposed in the council of Nieda, to oblige priests married *before* their ordination, to leave their wives. It was *this* resolution which Paphnatius opposed, observing, that so severe a yoke, imposed on ecclesiastical persons, was beyond the strength of many among them, and that moreover it was observing chastity to live with one lawful spouse.

Edward. I confess this does not seem to me to be greatly in favor of celibacy.

Odilon. Be so good as to hear me to the end : "It is sufficient," added Paphnatius, "if, according to *the ancient tradition of the Church,* those who were single before their ordination, continue so after it; but those, who when laics, had already taken a lawful wife, ought not to be separated from her."

Ulric. The testimony of Socrates and Sozomen appears to me of little weight, as those two historians belong to the fifth century.

Odilon. But why then should their testimony seem so

important, when invoked to prove, that an insupportable yoke should not be laid on ecclesiastics, by forcing them to renounce their wives taken before ordination? Must we not allow the same confidence to those authors, when they relate that Paphnatius agreed, that those who were single before ordination, should continue so after, according *the ancient tradition of the Church!*

Edward. I acknowledge that no objection can be made against this authority; and, it follows, that the celibacy of the clergy was known in the first ages. But how does it happen that the introduction of this law is attributed to Gregory VII.?

Odilon. He did what so many others had done before him; that is, he endeavored to re-establish relaxed discipline, which was not generally well observed in the church; and his zeal, in this respect, was crowned with success. But do not let us wander from the subject, nor forget, that as early as the *fourth* century, the celibacy of the clergy was considered as an establishment consecrated by *ancient custom*, and the *ancient tradition* of the Church.

Edward. But may not this celibacy belong to those maxims that were borrowed from Paganism? I think Middleton has already made this reproach against the church of Rome.

Odilon. It is notorious, that the ancient Greeks and Romans not only imposed a temporary celibacy on those, who exercised certain religious functions, but also exacted the same abstinence for life, in a particular class of persons. Read the passages all drawn from profane authors, which Feller quotes on this subject in his *Philosophical Catechism*, tom. iii. p. 219; in that work particularly, you will find a most complete refutation of all the objections against the celibacy of the clergy: but, as you like to search into antiquity, why do you not go still higher?

Edward. What do you mean?

Odilon. That you might as well derive celibacy from the Jews as from the Pagans. We find, indeed, in the Bible, the genealogical tree of Aaron; but you certainly will not find that of the two sons of Moses, begot before his vocation; and the same silence is observed on the subsequent marriage of that patriarch, and the children who may have sprung from it. We know also that the Essenians lived in celibacy. But why seek so far? On the question of the disciples, "It is not
3*

proper then to marry?"* Jesus Christ merely answered;
" All do not understand this word, but those only to whom
it has been given."† St. Paul, 1. vii. Corinth. expresses
himself more at large on marriage and celibacy; and you will
find in the Apocalypse, chap. xiv. v. 4, what great esteem
St. John had for this state. Why therefore have any difficulty in giving Judaism the preference in this matter over
Paganism?

Edward. Grant, however, that this law offends nature, and
that religion and morals would be equal gainers by its abrogation.

Odilon. I confess, I did not expect this objection. Tell me,
then, do you think the same of the law of a country which
forbids and impedes the marriage of soldiers, or which, in
some countries, forbids it to all placemen who cannot prove
they have a certain fortune, or at least that they will acquire
it by their marriage?

Edward. The State has surely good reasons for this; and,
besides, I imagine that it is considered, that the persons you
mention may find other ways of indemnifying themselves for
the severity of the law in this respect.

Odilon. Come, this is a fair avowal and very honorable to
the Catholic clergy: it proves, that it has not been mentioned
that they would *indemnify* themselves in such a way. But,
pray tell me, ought not this law of celibacy to be called much
harder and more inhuman, when it restrains soldiers, exposed
by their profession and daily intercourse to innumerable
temptations, than when it obliges persons formed by education, by the sanctity of their character, the nature of their
studies, and their separation from the rarities of the world, to
a great habit of commanding their senses, and watching their
passions?

Edward. Your observation is just, and I now agree with
you on this point; but you will allow at least that the abolition of this law would produce great advantages to religion
and the state. Luther therefore was right in suppressing it,
and in allowing the clergy to marry.

Odilon. I could never find in the works of that reformer,
any proof that he *positively* abolished celibacy: this came on
of itself. If I am not mistaken, the first priest, among the

---

* Non expedit nubere?
† Non omnes capiunt verbum istud, sed quibus datum est.

new partizans of Luther, who married, was Bernhardi, rector of Kemberz in Saxony. His marriage was celebrated in 1521, and this example soon followed by others, was at length imitated by Luther himself, 11th of June, 1525; a step that was disapproved even by many of his friends. When afterwards, all those great personages Bucer, Zuingle, Œcolampadius, &c. took wives, the satirical Erasmus said; "This is the way they mortify themselves! The Reformation seems to have no other object but to transform monks and nuns into bridegrooms and brides; and this grand tragedy will end like a comedy, where every body is married in the last act." But let us not forget that you spoke of the advantages which the abrogation of the law of celibacy would procure to religion and the state.

Edward. You have only to consider how population would gain by the marriage of the priests: and what an advantage to the state!

Odilon. I cannot at all conceive this great political advantage, unless such gratuities of men are wanted to make *food for powder,* as Falstaff calls his soldiers in Shakespeare. But if this be it, why then impede so much the marriage of soldiers, and other persons in certain circumstances? I remember to have read also in the *General Indicator,* for 1809, No. 172, that in several countries, marriage is impeded, or even prohibited, not only among those employed by the government, but even to young men of the laboring classes, if they have not a capital of two or three hundred florins. It is my opinion, that the abolition of this law, particularly in our times, would be very imprudent.

Edward. And why?

Odilon. Because our clergy is at present so stripped, distressed, and narrowed in their circumstances, that it would be absurd to exact of a man embarrassed how to provide a livelihood for himself, to maintain out of it a wife and family.

Edward. This melancholy truth is but too well established. In our church, also, a clergyman with any fortune is a phenomenon, and it is a common saying, that the inheritance of our pastors commonly consists of books and children.

Odilon. What great advantage then would the state gain by this? The English writer, Malthus, has published an excellent work on *the conditions and consequences of an increase of population:* he proves that it should absolutely be in proportion with the means of subsistence; and that, in general, a great population does not, in itself, form the happiness of a country, as the economists fancied. But did you not say, that the State had good reason for prohibiting or restraining marriage among the military ?

Edward. Yes ; for besides that marriage is little suited to a profession exposed to so many troubles, chances and risks, it must be allowed that the pay of a soldier is so small, that his marriage would only increase the number of beggars.

Odilon. I have already observed, that the latter point, especially in these times, is also applicable to the clergy. Besides, do you not suppose that the church had good reasons, likewise, for introducing the precept of celibacy from the beginning of its formation, and for preserving it during so many ages ?

Edward. I should like to know these reasons ; for, I declare to you, that I still stick to the opinion, that the abolition of this law would be very beneficial to religion, if it were only, that the clergy, being thus more closely connected with the State, might cease to form, as it were, a separate body.

Odilon. What you consider as a disadvantage to religion, is precisely the contrary. I will not even quote St. Paul, who says, " He who has no wife is careful of what concerns the Lord, and how he may please God ; but he who has a wife is occupied with the concerns of the world, and how he may please his wife, and is divided between them !" I will merely fix your attention on one consideration ; which is, whether you do not think that many occasions may happen, where a married clergyman would be placed in the alternative, either of sacrificing his principles, his conscience, and duty, or the happiness of his family, by exposing it to the attacks of a powerful adversary.

At these words, Ulric of Stetten took up the conversation, and said : " 'The great number of complaints that have been raised against the nepotism of Catholic priests, prove sufficiently that they do not neglect the fortune of their families."

Odilon. I grant that many among us have deserved that reproach ; but it never can be urged against us so often as against men burdened with a family, and who are entirely dependant, besides, on the kindness and pity of others. I will say nothing of another very essential point, because I am convinced you are perfectly aware of it from your own experience.

Edward. Explain yourself more clearly.

Odilon. If a clergyman wishes to render himself useful to religion and science, by learned works, are the great and insurmountable difficulties he has to struggle with, if burdened with a family, nothing ? A very distinguished Protestant, who cannot be accused of any partiality for the church of Rome, has publicly avowed this in our time.

Edward. What is his name ?

Odilon. The late Dr. Walch of Gottingen. Read what he says on this subject, in the introduction to his translation of Mosheim's Ecclesiastical History, p. 149 and 151. But I only meant to speak of the great disadvantages which result to religion and the ministry, from the inevitable state of dependance to which a clergyman with a family is exposed.

Edward. Yes, and I imagine more than one example might be given of it.

Odilon. But these inconsistencies, great as they are, are not the only ones. What would become of confession, that Divine institution, if priests married ? Would the penitent have a sufficient security for their discretion, on those occasions in which a wife has frequently so much empire over her husband ? And as the preservation of confession is a security for that of religion also, do you think it could subsist long after the fall of the hierarchy, and with a married clergy ?

Edward. But Protestantism, with its married clergy, has lasted three centuries, and the Greek church, with the same regimen, much longer.

Odilon. When you mention the Greek church, do not forget that the hierarchy there properly belongs to unmarried clergymen, as the bishops, archbishops, and metropolitans are taken out of monasteries. It is besides very remarkable, that in the whole patriarchate of Constantinople, no Pope or Greek priest who is married, is allowed to hear confessions, except in cases of urgent necessity.* The inconveniences of confessing to a married priest must of course have been strongly felt.

As to Protestantism, it should first be well ascertained, whether it has not degenerated to such a degree, that nothing remains but the name. At least, you will allow yourself,

* Lett. edif. et cur. tom. xi. p. 46

that from the examples I have already quoted, it has undergone such considerable alterations, both in doctrine and
exterior discipline, that if Luther and Melanchton were to
rise again, they would no longer recoguize this church, the
work of their hands.

Edward. Let us pass over this. It is certain, from what
you have said, that those, who like Beaufort, have proposed
projects of re-union, neither knew Catholicism nor Protestantism, without mentioning other great difficulties which
are impediments, on every side, to the success of this great
business. I am extremely anxious, however, to know,
whether you yourself, after all, consider a religious re-union
as utterly impossible.

Odilon. I really cannot see what sort of re-union could
possibly be effected.

Edward. As toleration has almost entirely dispelled the
ancient spirit of party, I think a re-union should not be absolutely impossible: all depends on the manner of setting
about it.

Odilon. It is precisely this, which, in my opinion, presents
almost insuperable difficulties. Which of the two parties
could possibly give into such a re-union, as is called *absorbent,*
by which one would pass into the ranks of his adversary,
and sacrifice its ancient doctrines, exterior worship, and
ecclesiastical constitution?

Ulric. My opinion, in this respect, is the same as yours.

Edward. But might not something be ceded on both sides,
as is commonly done in all treaties, after the heat of the com-
bat is a little cooled?

Odilon. This, if I am not mistaken, would be what they
call a *temporative* re-union; but then the question would
recur: what, and how much must be ceded? The Catholic
neither will nor can abandon any part of doctrine; and, if it
be said, that the Protestant, according to the indifferentism,
which has taken root in his church, should have little concern for doctrines that have ceased to be his, or which at least
do not interest him as formerly, still it would not follow, that
this Protestant would be disposed to adopt all those of the
Catholic church. Supposing even that the latter were disposed to yield on some points of pure discipline, nevertheless,
she neither would nor could, in any way, give up her

worship, or hierarchial constitution; and it would be difficult to conceive how modern Protestants could be brought to accept of either.

Edward. But supposing every individual to be allowed his own way of thinking on points of doctrine, might not a re-union be confined merely to a common and uniform mode of external discipline.

Odilon. I have reason to think that Beaufort, and some other projectors, of his way of thinking, really conceived a re-union of this sort, called a *conservant*, and which squares so well with the actual spirit of indifferentism. But what would then become of that *unity of the faith*, so much recommended by the apostle, and the object of so much solicitude during so many ages? The church of Jesus Christ would be nothing but an amalgamation of the most heterogeneous elements, a monstrous body, composed of Catholics, Lutherans, Calvinists, Jansenists, Arians, Semi-arians, Macedonians, and Socinians. Could they ever unite in a common worship? The Socinian, Arian, and Macedonian, who deny the Divinity of Jesus Christ and of the Holy Ghost, could they adore them with us, without incurring the reproach of idolatry and hypocrisy? Even supposing the ancient prejudices against the Catholic worship, are not only weakened, but that several Protestants are even favorably inclined towards them, still a crowd of obstacles appear, which this *conservant* re-union could hardly ever get over.

Edward. You have no hope then of ever seeing a re-union of the separated churches?

Odilon. Nothing is impossible to God.

Edward. If I understand you rightly, you think there are so many difficulties in it, that nothing but a miracle can overcome them.

Ulric. We are no longer, unfortunately, in the age of miracles.

Odilon. The Divine power and mercy are not confined to certain epochs. God, when he pleases, can act as in the time of our fathers, and perform still greater miracles; but this is not what I meant to say. Yes, I do consider this union as impossible in itself; but, at the same time, as easier and more practicable than ever, provided it be left to God alone; he can smooth all the ways at his pleasure, and as he did formerly, bring back into one fold the strayed sheep of Israel.

Edward. What are these frightful impossibilities?

Odilon. In this respect, I am entirely of the opinion of Tabaraud, when he says: "If God himself does not conduct the hands of those who labor with a religious view in the execution of a work so full of humanity, as the reunion of the churches, it would be vain to hope for success." It is certain, also, that several Protestant divines, as eminent as Plarick, Marozel,* and others, must have thought with me, that these difficulties were insurmountable, since they conceived, that far from being advantageous to both sides, such a re-union would rather be prejudicial; and, therefore, that it would be better for each to continue in his old way, as before, merely uniting with his separated brethren, in reciprocal feelings of toleration and friendship.

Ulric. You will allow, however, that this is by no means applicable to the Lutherans and Calvinists, since (thanks be to toleration) they have renounced those miserable controversies.

Odilon. Believe me, we had better let this toleration alone. That which truly deserves the name, knows how to distinguish truth from error; and, while it rejects the latter, can endure it with patience. False toleration, on the contrary, is only that frigid indifference which makes us think, that God considers in the same view all opinions whatever on his attributes and on religion.

Ulric. Be it indulgence merely, or that indifference you mention, it is not less certain that, since the two parties have given up their ancient disputes, they have drawn together spontaneously to such a degree, as almost to form one and the same body.

Odilon. Nobody better than you, sir, can inform me what *species* of union this is, and which of the two parties has gained or lost the most by it.

Ulric. But if these eternal polemical discussions between the Catholics and Protestants were once sincerely given up, should we not see them following each their own way in sentiments of harmony, concord, and love?

* Words of Peace to the Catholic Church, by Plarick, 1809. Sermon of Mazorel, in which he maintains, that the re-union of the Roman and Protestant Churches, far from promising any advantages, would positively produce the contrary: 1808.

Odilon. In my last unfortunate emigration, I took two of my religion with me. An accident forced us to go to the next village on foot. The youngest of us, full of the idea of his strength, lively and nimble, rather flew than walked; he soon got a-head of us; but, to his cost, as we soon heard. As to us, more in years, and moderate from long habit, we could never come up with our young fellow-traveller.

Edward. Have the kindness to explain your meaning more clearly.

Odilon. I beg you will excuse me. As we are here at a quiet and friendly meal, I must not disturb it by any thing that might be disagreeable to any of the company.

Edward. Do not be afraid, but tell us whatever you think. Truth should never displease any one, and if any of us is in an error, I am sure he will thank his antagonist for setting him right, and putting him in the right road.

Odilon. I submit. If, in the 17th century, and even the first half of the 18th, the mutual animosity had not been so violent; or if the pacificators of that time had displayed as much prudence and zeal, as those of our days, I am persuaded that an approximation would have been easier then than now; for, at present, you have got so far before us, that with the best will in the world, and even supposing the thing were allowed, it would be impossible for us henceforward ever to come up with you.

Edward. But how! are you not much nearer us now than formerly, and our intentions, though they appear in a milder shape, are they not the same?

Odilon. I am far from thinking so. It is true there were formerly, among us, some indiscreet zealots, whose intentions respecting religion were, however, very good, who often delivered maxims by no means approved by the faith of the church, or on which at least it had decided nothing. We have had others who gave in to more than one species of exaggeration. But, to speak only of our own times, I know some writers among us, who to gain the approbation and applause of the journalists and critics of Protestant Germany, made advances in more than one article, and yet with very bad success.

Edward. How do you mean?

Odilon. I remember to have read in one of your most

4

popular critical papers, that no attention should be paid to
these kinds of advances on the side of the Catholics, because
in reality they continued the same; that they must not be
attended to, or considered as *enlightened*, until they had given
up the doctrines of transubstantiation, of our faith, the only
part of salvation, as well as the infallibility of the Church,
purgatory, the mass, and a visible head of the Church. I
could quote, in confirmation of this, several other passages
drawn from the writings of your most eminent divines; but
they would be superfluous, as you cannot be ignorant, that
according to the judgment of your own writers, we are not
near enough to them yet with respect to our principles and
doctrine.

Ulric. Yes, and it is truly the height of ridicule; for, in
this way, the Catholics could only be considered *enlightened*,
by ceasing to be Catholics.

Odilon. If indulgence were not become one of the most
necessary qualities of our days, one might pass one's time in
laughing at a great many things.

Edward. I think I heard you say at the same time, that,
though become more moderate, our sentiments were still the
same, and that consequently the re-union in question appeared
more difficult than ever? Have the kindness to explain yourself more clearly.

Odilon. If I understood you right, you seemed astonished,
that, though time had weakened the animosity of the two
parties, and had brought us nearer the Protestants, who were
still in their old position, I maintained, nevertheless, that the
re-union would have been less difficult two centuries ago,
than at present; however, you are now convinced that you
were mistaken with respect to the Catholics.

Edward. I was; but, will you also maintain that modern
Protestans do not resemble those of former times?

Odilon. Formerly, when with respect to principles, the
Protestants were not so far separated from the Catholics as to
authorize Erasmus, I think, to say *that the old and simple
disputes of the schools had been reduced into articles of faith*, it
would not have been impossible perhaps to effect a reconciliation and a re-union. But now, that the Protestants have so
far deviated from their *primitive* constitution, that Luther
could no longer recognise *his* church, I think I may positively

maintain that the difficulties of a re-union are become equivalent to an impossibility.

Ulric. What! we have ceased to be Protestants?

Odilon. I cannot help saying so, and I can assure you this sentence would be very mild, in comparison of that of an estimable divine of your own church, who had examined the whole state of the question with scrupulous attention, and who has proved all he asserted.

Ulric. What is his name, and what has he asserted?

Odilon. It is Du Trembley, in his " Present State of Christianity," an excellent work, and which I cannot recommend to you too much. He not only there asserts that modern Protestants have ceased to be so ; but he says downright, that they depart entirely from all that Christians have believed since the time of the Apostles, and that a Mussulman who admitted the miracles of Jesus Christ, would be nearer the Christians, than the doctors are of modern Protestantism.

Ulric. And still we are always boasting of being Christians and Protestants!

Odilon. Yes, but it is like Bayle, when he said to the Cardinal de Polignac: " I am a Protestant, for I protest against all that is done and all that is said ;" or, like the picture of Protestantism which Rousseau drew, when he used to call it a protestation against every thing that reason cannot comprehend. But the history of the Reformation is sufficient to inform you, that this is not primitive Protestantism.

Edward. As the primitive spirit of Protestantism, that is to say, individual examination, and the right of only accepting what is founded in Holy Scripture, still reigns among us; as the Bible, translated by Luther, is still in our hands, and is used in the public exercise of our religion ; as the hymns composed by him are still sung in our churches, and as the principal articles of our whole religious establishment still correspond with those which were prescribed by the first reformers ; as Luther's catechism has never ceased to be the basis of our religious instruction, and as our pastors, in short, are still restricted to the acceptation of the symbolic books, I really cannot see, how any one can pretend that we are no longer Protestants, and that if Luther returned among us, he could no longer recognize his church.

Odilon. I allow that these objections would be very forcible,

if they could not be answered; but, I persist in thinking myself authorized to maintain, that Protestantism, especially
during the last half century, has insensibly degenerated from
its first institutions, so far that Luther and Melanchton could
no longer recognize it.   Hence Grégoire, in his "History of
Religious Sects," has not hesitated to say, "Modern Protestants hardly resemble those of the sixteenth century in any
thing; for the identity of the name does not establish the
conformity of doctrine.   If Luther and Calvin were to return
on earth, they would be very much surprised not to be of the
religion of those who have borrowed their denominations from
them."   This opinion is conformable to that of all those who
are acquainted with the ancient doctrine of your churches,
and its actual state.

Edward. I cannot conceive how such an opinion could be
given.

Odilon. Allow me to make a single provisional question.
To whom must we refer in these matters? To the people, to
laics, or to the doctors of the law, who have made a particular study of it, and whose duty it is to teach it?

Edward. To the latter undoubtedly; but you will gain
nothing by this confession on my part, since I have just told
you that our pastors are still restrained, on oath, to conform
their instructions to the symbolical books of our church.

Odilon. I have no doubt that they form this engagement,
but do they keep it? "In the reformed churches of France,
Geneva, and Switserland, as well as in the Lutheran
churches," says Tabaraud, "the ancient confessions of faith,
which establish their doctrines, are still of importance to those
who are candidates for a professorship, and are still considered
as the preservers of faith and worship."

Ulric. Well! this is precisely what I have just said.

Odilon. Hear the end.   "The way of understanding,
interpreting, and defending the dogmas of Christianity, has
undergone great changes in the new philosophical methods."

Ulric. The way of treating a thing makes no change in
its essence.

Odilon. Even granting that Tabaraud has not said all in
this passage, I should still be convinced myself, that the doctrines and principles of your modern divines and doctors, are,
in all their writings that I have read, so unlike those of the

founder of your church, whose way of thinking on several fundamental points was still conformable to ours, that he could not possibly admit them among his disciples and successors.

Edward. And how would you undertake to prove this?

Odilon. You remember what I said with respect to confession and the sacraments, of which Luther acknowledged three, and you only two. I shall now merely quote the opinion of that reformer on an article just as important. "We admit," said he, eleven years after the beginning of his reformation, "that much good, nay all that is good, in Christianity, is to be found in the Papacy, whence it came to us; that is to say, we confess that there is in the Papacy the true Holy Scripture, the true Baptism, the true sacrifice of the altar, the real keys for the remission of sins, the real apostleship, the true catechism, namely, the ten commandments, the articles of faith, the Lord's prayer, &c. I say, that in the Papacy is true Christianity, yes, the true model of Christianity, and several great saints.—But, if Christianity exists under the Pope, it must be truly the body and members of Jesus Christ. If Christianity be his body, it follows that it possesses also the real spirit: the Gospel, Baptism, the Sacrament, the Keys, the Apostleship, Prayer, the Holy Scripture; in a word, all that Christianity ought to have."

Edward. This is certainly a very remarkable declaration.

Odilon. You know, besides, as well as I, that, though on other occasions Luther allowed himself to be carried away so far by the inexcusable violence of his temper as to lose all bounds, and assert that the Catholic Church was founded by the devil, and that its doctrine was a diabolical doctrine, still it is not less true, that in the principal dogmatical book of the Protestants, a book obligatory on all their pastors; in a word, in the 21st article of the Confession of Augsburg, it is said, that in all principal points, the doctrine of Protestants agrees with that of the Roman Church; that they only meant to suppress some *abuses* of that church, and that its doctrine may be considered as conformable to the word of God.

Edward. Yes, these were the opinions of that time, and could not be otherwise; for the particular expressions of Luther, in this respect, could only be considered as the temporary eruption of violent passions.

Odilon. You must allow, however, that there is a great

4*

contrast between this very remarkable, and the later maxims of Protestant divines, who have gone so far as to maintain, that in a church so much degenerated as the Catholic, it was very difficult to effect one's salvation.

Edward. These sorts of expressions must also be classed among those that were produced by that period of acrimony and contention between the two parties; but I imagine you will find nobody that thinks or speaks in that way at present.

Odilon. I admit, that in our days, you have set open the gates of Paradise so wide, that notwithstanding the express decision of St. Peter, Acts iv. 12, the Pagans themselves and the Jews may enter in ; but it is not less true, that with respect to Catholics many of your divines still think as in those days of exasperation.

Edward. I can hardly believe it.

Odilon. Two of your most celebrated divines, Miller and Less. have expressly said, "That it was impossible that so respectable a church, as the Evangelic, could ever be re-united, in any way, with such usurpers as Catholics ; and that the name of Christianity might better be given to Islamism, or even to Paganism, than to what is now taught as such at Rome." What a distance from this opinion to that of Luther !

Edward. I confess, I by no means expected such strong expressions ; but let us choose another subject.

Odilon. You know, and probably better than I, that in your church, every kind of attack is made on our doctrine of the infallibility of the church.

Edward. I know, and I think with very good reason ; for if the church could not err, so many errors, which we cannot mention at present, would not have crept into it. Such must also have been Luther's opinion ; for otherwise he would never have separated from an infallible church.

Odilon. Hear what he wrote in 1532, against those who denied the real presence in the Eucharist, and whom he called *spirits of cabal*: "This article is not a doctrine foreign to Scripture and imagined by men; but is clearly founded in the gospel, on the precise and indubitable words of Jesus Christ; it has been uniformly believed and preserved from the beginning of the Christian Church down to this hour, as is proved by the works of the Holy Fathers of the Greek and Latin churches: add to this, daily practice and experience to the present moment: which testimonies of all Holy Christian churches should be sufficient for us, without any other proof, to remain firm on this article, and not to hear or suffer any spirit of cabal concerning it. For it is dangerous and terrible to hear or believe any thing contrary to the unanimous testimony, faith, and doctrine of the whole Christian church, and 'to what has been maintained in the whole world, and uniformly, for more than 1500 years. If it were a new article, and had not been so uniformly preserved throughout all Christendom, in the whole world, and from the beginning of the Holy Christian church, it would not be so dangerous or terrible to doubt of it, and to dispute its validity. But since, from the beginning, and as far as Christianity extends, it has been uniformly maintained, he who doubts of it is as culpable as if he believed in no Christian church; and not only does he condemn the whole Christian church, as if she were a cursed heretic, but even Jesus Christ himself, with all the apostles and prophets, who founded and have so strongly attested this article; *I believe in one Holy Christian Church;* Jesus Christ has said, Matthew xxviii. *I am with you to the end of the world:* and St. Paul to Timothy, ii, 3: *The Church of God is the column and foundation of the truth."* In another place, he uses, concerning the church, the very terms commonly employed by Catholics: *" God cannot lie, therefore the church likewise cannot err."* But it is useless to cite any more passages on this subject.

Edward. Those are certainly very important texts, and sufficiently prove what a regard Luther had at that period for the power of the church, for its infallibility, its tradition, and the general uniformity of its doctrine: however, he must have altered that favorable opinion very much, as later, he accused that same church, whose infallibility† he had acknowledged, of having fallen into several errors.

Odilon. That may very well be, though I have no recollection of the passages in which Luther is supposed to have revoked his former maximg in this respect. But supposing it, have we not many instances to prove that Luther's opinions were but too often governed by his passions? As long as the church did not condemn him, it was infallible; but when it did, it appeared to him full of errors.

* Opera, tom. v. fol. 490.   † Op. tom. vii. fol. 417.

Ulric. This I grant; but will you seriously maintain that the church can commit no error?

Odilon. If you had examined the motives alleged by Merz, on this subject in his sermons for 1776, 1778, and 1784, you would think very differently.

Ulric. What! that controvertist, Merz! I know he is in great repute in your church, but not so in ours.

Odilon. You know, one may love Plato and Aristotle, but we should, above all, love truth. Thus, wherever it appears in that writer, we should cherish it, however bitter it may otherwise appear. Nevertheless, I shall give up his testimony, and confine myself to ask you, by what articles this accusation of errors in the Church will begin and end? Luther retracted his opinion, in favor of the infallibility of the Church, and accused it of error; but this was only in points of doctrine, that did not agree with his opinions. In later times, this Church and he himself have been accused of error in articles, to which he still strongly adhered, such as the expiatory death of Jesus Christ, the Eucharist, and Baptism; and since that epoch, the same has been done with respect to the divinity of Jesus Christ, that of the Holy Ghost, and the Trinity; this way of proceeding will continue, till in the place of all Christianity nothing will be seen but pure naturalism.

Edward. Have we not the Holy Scriptures? It is in as much as the Church maintains and preserves the doctrines contained in it, that Luther acknowledges and proclaims the infallibility of that Church, as may be shown from the very passages you have quoted.

Odilon. Very true; but he acknowledges, at the same time, that the Church is the authentic interpreter of the passages of Scripture, and arbiter of the doctrines that must be believed according to Scripture; for without that, he could not have invoked the uniform belief of the Church, as well as the decisions of the Fathers; and this profession of faith by Luther, which I willingly support on this occasion against his modern disciples, is very conformable to the essence of the thing.

Edward. How is that?

Odilon. The Scripture, as you know, is susceptible of several interpretations, not only in the difficult passages, but even in those that appear the clearest. Would you believe it? Dr. Thiess has reckoned eighty-five different explanations of that plain parable of the unjust steward, in St. Luke xvi., and he has reckoned up one hundred and fifty on chap. iii. ver. 20, to the Galatians. You may convince yourself of this, by reading his work on the incompatibility of the spiritual and profane power, p. 17, note 14.

Edward. And what consequence do you draw from this?

Odilon. The most natural and, at the same time, the most necessary; namely, that if we do not wish the Scripture to become useless, and even dangerous, but, on the contrary, an immoveable rule of faith and life, it must absolutely be accompanied by a tribunal, to decide on the sense of it; and this tribunal, for that purpose, must be invested with an infallible authority. This has been the opinion of the most distinguished and eminent doctors of the Church, in all times. "We do," says St. Augustin, what pleases the whole Church, which is approved by the authority of the Scriptures themselves, that, as the Holy Scriptures cannot deceive, every one who fears he may be deceived by the obscurity of a question, may consult that same Church which the Holy Scripture points out, without any ambiguity."[*] The saints Jerom, Cyrill, Basil, and Gregory of Naziunzen, all hold the same language; in the Councils, which condemned the heresies of Nestorius and Eutyches, recourse was not had to the interpretations and commentaries of authors, but this general exclamation was heard: "This is the faith of our Fathers! this is what we all believe!"[†]

Ulric. All these testimonies are not the most ancient.

Odilon. Well, let us go back a century, and we shall find in St. Athanasius, that at the Council of Nicæa, the word *consubstantial* was principally admitted and consecrated, because the preceding Fathers of the Church had already employed it; and Eusebius of Nicomedia, on signing it, appealed to the testimony of the ancient Fathers. If we ascend still higher, that is, to the third century, we find Clement of Alexandria, who, in the 7th book of his *Stromata,* formally asserts, that all those who admit any other explanation of the holy books, than that of the Fathers, are in error. Tertullian,

[*] Hoc facimus quod universæ Ecclesiæ placet, quam ipsarum scripturarum commendat authoritas, ut quoniam S. scriptura fallere non potest, quisquis falli metuit hujus obscuritate quæstionis, eamdem Ecclesiam de illâ consulat, quam sine ullâ ambiguitate sancta scriptura demonstrat. St. Augustin, lib. I. cap. xxxiii. contra Crescon.

[†] Hæc est fides patrum! omnes ita credimus!

in the same age, and Irenæus in the second, give the same opinion, and you will find it thus established, passing from age to age, down to the Council of Trent.

Ulric. O! the Fathers! what is there they have not maintained?

Odilon. I will not call upon you to specify the singular imputation; but I remember to have read on this subject, a most important passage in one of your most learned and generally esteemed writers.

Edward. Will you name him?

Odilon. Lessing.

Ulric. Lessing! what, a man who joined the greatest condition to the most judicious and unprejudiced way of thinking, can he have pleaded the cause of a Church and its traditions?

Odilon. Yes, and so far, that it was not the Bible, but the Church and tradition which he considered as the rules of faith.

Edward. The freedom of Lessing's principles is so well known, that you must allow me to doubt of the truth of such an assertion. Perhaps the meaning of his expressions has been ill understood, or explained differently from what he intended.

Odilon. I will make him speak himself from his "Posthumous Theological Works:"—"The whole religion of Jesus Christ was practised, and still none of the Evangelists and Apostles had as yet written; the Lord's prayer was recited before St. Matthew consigned it to writing; for Jesus Christ himself had taught it to his disciples. The formula of Baptism was used before the same St. Matthew made mention of it, for Jesus Christ himself had prescribed it to the Apostles. Consequently, if the first Christians were not obliged to wait for the writings of the Apostles and Evangelists in those points, why should they be confined to that obligation in other articles? After having prayed and baptized, conformably to the orders of Jesus Christ, orally transmitted, how could they refuse to follow the same method with respect to all the rest of Christianity? But, it will be said, if Jesus Christ fixed these points by word of mouth, why did he not do the same with respect to all that the Apostles teach of him, and that the world was to believe? As if the authors of the New

Testament had ever pretended to consign to writing all the actions and all the words of Jesus Christ; as if they had not said expressly the contrary, with the intention, no doubt, of leaving something to tradition! Is it not enough, that the first Christians believed in a sort of symbol of all the points of doctrine, drawn out by Jesus Christ himself, and which they called *rule of faith?*"

Edward. I frankly declare, I never should have expected such an expression from a man like Lessing.

Odilon. This is not all: that author goes so far, that he does not hesitate to say of this formulary of faith, derived from the oral instruction of Jesus Christ and his Apostles, and not taken later out of the writings of the Evangelists or Apostles, and preserved in the Church by tradition, that without it, the Scripture was nothing.*

Lessing, in another passage of this very remarkable work, explains the same principles, disowned by modern Protestants, who reject the testimony of the ancient Church and its Fathers, but so conformable to those of Catholics; he explains them, I say, by the following words of Irenæus: "we have learnt the dispositions of our salvation, by no others than by those, through whom the gospel came to us, which they first preached, and then transmitted to us, in their writings, by the effect of the divine will. But if the Apostles had not even left us any writings, what then could be done, but to follow the order of tradition?"† "It is impossible for me," says Lessing,‡ "to shut my ears on purpose, when all antiquity declares unanimously, that our reformers have pruned and thrown away too many things, under this name of tradition, which sounded so ill to them. They should have granted, at least to what Irenæus understands by that word, the same divine authority, as they thought fit to grant exclusively to the Scripture."

Edward. Very well; but though, according to all these quotations from Lessing, we may be forced to acknowledge, that from the beginning of Christianity, the Bible was not considered as the exclusive rule of faith and morals, but that

---

* Lessing's Posthumous Theological Works, p. 6. 75.

† Non per alios dispositionem nostræ salutis cognovimus, quam per eos, per quos evangelium pervenit ad nos, quod quidem tunc præconaverunt, postea vero per Dei voluntatem in scriptis suis nobis tradiderunt.—Quid autem, si neque apostoli quidem scripturas reliquissent, nonne oportebat ordinem sequi traditionis? Irenæus.

‡ Posthumous Theological works of Lessing, p. 126

tradition was added to it, it does not yet follow that the
Church is infallible in her decisions on those two points.

Odilon. If this were the case, it would be better to reject
at once all sort of rule, and abandon the decisions on the objects of faith and justice, to the free interpretation of each
individual. For if by the admirable art of the new expounders (*exegetæ*), the Holy Scripture is become so dubious, that
one single passage may admit from eighty to a hundred and
fifty different interpretations, without the Church on her side
having the means of deciding authentically and infallibly on
these objects, I beg you to tell me on what can we fix?

Edward. I allow that these observations are perplexing; but
the judgment of the church is still a mere human judgment.

Odilon. Yes, but supported by the promised assistance of
the Divinity. A very learned Protestant divine, therefore,
has said very judiciously on this subject; " With the character
of unity, which the church should inviolably maintain
(Ephes. iv. 3–6), it may also pretend to universality and in
some sort to infallibility, (St. Peter i. 19).* I imagine, that
after this, you will think the opinion of Lessing sufficiently
founded.

Ulric. I confess it is rather surprising; but, at the same
time, I think you do us an injustice, if you think that modern
Protestants have no regard for the unanimous agreement of
the ancient church, and the opinion of its Fathers. On the
contrary, we have the highest consideration for them, and
look upon them as most credible witnesses of the faith, in
fixing the authenticity and canonical belief of the scriptural
books, as you may easily convince yourself, from all the
works which Protestant divines have written on the canon.

Odilon. With respect to that, I remember that one of your
most celebrated divines, who has written a great deal on the
canon, has delivered an opinion perfectly conformable to that
of Lessing.

Edward. Sember, perhaps?

Odilon. The very person. In Hirsching's Historical Elements, book xxii. p. 293, he uses these expressions: " It is
a proof of ignorance in history, to confound the Christian religion with the Bible, as if there had been no Christians before
it existed; as if particular persons could not have been good
Christians who knew only one of the gospels, or some Epis-

* Theiss, on the incompatibility, &c. p. 92.

tles only of the whole collection. A complete New Testament could hardly be had before the fourth century, and nevertheless, faithful disciples of Jesus Christ were always found with more or less strength in their principles and sentiments, accordingly as they have detached themselves more or less completely from ancient Judaism." Is not this a new argument of great importance in favor of ecclesiastical authority and tradition, as a source and rule of faith?

Ulric. Since you mention Sember, you must have observed by his writings, that our modern divines invoke the testimonies of the Fathers of the Church, where there is question of the authenticity of the holy writings.

Odilon. Very true; but if the testimonies of the Fathers, in this respect, seem to them of so much weight and so worthy of belief, why do your divines of a sudden refuse them all credit, when those same Fathers unanimously declare doctrines contrary to those of Protestantism? Such was precisely the conduct of the *remonstrant* divine Limborch, who, after having rejected every sort of tradition in his "Christian Theology," invoked it afterwards, as well as the opinion of the Fathers, when it was question of deciding what were the canonical books acknowledged by the Church. I cannot conceive how such contradictions and inconsequences could be overlooked. Moreover, it is not only with respect to the canon and authority of the sacred books, that you regard the tradition of the church; for I have remarked also that provided your doctrine is not concerned, you admit several things, the truth of which rests solely on that tradition; and this, in my opinion, still further increases the inconsequences I have just mentioned.

Ulric. For my part, I do not know that you can reproach me with a single instance of this.

Odilon. Pray, tell me, on what mountain did the transfiguration of Jesus Christ happen?

Ulric. Every body knows it was on mount Thabor.

Odilon. St. Matthew, who relates this history, merely speaks of a *high mountain*, and St. Peter, who alludes to it, calls it the *sacred mount*, without naming it. How then do you know it was Thabor, unless by that tradition, of which the first reformers allowed some ruins to subsist, and which Lessing still respected, but which has been entirely destroyed in our days.

5

Edward. Let us leave this subject, not to wander too far from the principal topic under discussion : it is sufficient to be convinced that on this point we have widely deviated from primitive Protestantism, and that the opinion of Lessing is much more conformable to it.

Odilon. Would you allow me to make a few more observations on this matter?

Edward. You will do us a favor, and the more so, as the great deviation of modern Protestants from the principles of the first reformers will better appear and the alarms of some persons respecting a religious re-union will vanish entirely.

Odilon. Another important point is, the mass; and it is quite incomprehensible to me, how Protestants can have deviated in this respect, so much as they have, from the maxims of the founder of their church. You have seen with what energy Luther declaimed against those who denied the true and real presence of the body and blood of our Lord Jesus Christ in the Eucharist; that he called them *spirits of cabal,* and invoked against them the unanimous, and uninterrupted testimony of the church.

Edward. Yes; and I allow that with respect to the Eucharist, modern Protestants depart greatly from his opinion, since a very great part of them come nearer to the principles of the Calvinists, which are ever to be found in their elementary religious book. But as to the mass, your objections seem to me of no weight, since it was abolished by Luther himself.

Odilon. Hear what he says in his Commentary on the Psalms : " What is the bread and wine sacrificed for Abraham? This sacrifice is in allusion to the priesthood of Jesus Christ, in that time till the last judgment, when he sacrifices, in Christianity, the hidden sacrament of the altar of his sacred body and precious blood." " Jesus Christ," says he, in another place, " in order to prepare a people dear and agreeable to the eyes of God, abrogated the whole law of Moses, and that this might not give rise to schisms and sects, he instituted for his people, one only law, and one only form, that is, *the holy mass;* for though baptism be also an external form, it only takes place once, and is not like the mass, the exercise of *our whole life;* for this reason, there was to be no other external manner of serving God, *than the mass,* and where that is celebrated, there is found the *true* worship of God." (Op. tom. i. p. 96 to 330. a). But as to this, you will find in the celebrated work of Arnauld, convincing proofs that from the time of the Apostles down to Berengarius, no one expressed a contrary opinion, and that not only the Greek church, but also that of Egypt, of Armenia, and all the other schismatical churches agree with that of Rome, in the belief of the real presence of the body and blood of Jesus Christ in the holy Eucharist.*

Edward. I confess I did not expect such a declaration from Luther.

Odilon. Luther did more than this; he frankly declared that to brave the Pope, he would willingly have denied the real presence ; but that the words of the institution of this sacrament were too clear and precise. Thus, speaking of the sacramentarians, he said, in his way, that they were *bedevilled, thoroughdevilled, and overdevilled.*† I allow, however, that the Protestants began but too soon to change their opinion in this respect; but Luther persisted in his, even after masses were abolished.

Edward. Nevertheless, Luther strips the mass of all idea of a sacrifice.

Odilon. I have already observed that it happened but too often to Luther not to agree with himself; his habitual vehemence, the heat of dispute, and the circumstances of the moment, sometimes made him hold a language quite contrary to his former opinions. For example, after having shown himself very favorable to the communion in one kind, he thought proper to say, in his work on the mass, that if a Council ordered the communion to be taken in both kinds, he and his disciples would only take it in *one* or *none*, and that they would curse all those, who, in conformity with this decree of the Council, should communicate in both kinds. You will, therefore, have no difficulty in comprehending how the same Luther, who once considered the mass as *the true Divine worship*, at another time, not only did not look upon it as a sacrifice, but even entirely suppressed it.

Edward. Your observation is but too true.

Odilon. He informs us himself, and with great candor,

* Arnauld, " Perpétuité de la foi de l'Eglise catholique ;" 1701, 6th edit. p. 18—28, et seq.
† Tabaraud, p. 91, on the passages cited. It was these extravagant expressions of Luther, which probably made Bayle say : " Two sectaries who quarrel, hate each other more than the trunk from which they separated." The history of the Reformation offers many instances of it.

why he contradicted himself so often. "I abolished," says he, "the elevation of the host, in order to brave the Pope, and I preserved this elevation such a length of time, merely to brave Carlstadt. If it should be decreed to be impious, we ought to preserve it; but if it were commanded as necessary, we should reject it." I leave these strange expressions to your own judgment.

Edward. All this only shows but too plainly how much passions and circumstances governed his opinions. But, for this reason, would it not be right to take as a rule, those commentaries of his which are of the latest date?

Odilon. Would you believe it? it is precisely these commentaries, these explanations, which speak most in my favor; they evidently show to what point modern Protestants have deviated from the principles of their founder, to whom they are going again now, or now for the first time, to erect a monument.

Edward. What may be the date of these explanations?

Odilon. I will not mention, that in 1533, that is thirteen years before his death, he gave the following declaration, certainly very remarkable: "There remained, in the Catholic Church, under the Pope, holy Baptism, the text of the holy Gospel, the holy pardon of sins, the Holy Sacrament of the altar, which is distributed at Easter, and even during the course of the year; the ordination of pastors, the custom of presenting the crucifix to the dying, prayer, the Lord's prayer, the ten commandments, &c. Where such articles remained, there also remain the Church and some saints; for there are the order and the fruits of Jesus Christ, except the privation of one kind; Jesus Christ, therefore, certainly remained there, near his own, with his Holy Spirit, and preserved in them the Christian faith.*

Edward. This passage would indeed be very conclusive, were it not rather of too old a date.

Odilon. And, therefore, I said, that though strongly in my favor, I would not avail myself of it; and shall confine myself to a declaration by Luther, made in 1546, the very year of his death, against the 31st article of the Louvain divines: "In the most holy sacrament of the altar, *which must also be adored,* is offered, and truly and really taken, the body and blood of our Lord Jesus Christ, both of them by the worthy

* Op. Altenb. tom. vi. p. 97.

and unworthy."[*] Consequently, nothing could be more unfounded than the reproach made to Luther by Calvin, of his having contradicted himself on this point.

Ulric. Calvin, you say? And what could he object?

Odilon. He declared, " that nothing was more absurd than to admit the real presence of Jesus Christ in the bread, and not to adore it." But his maxim, good in itself, was by no means applicable to Luther, who, as you have just seen, formally *exacted this adoration.* Now, Sir, with your hand on your conscience, is this the belief of your *enlightened* divines and ministers at this day?

Edward. I cannot deny but that the number of them, who think like Luther on this point, is at present very small.

Odilon. There are some other important articles, and which will surprise you, perhaps, even still more than this.

Edward. You excite my curiosity exceedingly.

Odilon. You know what you think at present of the invocation and worship of saints.

Ulric. Ah! as to that matter, I flatter myself the first reformers had positively the same opinion as we; and you will allow, Sir, that it is an absurdity to invoke the assistance, protection, and mediation, of one to whom our position is unknown, and must be so, who cannot hear us, and is unable to help us; and this was certainly the opinion of the first reformers.

Odilon. You must allow me to suspend my opinion on this pretended absurdity, till you have clearly informed me what is the state of another life, and especially that of a blessed spirit, removed from this, what it can do, and what part it takes, or does not take, in what happens here below. I suspect this subject would present you with many difficulties and unforeseen contradictions; but what is certain is, that, respecting the invocation, mediation, and assistance of the saints, Luther did not consider the doctrine so absurd as you seem to imagine. What is more, he declared himself in favor of it, in a very clear and precise manner.

Edward. The proof of this would astonish me much.

Odilon. I will give it you, by quoting some very remarkable passages. In his instruction on some articles, attributed

---

* Op. Jenens, tom. viii. p. 381 ; Altenb. tom. viii. p. 498 ; Tabaraud, on the *Re-union,* p. 76.

to him by his adversaries, Luther says: "Some are foolish enough to think that the saints have the means or the power to do a thing, while they are merely mediators, and all is done by God alone; they must, therefore, be invoked and honored, with the view of invoking and honoring God himself."[*]

Edward. This, I confess, is very striking.

Odilon. But what will you think, when you have heard what he says immediately before that passage. "With respect to the saints, I say, and I maintain, with all Christendom, that they must be honored and invoked; for who can deny, that in our days still, God visibly performs miracles, near the precious bodies and tombs of the saints, in the name of those saints?"

Edward. This declaration would be most astonishing, did it not belong, as I conclude, to Luther's first opinions, which he afterwards altered.

Odilon. That is true; he wrote those words in 1519, and, since that period, the 21st article of the Confession of Augsburg rejected the invocation of saints, confining it to *a simple remembrance.* But what can you think of a man, who knows his own mind so little as to give up a maxim, which he declared was that *of all Christendom?*

Ulric. It seems to me in general, that in the beginning, Luther, and the reformers who followed him, were not at all in unison with themselves.

Odilon. You are perfectly right, and you have also, on your side, a modern Protestant writer, who, however, defends Luther with great ardor on another article, not less important, and which drew on him reproaches, as well founded, in my opinion, as the preceding.

Ulric. Whom do you mean?

Odilon. Sartorius, author of the "History of the War of the Peasants." He says, p. 42, "Luther did not know the road he had to go over; and of course frequently ran against obstacles he had never foreseen. He had no idea of one of those plans conceived by a comprehensive mind, and then executed with vigor."

Ulric. Nothing truer was ever said.

Odilon. It is not necessary for me, I imagine, to point out

[*] Op. Jenens, tom. i. fol. 163. a.

the unhappy situation of a religion, the founder of which did
not even know *the road he was to go over;* however, this circumstance helps to explain several important expressions of
Melanchton, which have been too little attended to.

Ulric. What expressions do you mean?

Odilon. In 1532, that is, after the Confession of Augsburg
had been already presented, Melanchton still expressed himself in this manner: "Many things of the greatest importance are not yet decided; we must consider of the means of
explaining the dogmas without any noise; I wish for this,
and that it may take place soon." The following year, these
affairs not being yet settled, he wrote as follows: "Who
occupies himself with the care of tranquillizing timid consciences, and with the discovery of truth? How culpable
are we not to think of healing those souls tormented with
doubts, by explaining our doctrines with purity and simplicity, and without having recourse to sophisms? all this
agitates me dreadfully."* And when, afterwards, in 1537,
he was reproached with his inconstancy, at Schmalkalden,
he acknowledges, "that from the fault of clergymen, many
defectuosities were to be complained of, and that, from the
beginning many things had been done without judgment and
reflection."

Edward. Let us quit this subject, which takes us off from
the principal topic. Did not you speak of other important
points, concerning which modern Protestants have adopted
opinions entirely different from those of old?

Odilon. I did so, and I could very easily produce various
other points of doctrine, on which Luther, at least in the first
years of the Reformation, thought exactly like the Catholics,
and from which his successors have deviated entirely; as,
for example, purgatory, relics, &c.† But I know some articles
much more important still than those.

Ulric. What! Luther was of the opinion of the Catholics
as to purgatory and relics!

Odilon. Most certainly. It is true, in one passage of his
writings, he declares that purgatory *is an invention of the
priests, a downright imposture, a fire-work;* but elsewere he

* Epist. lib. iv. 134. 140. 170.
† Op. Luth. Wittenb. tim. v. fol. 161; tom. vii. fol. 7. On. Jenens;
tom. 1 fol. 86; tom. viii. in conc. deconvers. 5, Pauli; et tom. i. fol.
165, a.,

maintains *that we must firmly believe it, and that we should
help the souls of the deceased by prayer, fasting, and alms:* he
even defends this opinion with great energy. As to relics,
after having said, at one time, that those of dead saints *were
good for nothing, and that a bit of a fellow that was hanged,
was just as good as a bit of* St. Peter *and St. Paul,* he declares
elsewhere, *that even now, God performs miracles near the tombs
and bodies of the saints.* He asserts, moreover, *that every
man, town,* and *people, have their tutelary angel,* and speaks
in this respect just like a good Catholic. It is not necessary
for me to inform you, how widely Protestants differ from all
these opinions at present.

Ulric. These expressions belong to a period when popery
still exerted its ancient influence a little over Luther; but this
influence vanished, as his ideas became enlightened. As to
Calvin, it was quite another thing.

Odilon. That may be. But might not this proceed from the
want of steadiness, which prevailed in Luther's ideas and
sentiments? And are we not authorized to adopt this opinion, from the certainty we have already acquired, that even
a little time before his death, his way of thinking on very
essential articles, was far from being so *enlightened* as you
think?

Edward. It was your intention, if I am not mistaken, to
speak of some other important articles.

Odilon. Yes, of those where modern Protestants have entirely abandoned the opinion of their ancient brethren.

Edward. And what are those points?

Odilon. You know what Christians have thought from the
first origin of the church, of the symbols or profession of the
Christian faith. Luther does not hesitate to notice it, in order
to prove, that under the papacy, as he expresses it, the
Christian church had maintained itself, and that the *credo,*
Lord's prayer, and ten commandments, were still to be found
in it. This reformer even translated into German, the ancient
symbols of the apostles, with those of Nicæa and St. Athanasius, and he very carefully adds, in his preface, that he
had done this, in order to show that he followed the opinion
of the ancient Christian church.* The Confession of Augsburg also appeals expressly to the symbols of the apostles and

* Op. Altenb. tom. vi. fol. 1255.

of Nicæa, and solemnly declares its conformity with them in faith and doctrine,

Edward. I am very anxious to hear what you will oppose to this.

Odilon. You certainly know the German translation of Beaufort's letter to the archbishop of Besançon, which appeared at Bremen and Aurich, in 1808?

Edward. I have heard of it, but as I had read the original itself, I did not trouble myself about the translation.

Odilon. In that writing, Beaufort asserts *that all the churches have the same profession of faith;* on which the translator, who appears to be a divine, without declaring, however, whether his is Lutheran or Calvinist, makes the following observation: " This is false; for Protestantism has long ago renounced the symbols of Nicæa and of St. Athanasius, which, besides that they only present dogmas, and no morality, moreover damn those who think differently, as if the authors of those symbols spoke in the name of God."[*] Well, Sir, what do you say of this public declaration? Is not the source of morality in doctrine? and the latter, instead of being exclusive, as this commentator dares assert, is it not the principal support and sanction of morality? Rousseau, whose testimony surely you will not reject, says in his Emile, tom. ii, p. 202, in a note, " Philosopher! thy morality is beautiful, but pray show me its sanction!" Does the church act unjustly, and does it usurp the divine authority, when, according to the command of Jesus Christ, it excludes from its community those who will not hear it, or when, after the example of St. Paul, it throws an anathema on those who preach another gospel, than that preached to us by the apostles? . . . Tell me, Sir, what do you say to this precise and solemn declaration of a modern Protestant divine?

Edward. It is as shocking as surprising.

Odilon. Others have put in practice the declaration of this writer, and it would be easy for me to put before you several of your catechisms, in which you would seek in vain for any traces of a profession of Christian faith. How much then do modern Protestants differ from the sentiments of their an-

* In 1783, the English, in America, formally abolished the Nicene Creed, and the profession of the Trinity. See the Philos. Catech. tom. ii. p. 33, note). I cannot tell, whether, in this business, the Americans imitated the Germans, or the latter took the former for their model.

cestors! Thus, one of your most esteemed divines, speaking
of those fundamental points, in which there is an agreement
of opinion between you and us, seems to have felt himself
that it would be impossible to assert with truth, that the belief, adopted from the beginning, by the whole Christian
world, is still that of Protestants.

Edward. And how so?

Odilon. Why I think that Dr. Plank, *in his Words of Peace
to the Catholic Church*, p. 24, *second principal article*, might
have united brevity with clearness and precision, by saying
that Catholics and Protestants adopted the same symbol of
faith, whether that of the apostles, or that of Nicæa; for there
could be no question of the symbol of St. Athanasius, since
it is not generally received, and Pithon and Antelme attribute
it to Vincent of Lerins, while Quesnel says Bishop Vigil of
Tapsus was the author of it.

Edward. What way did Plank adopt them?

Odilon. Too well informed of the opinion of modern Protestants respecting these two symbols, his equity and love of
truth would not allow him to say, downright, that the two
churches still received them at present, and equally professed
all the articles contained in them. For this reason, having
recourse to the most vague circumlocutions, he says: " That
the human and supernatural history, the terrestrial and celestial life of the divine founder of Christianity, are an object
of faith, with both parties; and that the facts drawn from the
supernatural and future world, which Jesus Christ himself
has mixed with his doctrine, have the same force of truth for
Protestants as Catholics, " *inasmuch as those facts can be guaran-
teed by the authority of Christ and his apostles.*" It will not
require any great effort, I imagine, to show how little precision there is in all this passage, nor how many subterfuges
such an exposition of faith authorizes, which is nevertheless
to re-unite the two parties; nor do I think it necessary to observe how many essential articles of these two symbols are
here wanting, nor, considering particularly that of Nicæa,
how we could hinder the Arians, semi-Arians, and Macedonians, from declaring, in consequence of this exposition, that
they also share the belief of Catholics.

Edward. This passage really appears to me to be a tacit
avowal of what induced the translator of Beaufort to declare

so openly and abruptly, that for a long time past, Protestan tism had renounced the symbols of the apostles and of Nicæa.

Odilon. Can you have any doubt now of the great distance which separates modern Protestants from their ancestors?

Ulric. I have an observation to make that will destroy at once all your objections; but I should like first to know the other article you meant to speak about. What is it?

Odilon. Nothing less than the Bible itself, and its divine authority.

Edward. The Bible and its divine authority! Never, Sir, never will you convince me, but that, from the origin of Protestantism, it has always been considered as the only rule of faith and morals.

Odilon. As long as you speak of the past, we shall agree entirely; a thousand facts will plead for you; but pray observe, it is of your present way of thinking, in this respect, that we are now treating.

Edward. And why do you insist on this restriction? Is not the Holy Scripture still the basis of all our religious instruction? Is it not from it alone, and without any regard for the church and tradition, that we derive all our proofs, in order to establish the doctrines of faith and the maxims of morality? Is it not on its texts that we preach every Sunday; and, in short, is it not its authority which we constantly invoke on every point?

Odilon. You have here opened, and probably without suspecting it, a vast field for the proofs that I have to give in favor of my opinion. Yes, from the knowledge which I think I possess of the actual state of Protestantism, I assert, that the authority of the Bible is no more considered in it, than that of the symbolic books. It is true, your ministers are restricted, by oath, to take it for the basis of their faith and instructions; but, in a hundred of your learned divines, one could not find ten perhaps who believe and teach conformably to the symbolic books. From all that I have said hitherto on the doctrines professed by the first reformers, and that which is preserved by you, in our days, I think myself fully authorized to exclaim with Lessing—"Formerly, my dear children, formerly."

Ulric. What is the meaning of that?

Odilon. Lessing relates, somewhere, that a traveller landed

in an island, found some children there, born of European
parents who had lately died. Having asked them, whether
they were Christians, the children answered Yes, without any
hesitation, but at the same time were unable to tell a single
thing that they had learnt from their parents. Being questioned more closely, they at last produced the empty binding of a
catechism, saying: "It is all in there." "Formerly, my dear
children, yes, formerly, all was in there," answered the traveller. You can easily make the application of this sort of
apologue without my assistance. But let us leave this; I
should be sorry to hurt your sensibility on this point.

Edward. No, no; you will even oblige me very much by
telling me all that you think on this subject, and as I am
persuaded you would not complain of me, if I should prove
you are mistaken respecting the fact you attribute to us, it is
right I should show the same justice, if you can demonstrate
how far we have deviated from our first opinions. If I recollect right, *those words of peace,* which you quoted, say likewise, that the two parties agree on the Bible, as the source
of religious truth; and, if it be so, how can you then pretend
that modern Protestants have deviated from the principles of
their predecessors?

Odilon. Very good; I will not consider the little precision
with which this source of *knowledge* is mentioned; I will only
say, that it is not even proved that the authors of the Protestant profession of faith were in perfect harmony with the
partisans of the ancient doctrine, as the learned author cited
pretends, since the hard maxims of Luther on several books
of the Holy Scripture have never been adopted by Catholics.
But, supposing that the two parties thought the same, respecting the Bible, it is not less true that that author himself
did not fear to say—"That modern Protestant divines, by their
new ideas on revelation, had deviated very much from those
of their ancestors."

Edward. Yes, but he adds; "They have preserved the
fundamental idea of what is divine in it, merely rejecting
what is immediately divine and supernatural."

Odilon. I can assure you I could cite a multitude of proofs,
perfectly conclusive and calculated to excite the deepest com-
passion, and all drawn from your own authors, to convince you
how little this *fundamental idea of what is divine* is maintained
by modern Protestants, with respect to the Holy Scripture:
but what would this *divine* be, if the *immediate* and *super-*

natural were separated from it? It is certain that the Holy Scripture would then be no otherwise divine, but as when we say the *divine* Homer, the *divine* Plato, or the *divine* discourses of a Masillon, a Mosheim, a Saurin. Most assuredly, these were not the ideas of the first reformers on the Holy Scripture, any more than they are ours, and it is evident that modern Protestants have deviated excessively from the opinion of their fathers on an article of such high importance.

Edward. But you meant likewise to make some objection against the credit which I said the Holy Scripture has among us, at this very time.

Odilon. Yes; you say that the Bible is still the basis of your religious instructions; and you are right, if you only mean that texts are still drawn from the sacred books, in order to clothe religious instruction, with at least a sort of Christian covering. But if you mean that the divine revelation of the Holy Scriptures is still generally believed among you; that its doctrines are considered as the only decisive rule of faith, and consequently have supreme authority, you have just heard the formal avowal of one of your most celebrated divines, respecting your opinion of the supernatural and divine inspiration of the Holy Scripture, as well as its divine authority, and therefore you see how much your modern divines have deviated from the ancient. But as to the maxim still followed of admitting the Bible as the fundamental basis of religious instruction, I can give you many proofs of the contrary. You have surely read two remarkable writings of the late Herder and Wolf, one on the confirmation of the hereditary Prince of Weimar, and the other on that of the Prince of Hesse?

Ulric. Who has not read them? They both obtained the most universal and most unequivocal applause.

Odilon. Very well! and do you pretend that those are religious instructions, founded on the divine inspiration of the Holy Scripture, and on its prerogative of being the sole and supreme rule in matters of religion?

Edward. No; but you know, that on this occasion, De Lue attacked Wolf's publication.

Odilon. I admit that De Lue, a Swiss, who is settled in England, and who happened at that time to be in Germany, raised his voice against this production, while the *whole* Pro-

6

thestantism of Germany kept the most profound silence : you know, silence gives consent.

Edward. In our times, all polemical discussions are avoided as much as possible . . . But I beg you will continue.

Odilon. You said, that with you, proofs are drawn from the Scripture alone, and without any regard to the Church and tradition. As to the latter, I make no objection ; but have you not, in place of that Church and tradition, another principle of knowledge ?*

Edward. What is that ?

Odilon. Human reason! and though one of your most esteemed divines, Jacobi, superintendant of Celle, has exclaimed loudly against this *rational idolatry,* since it is impossible to decide to what man we should give this prerogative of reason, it is not less true, that in our times, this tribunal is become supreme, with you, in matters of religion. The Holy Scripture is obliged to yield to it ; submitted to the new exposition of your *Tellers* and *Pauluses,* it is incessantly handled and turned about, till its decisions are approved by this magisterial reason. Yes, the way in which these new expounders treat the Bible, is so extraordinary that it has hurt you very much in the eyes of foreigners.

Edward. Are you quite sure of this ?

Odilon. Take the trouble to read the excellent work of Trembley, entitled, " The present State of Christianity," and you will find a multitude of proofs in favor of my opinion. You will tell me perhaps that Trembley is from Geneva ; but I shall answer that he is an author thoroughly acquainted with the literature of our country.

Edward. Yes, this disorder is unfortunately pushed too far ; however all Protestants are not partisans of this new exposition.

Odilon. You said, moreover, that there was preaching, every Sunday, from texts of Scripture : be it so : but in what way is this very often done ? To speak the truth, the Bible, in these sermons, acts so poor a part, that passages drawn by chance from the first profane writer at hand, might be substituted for it ; for nothing is heard but maxims of moral philosophy, entirely freed from any positive doctrine. So I remember, one of your celebrated newspapers, a few years ago,

* *Principium cognoscendi.*

proposed reading the gazette in the pulpit, in order to induce the faithful to frequent the churches; and I am obliged to tell you, that even this extravagance found an apologist in one of your most noted divines.

Edward. This is melancholy, to be sure; but fashion changes, and the eloquence of the pulpit is subject to it like other things. Have you not had ridiculous preachers in your Church? Believe me, these new-fangled doctors, who entertain the people with scholastico-philosophico-moral absurdities, will pass away like their predecessors.

Odilon. I hope so from the bottom of my heart: but from the way things are going on, I have every reason to fear the evil will increase from day to day. But what do you say of the new exposition introduced among you, of that system of complaisance or accommodation, which I have reason to think, is become general among your divines; and, by virtue of which, all that one cannot conceive, or all that is opposed to the philosophical system now in vogue, is thrown out at once, and all that can be said respecting Jesus Christ and his apostles, is treated as nothing but a condescension, which they were forced to have for the prejudices and opinions of the Jews?

Ulric. But St. Paul himself favors this sort of accommodation, in his first letter to the Corinthians, where he says, that he became a Jew with the Jews, in order to gain them, and that thus he was become *all to all.*

Odilon. St. Paul never spoke nor acted in this manner, when there was question of the truths of religion, or of the duties it prescribes.

Ulric. Do not the writers of the New Testament themselves apply to Jesus Christ and his actions, passages of the old law, which have evidently no connexion with him?

Odilon. I admit this; but they alone could be authorized to do it. Besides, it seems to me that you confound together two things of a very opposite nature; for there is a great difference, for example, between quoting sayings to the purpose, or words of some prophet, as recollections or comparisons, and declaring that truths published by Jesus Christ and his apostles were mere condescensions in favor of the prejudices of the Jews.

Ulric. Your observation seems just.

Odilon. But, however, supposing this system of accommodation to be admitted, what reliance could be placed on the decisions of Jesus Christ and his apostles? Where are the boundaries to stop at? This notion of condescension for Jewish prejudices were first applied to what is said in the gospel respecting possessed persons. When it was found that this sort of commentary met with success, they did not hesitate to go farther, and at length went so far as to declare, that what is said of the expiatory sacrifice of the death of Jesus Christ, was only meant in general out of complaisance to the ideas of the Jews, and to their doctrine on sacrifices. When our Lord Jesus Christ announced and declared himself to be the Son of God, is this precise declaration to be treated also as an act of complaisance for the ideas which the Jews had formed of the Messiah, whom they considered as the *schechina,* and first emanation of God? By thus advancing progressively towards naturalism and atheism, the dogmas even of the existence of God and of a future life, will come to be classed in the category of the respect that was due to those same Jewish prejudices; and might I not here instance the terrible example of one of your writers, who was not afraid to publish, that at bottom, Jesus Christ was nothing but an atheistical philosopher? Once again, I ask, where are the boundaries to this method of proceeding?

Edward. What you have just said is but too true, and I have too often found myself obliged to conform my ideas on this subject with yours. Nevertheless, I trust, that by proceeding with sounder views in the exposition of Scripture, this evil will be obviated, and the proper boundaries at length be fixed.

Odilon. Your hopes are vain, without the assistance of ecclesiastical authority and tradition. Judge yourself: if Protestants rely solely on the Bible, if each of their doctors has the right and liberty of explaining it in his own way, why should not the Arians and Socinians, for example, enjoy the same privilege? A Protestant philosopher, universally esteemed, was fully aware of the force of this objection.

Edward. Who was he, and what did he say?

Odilon. The English philosopher Locke, who, in his "Reasonable Christianity," p. 68, says, "You Protestants, who find in Scripture transubstantiation, the ubiquity of the body of Jesus Christ, and absolute predestination, you are obliged to believe them; but if I reject those doctrines because I cannot find them in Scripture, you have no right to attack me, to cry me down, or to condemn me as a cursed heretic, devoted to the devil and his satellites. This, to me, is a downright paradox." But you would do well to read the whole of this remarkable passage.

Ulric. Locke was right in calling the conduct of those paradoxical, who accuse every man of heresy that understands Scripture differently from themselves, or who draw maxims from it, different from the doctrines of such or such a church, since none of those churches have a supremacy over the others. But this rule might be good in the time of Locke. The world at present has got very clear of these absurdities or paradoxes. Every one may now interpret Scripture as he likes, and deduce any doctrines he chooses from it.

Odilon. This is undoubtedly a very convenient privilege; but what will be the result? Will not your church become a prey to every error, and to the most audacious opinions? It seems to me, that this is an invincible argument in favor of ecclesiastical authority and tradition; and what is going on among you sufficiently confirms it.

Edward. I should have thought, however—

Odilon. I have not quite done yet. I have read in an elementary biblical work of one of your first divines, that the Bible contains *faults* and *errors.* If this be admitted, how can it be a sure rule of faith and morals? Another of your theological writers has not scrupled, not only to rank the prophets of the Old Testament with the *wise men* of other nations, but has represented them like so many Indian jugglers, who made use of the pretended inspirations of Moses, and the revelations of the prophets, to deceive the people. This writer goes still further, and extends this opinion even to the prophecies of the New Testament; he treats all those who have still any regard for them as enthusiasts and simpletons; calls all the predictions concerning the person of the Messiah nonsense; accuses the prophets of being cunning *deceivers;* and says, in fine, *that the belief in those prophets brought and has preserved incredulity on earth.*[*]

Edward. This, it must be allowed, is horrible. But have you not also had among you, and in great quantity, such enemies of religion?

[*] Detailed explanations of all the predictions concerning the Messiah. Altenburg and Erfurt, 1801.

Odilon. Yes; but what is the situation of the writer I have just mentioned? He is the rector of a country parish, in the grand duchy of Hesse Darmstadt, whose name is S * * * *, as was publicly declared in a review of this shocking work; and, to complete the picture, you must know that the person who reviewed it, says in his turn, that it is a very commendable book, as it contributes to dissipate the shades of ignorance, of blindness, and of folly.*

Edward. You are too just, to form your judgment of the whole body of Protestant divines, from a single antichristian fanatic, who happens to be among them.

Odilon. I admit the justness of your observation in general; but I should like to know if you are really convinced yourself, that the majority of those divines think much more properly about the Bible, than the one I have just mentioned. The manner they adopt with respect to the sacred books, is not favorable to your opinion of them; and another writer, in a work in which the most sacred truths of our religion, baptism, eucharist, and prayer, are rejected, dares to say, *that the inspiration of the Holy Scriptures is a chimera, that the Bible, and above all, the New Testament, that spoke which stops the progress of light, being no longer suitable to our times, are become perfectly useless;* and, take notice particularly, he appeals, on this point, to the testimony of *great Protestant divines.*† It seems to me, that after such extraordinary expressions, so contrary to the doctrine of primitive Protestantism; but in support of which, however, the testimony of your most celebrated divines can be invoked; it seems to me, I say, that Luther and his co-operators, would hardly recognise the religious society which they founded.

Ulric. But do not forget, Sir, that these are unknown writers, who have not even dared to declare their names: I know no court but the Inquisition that admits the testimony of anonymous persons.

Odilon. Well, then, I will produce something now less objectionable in your eyes. You are well acquainted, no doubt, with the *Agathodemon* of the celebrated Wieland, a work which appeared with so much success at Berlin in 1799.

Ulric. It is a master-piece, worthy of a writer of such reputation.

* Allgemeine Deutsche Bibliothek, 69. See pages 228 and 238.
† New Aphorisms at the Tomb of Theology, 1801.

Odilon. Do you speak seriously ?   You cannot then have
observed, that in that work, Jesus Christ our Lord, called by
St. Paul, *the author and consummator of the faith,** is there
styled, *a noble Jewish magician,* who never conceived the
idea, himself, of becoming the founder of a religion, and
whose *institute* only assumed the form of a new religion, by
time.   Well, how do you like these expressions of your
renowned writer?   Jesus Christ, the adorable through eternity, represented as a *wonder-worker,* as a philosophical
magician, like Jamblichus, Porphyrius, and other such disciples of the modern Platonic school !

Edward. A horror! an abomination !

Odilon. And as the moral character of Christ probably
appeared too unimpeachable to the *celebrated* author, and he
could not accuse him, all at once, of being an impostor, he
is satisfied with styling him *an enthusiast, who had not the
direct intention of deceiving, but was so himself, before he became an occasion of error to others, since he really thought he
was what he gave himself out for, the envoy of God, and the
minister of his will ; that he never had any other idea than of
acting for the love and glory of that same God, and that his
success did not even answer his first expectations.   That his
apostles and disciples were men of a thick and confined understanding, who, indeed, did not want for good intentions, but
who were by no means organized so as to comprehend their
master, and to rise to the height on which he was placed,* &c.*
Read the 4th book of that work, from page 335 to 355, in
the 32d volume of Wieland's Works, and then tell me, if it
be possible to attack Christianity in a more cunning manner,
or to shame it with more impudence than this writer has
done.

Edward. I am quite distressed; if Christianity were nothing
but the crutch of the paralytic, and could not stand without
it, woe to him who could have the cruelty to break that stay !

Odilon. Hear the witnesses I still have to produce; they
are neither *unknown* nor *anonymous.*   Lüders, in his Ichno-
graphical History of the principal nations of the old world,
which appeared at Brunswick, in 1800, says, "The Jehovah
of Moses was not at all that kind and amiable being which
Abraham venerated ; he was neither the creator of the world,
nor the father of men.   He was one of those gods the number of which could not be determined ; a god, against whom

---

* Auctorem fidei et consummatorem.

every feeling heart was shut, and from whom every thinking mind withdrew." In another passage, he adds, "The Mosaic religion was a religion without morality, without humanity; it could not conciliate itself with any free and open investigation of the principal concern of man; and, above all, it was a stranger to that sublime and delicious idea, which affords us a fortunate existence beyond the grave." Who would not think that this writer had never opened the Bible? Tell me, are these Protestants, those Protestants who, in their attacks against Catholicity, never cease, notwithstanding, to speak of Scripture? And as Christianity, as we see in the person of Jesus Christ himself and his apostles, rests essentially on the revelation of the old law, can I still give the name of Christians to such blasphemers, even though I take no notice of their shameful and gross ignorance!

Edward. I confess, without reserve, all this shocks me exceedingly. Besides, I suppose this writer speaks hardly any better of Christianity.

Odilon. No doubt, for our Lord Jesus Christ says, "If you do not believe the expressions of Moses, who wrote of me, how will you believe my words?"* "It is not," says this author, "the purity and elevation of the morality, but the multitude of the prodigies in the history of Christ, which filled the heads of the partisans of the new sect; it was this history which drove the martyrs on the scaffold, and these martyrs were almost all very immoral men. Judaism and Christianity were melted down together into a re-union, which has now lasted near two thousand years. From that time, the enjoyment of the most innocent pleasures of life was considered as a most criminal sin against Heaven; and even the very idea of virtue was lost among men." When we read such things, must we not allow that the Protestants of the last edition know Christianity perfectly, as well as its history, and especially know how to appreciate it?

Edward. Your reflections are too true, and I cannot sufficiently express to you how painfully I am affected by expressions of this kind.

Odilon. I can give you some more testimonies of *known* and not *anonymous* authors. One Janisch, in a work printed at Berlin, in 1801, the title of which is, "A general View of the developement of the human race," turns Jehovah into

* Si Mosis litteris, qui de me scripsit, non creditis, quomodo verbis meis credetis?

a *fetiche*, or household god of the family of Abraham, which David, Solomon, and the prophets, afterwards exalted to the dignity of the creator of heaven and earth. Buchholz, in his *Historico-political Dissertation*, entitled "Moses and Jesus," also printed at Berlin, in 1803, makes Jehovah one of the *lares* of the same species; and though Jesus Christ himself frequently appeals to Moses, yet Janisch represnts the latter as a very ordinary impostor, who, on the least doubt being raised against his doctrine and his pretensions, was able, by his *terrorism*, to change falsehood into truth, and that for this purpose, the Levites were the undaunted *satellites* and executioners of that legislator. I pass over other expressions of the same kind, in these writers, and in several others among the Protestants. This is sufficient to prove how much modern Protestants have deviated from their primitive religion, to approach nearer to naturalism.

Ulric. Your proof does not appear to me complete; for, I must observe, that your authors, though *known*, do not belong to the class of theologians; and I am very sure that the latter think very differently. Have you not had also among you, Fanatics, Deists, Naturalists, and Atheists? What would you say if an argument were drawn from this against Catholicity?

Odilon. Your observation is very just; but unfortunately you are not without theologians of the same sort. I admit, that of the three writers I have just mentioned, Dr. Buchholz was only a man of letters, living privately at Berlin, and probably of the class of philosophers; for our masters of arts, of former times, now all call themselves doctors. The other, that is, Lüders, is a professor at Gottingen, and I know he does not belong to the theologians. Consequently, the shocking expressions of these two writers, which shew also such a superficial knowledge of theological studies, cannot in this respect excite much surprise. But Janisch, the same who afterwards drowned himself, has a right to be reckoned among theologians, for he was a preacher at Berlin.

Ulric. Forgive me for saying you go a little too far in drawing this consequence. A man may certainly preach well, and have studied theology enough to mount the pulpit, without deserving, for all that, the title of theologian, in the proper signification of that word.

Odilon. As to that, Sir, I have on my list the names of some persons, whose opinions are hardly better than those of our three authors, and to whom you will certainly not refuse the quality of theologians, in the most strict sense of the word : open the *General Library of Theological Literature*, edited by Schmidt and Schwarzen, for the year 1801.

Ulric. Well!

Odilon. See what these two writers assert. " It is probable that Moses only acquired a better and more particular knowledge of the God of Abraham, through Jethro, his father-in-law, who was an Arabian priest : it is likely, that Mount Horeb, being undoubtedly the seat of the God of the Arabian Abrahamites, Jethro, presiding over the feasts there celebrated, would have conferences with Moses, who there saw, or thought he saw, real prodigies ; and that Aaron, a member of the college of the priests of Horeb, alone repeated these prodigies in Egypt : and it was probably also on this mountain, that one of those priests gave Moses the tables of the law." Can such commentaries have any other tendency than to discredit divine revelation, as well as the legislation of Moses, and represent them as the work of imposture and imbecility ?

Ulric. Some indulgence may be allowed to young professors ; they commonly choose the voice of paradox to make a noise, and to obtain the applause of their pupils.

Odilon. Woe to those who sacrifice truth to such pitiful motives! But, this demon of the *new light*, who attacks the divine mission of Moses, has already begun to blow on the Jews themselves, and has driven some of them to the same extravagances.

Edward. This is the very last thing I should have expected ; for Mendelsohn, for example, though very enlightened, remains notwithstanding a thorough Jew.

Odilon. I learnt lately by the public papers, that a Jew of this kind, all shining with light, called Ben David, had maintained in a letter, that the God of Abraham, the all-powerful El-Schaddai, the supreme God, who revealed himself to Abraham and Moses, the God whom Job and David also knew by those denominations,* was, nothing more or less, than the goddess Isis of the Egyptians.

Edward. What a tissue of absurdities ?

Odilon. Nevertheless, I am convinced that this fine discovery was admired as of great importance, by many of his audience. But let us leave the Jews, I will only speak of

---

* Moses, i, 17 ; i Moses, ii. vi. 3.—Job v. 7. David, Psalm xxviii. 15.

your pretended Christian *enlighteners*, and I will quote one who will shelter me from all the reproaches you have made me on this subject.

Ulric. Who may that be ?

Odilon. One of the supreme pastors of your flock, Mr. Cludius, superintendant at Hildesheim. In his *Primitive View of Christianity*, which appeared in 1808, he expresses himself thus : " In the Christian religion, nothing belongs to it that regards the history of Jesus, nothing of all that he said of his person as Son of God, nothing of what he said of the kingdom of God, and of the destinies of his doctrine and his Church. It was necessary that Jesus should show himself with an elevated and imposing aspect, in order to make a better religion be adopted ; he was obliged to make himself pass for the Messiah, because the Messiah was expected ; and attribute his qualities to himself, and speak of his religion as of the kingdom of God. By this conduct, it only appears, that he allowed some of his actions to be magnified, or even to be exalted into prodigies, nevertheless without ever authorizing any deceit or illusion. Jesus never arrogated to himself any other title than that of an envoy of God, never did he exact divine honors." What do you think of these expressions?

Ulric. They give me the greatest surprise, and most certainly the synods of Holland and Swisserland would not have heard them with indifference ; but the Lutherans, in Germany, have the liberty of thinking what they like.

Odilon. I could make more than one observation on these two articles ; but I shall only ask, whether anti-christianism could be shown in broad day with more evidence ? Thus, Jesus *gave himself out* for what he was not ; thus his miracles were nothing ; and were only considered as such by the people and his disciples, who *exaggerated* his actions. Thus he imposed on them when in St. John, ch. v. 23, he proclaimed himself the Son of God, and required the same worship as that which is given to the Father. With such dispositions, and such expressions of your *enlightened* theologians, it is plain, that it would be merely hypocrisy and delusion to give the title of excellent moralist to our Lord Jesus Christ.

Edward. How do you conceive that ? I do not see how the last point depends on the others.

Odilon. Only judge for yourself; tell me, how can the title of an excellent moralist be given to a liar, an impostor, a perjurer even, who with death before his eyes, being summoned by his judges with the most terrible oath known to the Jews, to declare the truth, betrays it, gives himself out for what he was not, for the Messiah, for the Son of God,* and quits life, charged with such a falsehood, and such a perjury ?

Edward. No, the thing is impossible, inconceivable !

Odilon. And yet, (far from me all idea of blasphemy !)* he would deserve all those epithets if the imputations of the superintendant Cludius had any foundation.

Edward. My surprise is complete, and I know not what to answer to such shocking expressions. Too much ink is spilt, in our days, to be able to read every thing. Subjects are scattered through innumerable pamphlets. You must not therefore be surprised to find me so ignorant, and so stupified with all these errors. We see the daily progress of incredulity ; but we are unable to investigate all the sources of its rise and increase.

Odilon. I said before, that you no longer think like your ancestors, concerning the Holy Scripture, in its quality of sole rule of morals and faith : this assertion induced me to quote some commentaries of several of your most famous writers and divines.

Edward. Which are any thing but edifying.

Odilon. I will even abstain from speaking of the opinion of those first writers on the Bible ; for Janisch dared to say, that *pride, intolerance, and proselytism are the effects of that method of doctrine which is founded on Holy Scripture, and that the artificial magic of the sanctuary had at length disappeared.* I will only fix your attention on the way in which the biblical doctor and superintendent Cludius speaks of the New Testament.

Edward. Well!

Odilon. "According to the Gospel of Matthew, the doctrine is delivered with many foreign supplements and changes ; it cannot consequently serve as a rule of faith. The Gospel of John and his letters are not his, but the work of some Jew. Many blameable and contradictory things are found in them ; the doctrine of them is gnostic. Paul, in his

* Absit blasphemia verbis !

letters, still preserves his Jewish ideas, he continues to believe in the divinity of the Jewish religion, admits a real resurrection of the flesh, and no where points out the doctrine of a providence. The letters of Peter, of James, and that to the Hebrews, are like those of Paul: in general, the writings of the New Testament cannot form a well connected or well attested body of doctrine." What say you to all these fine things?

Edward. I cannot help being shocked at such expressions, especially from the pen of learned Ecclesiastics. But criticising and expounding having made enormous progress among us, it is very natural that a new way of viewing things should be the result; a way, which I confess, will end by doing infinite harm to religion itself.

Odilon. I shall also be silent on that temerity in explaining the miracles of the Old and New Testament by natural causes, and in attributing them to the ingenious contrivances of the operators and the imbecility of the people, though they are invoked by Jesus Christ and his apostles, and to which your ancient theologians themselves appealed to prove the divinity of Christianity; I shall only observe that these detractors begin already to be disgusted with the Scripture itself; that Scripture, which your first reformers prized to that degree, that they would neither hear nor admit any beside it.

Edward. I cannot reconcile this imputation with my preceding observation on the universal custom, which still prevails in our churches and schools, of admitting the Bible as the foundation of all religious instruction; and it is not probable that this custom can ever be abolished.

Odilon. You have just seen the contrary, however, in the expressions borrowed from Cludius and others. But read Augusti's Theological Journal, which is much read and in great circulation; for, to say it, by the bye, the theology of most of your modern doctors is nothing but a newspaper theology. Here is the article which you will find established, No. 9, p. 196 and 207, for the year 1801 : " Would it not be better if we had no written relation concerning Jesus Christ? The real knowledge of them is as uncertain, as that which is derived from oral tradition. It is probable that the pure doctrine of Jesus Christ has *certainly* not been received by the documents of the New Testament, or that at least several mistakes have been intermixed. Already, at the very

7

time these relations were formed, different opinions were in
circulation respecting the plan and doctrine of Jesus Christ,
and his meaning has often been misunderstood by the apostles. Besides, these documents contain many real contradictions; and, in general, a written religious constitution
does not always preserve its unity and agreement with itself:
it never becomes general amongst men, and sooner or later
grows old, and contributes to its own ruin." What do you
think of such a piece of declaration? what can you augur of
this new-fangled Protestantism, all the principles of which
are so diametrically opposite to those of the first reformers,
and to the opinions even of all Protestants down to the
days of error and affliction with which we are desolated?

Edward. If the documents of the Christian religion were
really such as Augusti has represented them, it must be confessed, they would be but little better than those of the Coran;
and I am astonished, that on this supposition, these old
writings are not thrown away as rubbish; there would even
be some consistency in this conduct. Ah! Sir, we have gone
far, very far indeed!

Odilon. We are not without frank and positive declarations in this respect neither. In a writing, published at Jena
in 1799, and entitled, *Explanation of the very important
Opposition fixed by St. Paul between the letter and the Spirit,*
it is said without circumlocution, that a positive religion was
also one of the prejudices of the apostles; that the relapse
of Lutheranism into popery could only be attributed to the
inadvertency that had been committed, in the very beginning
of the Reformation, in not suppressing entirely the document
of the New Testament; that the adoption of it was only a
source of fanaticism, and that we might do perfectly well, as
to religion, if that book were suppressed, and even if the
name of Jesus Christ were totally forgotten."

Edward. Horrible, abominable maxims, contrary to every
thing that bore the name of Christianity, in early times!
Yes, I now clearly see that our modern innovators wish to
reject the Holy Scriptures, and with it all positive religion.

Odilon. However, I think something is still wanting to
make these frank declarations quite complete.

Edward. What is that?

Odilon. To act in consequence of the principle, and to say
roundly, like so many ecclesiastics of both communions,

whom Robespierre and his set had *terrorized*: "Illuminated by the new lights, we *freely* declare, that we have deceived the people; and if we still mention the Bible, and a positive religion, it is only from hypocrisy, and because such an assertion gives us distinction and bread."

Edward. Indeed, you are quite right; but what I can never conceive is, that nobody should have taken notice of such frightful excesses.

Odilon. If you are curious to see how much modern Protestants have deviated, not only from the faith of their fathers, but even from that of all Christians; if you wish to sound to what depth they have fallen into naturalism and downright anti-christianism, read the excellent work of Trembley, which I have already mentioned; and you will find that by following the commentaries of your celebrated divines and expounders on the actions of Jesus Christ, it is impossible to help considering him as a senseless enthusiast or a juggler, and his disciples as the stupidest of men, or as the most shameless impostors.

Edward. This however would be the height of abomination! I agree that this new method of expounding may give occasion to errros and false views; but are you very sure that Trembley has not overcharged the colors, and exaggerated the humble picture you have just drawn?

Odilon. Judge for yourself. What qualifications can one give to Jesus Christ and his disciples, when one believes oneself, or tries to make others believe, what I am now going to tell you, from the works of one of your most celebrated divines? "When the shepherds, in the fields of Bethlehem, were illuminated by the glory of the Lord, they saw nothing in reality but the light of a lantern which was brought before them; when Jesus Christ walked on the waves of the sea, he was merely going along the shore; and if he laid the storm, it was only by managing the rudder with an able hand; when the miraculous feeding of several thousand persons is spoken of, it must always be understood that each one ate his own bread which he had kept in his pocket. The dead, who, it is said, were raised by him, were only in a lethargy; and he himself was not really dead, when the same prodigy was applied to himself. When he was supposed to have ascended into heaven, he slipped away from his disciples in a fog; and when Paul saw himself surrounded by a heavenly light, in the midst of which Christ revealed himself to him, it was only the lightning that had fallen near him." &c. After such absurdities, you will no longer be surprised at the unfavorable judgment which Grégoire passes on modern Protestantism.

Edward. What is this judgment?

Odilon. In the preliminary discourse to his History of Religious Sects, p. 56, he expresses himself as follows: "Among the Protestants and Calvinists of Germany, the neologists, or partizans of the new exposition, have hardly preserved any part of the belief of the first reformers. The Bible, in their eyes, is only an ordinary book of morality, from which they put away the prophecies and miracles." Grégoire, after having quoted several examples of his assertions, says in another place as follows: "The principles of Protestantism, which leave every one the faculty of interpreting the Bible, suppose also, that of believing what one likes, and of conforming one's conduct to one's belief." From all this he draws the same consequence, as I have already mentioned: "If Luther and Calvin were to return on earth, they would be very much surprised not to be of the religion of those who have borrowed their denomination from them." Hist. of Sects, tom. i. p. 316, 317. Ibid. tom. ii. p. 181.

Edward. What a melancholy truth!

Odilon. I am only surprised at one thing.

Edward. What is that?

Odilon. At the infinite trouble which your doctors still take, to torture violently, and contrary to all the rules of sound criticism, those passages of Scripture which they do not comprehend; in despising the authority of all Christian antiquity, to twist in their way those same passages which treat of the life and miracles of Jesus Christ and his apostles, to throw, in one word, all that is supernatural, into the regions of fable, for which they have even invented the term of *Christian mythology.*

Edward. And what would you have them do?

Odilon. Why they might have followed the example of Mr. Mauvillon, of Brunswick, who, being questioned by his friend, Mr. Knoblauch, respecting the natural explanation that might be given of the miracles of the New Testament, and particularly that of feeding the five thousand persons, Mr. Mauvillon answered: "You would settle all this much more easily, by saying, that nobody knows any thing of the fellows who tell such histories; that they are downright liars, and that all that is alleged in favor of their veracity, is a mere fable." Read, read the writings of your Ammons, Eckermanns, Gablers, Flügges, Pauluses, and so many others, who by the most extravagant commentaries on the Scripture, try to rob us Christians of our faith of eighteen centuries, and in particular, of that salutary belief of the ascension of Jesus Christ.

I have, therefore, read lately with great pleasure and consolation, the work of a young divine of Strasburg, called Himly, in which he defends, with great erudition, this true doctrine, against the *great lights of the new exposition.*

Edward. Ah! stop, sir, stop! The absurdity of these new interpretations of the Scripture can never be surpassed; and as it is impossible to think that men who have a grain of judgment left, that men whose profession it is to enlighten the world, are not sensible of such absurdity and extravagance, I can only find the true clue of their *conduct* in a satanic hatred against Christianity; though on the other hand, I cannot conceive this hatred, as these new divines pretend they are bringing back Christianity to its primitive purity.

Odilon. I will not say what I think. It is true, however, that so much latitude has been given of late to this pretension, that not only the *essential* dogmas are gone with their *amendments,* but even morality itself has been shaken in its foundations, and doors and windows have been opened to every vice.

Edward. Pardon me, for contradicting your opinion in this respect; for it is morality and not doctrine, that our divines have chiefly in view; and the preachers of that school confine themselves to mere moral dissertations, without troubling themselves with the dogmatical sense and spirit of their text. How, therefore, could they deliver doctrines subversive of morality? But what are these *essential dogmas* you mentioned just now?

Odilon. Read the " Review of the ancient and new dogmas of the christian doctrines," published by the superintendant Cannabich, in 1799; you will there find the belief of the Most Holy Trinity, to which all Christendom so strongly adheres, effaced from the number of our dogmas; and the author even points out the way in which this truth must be destroyed amongst Christians. .

7*

Edward. I cannot believe it !

Odilon. That clergyman, one of the chiefs of your Church, says : " The dogma of the Trinity may be removed, without scruple, from religious instruction, as being a new doctrine, without foundation, and contrary to reason; but it must be done with great circumspection, that weak Christians may not take scandal at it, or a pretext to reject all religion. We should, therefore, contrive to let this doctrine fall insensibly into that oblivion, by passing it over in silence, and changing, softening, improving, and finally by suppressing, by little and little, all the old formulas that favor it; and masters, on their side, should be ordered no longer to teach any thing positive on this subject, and to set no value on a doctrine which is purely speculative."

Edward. An excellent specific for the triumph of incredulity !

Odilon. You may easily conceive what will become of the Divinity of Jesus Christ, with all the fine subtilties of this doctor. But Mr. Cannabich is not the only partizan of them, and I shall now give you a profession of anti-christianism, so precise and solemn, that you will certainly have no reason to reproach its ambiguity. The " General Literary Gazette," in its supplementary sheet, No. 41, April 1811, giving an account of a sermon for Good Friday, says : " Moreover, the whole prayer is directed towards Jesus Christ, who said however : Thou shalt adore the Lord thy God and serve him alone. St. Matth. iv. 10. And thus we no where find that the apostles ever addressed their prayers to Jesus Christ; and it is God whom they implore on all occasions." So, this critic despoils Jesus Christ of his divinity contrary to the formal passages of the Holy Scripture which establish it: thus, it follows, according to him, that the adoration offered to Jesus Christ must be treated as idolatry, and be suppressed as soon as possible. According to the same rule, also, we cannot help blaming the behavior of St. Stephen, when he exclaimed : *Lord Jesus, receive my soul!* or St. John, when he said: *So be it, yes, come to me, Lord Jesus!* and St. Paul, in fine, when he *prayed three times to the Lord,* by which Jesus Christ alone can be understood, 2 Corinth. xii. 8. I ask you now, could anti-christianism be professed in a more public and more solemn manner?

Edward. What distressing doctrine !

Odilon. I have still a few words to say on Mr. Canna-bich, who treats another dogma with still less regard than that of the Trinity.

Edward. What, is he not satisfied with the denial of that fundamental truth!

Odilon. No; he also attacks original sin. "The Bible," says this new father of the Church, "does not speak of any original sin, nor of any corruption of human nature, by the sin of Adam. I know of no evil more melancholy and more dangerous, than this belief in original sin. It is consequently high time to efface and banish, at once for all, from our books of religious instruction, a doctrine so destitute of all foundation, and so dangerous, and which has been too long preserved for the honor of the human race."

Edward. It is impossible to promulgate doctrines more shocking and more opposite to the faith of all Christians; I really cannot understand such conduct.

Odilon. I understand it very clearly; for it is with respect to religious doctrine, in particular, that we may say the first step is all. Besides, I could mention another fundamental dogma of Christianity, *on the testimony of one of your most celebrated divines,* which Protestants appear to have abandoned, contrary to the doctrine of the first reformers, and of all Christians.

Edward. What dogma is that?

Odilon. That which is so precious to us all, the dogma of Christ, the Saviour of men by his death, the expiation of sin.

Ulric. The passages of Scripture, by which this dogma has been hitherto supported, being susceptible of diverse interpretations, it is quite natural there should be different opinions upon it.

Edward. Who is the celebrated divine whose testimony you say you would invoke!

Odilon. The same Doctor Plank, whom I have mentioned already. In the work we have examined, he mentions several articles, in which, according to him, Protestants and Catholics agree. I, therefore, should have expected to find this fundamental dogma, on which the ancient Protestants certainly thought like us. But what was my astonishment, to find, as supererogatory, this strange maxim: "Man having become a sinner, and guilty, and the object of the divine displeasure, can only become again susceptible of happiness and beatitude, by becoming a good man."

Edward. I believe, that with respect to the principles of this maxim, it is not only received by Catholics, and *us*, but also by the Jews, and rational Pagans.

Odilon. Yes; but observe that Plank, after having rashly allowed himself, as he went on, to accuse Catholics *of having so much observed this truth, that to many eyes it is become invisible,* is only accused here, in his turn, for the affectation with which he restrains the reparation required of man, to his will, to his faculties *alone,* contrary to this expression of St. Paul: "He gratifies us in his beloved Son, in whom we have redemption, *through his blood,* and the remission of sins."* Do not forget, moreover, that by this restriction, Plank contradicts a multitude of other passages, equally forcible, together with the formal doctrine of the first reformers, so scrupulous in this respect, that they gave every thing to *faith,* and nothing to *works.* In your new dogmatical treatises, you must, therefore, efface all that treats of the merits of our Saviour, and all that speaks of our faith in this merit. On this subject, I will quote you another very striking explanation, from a public paper, and the more extraordinary, as it is one of those which you honor with the title of the "Authentic Interpreter."

Ulric. Is it the General German Library ?

Odilon. No, it is the "General Literary Gazette of Jena." This periodical paper contained a review, in December, 1810, of a work entitled, "Religious Instruction for ordinary Christians," by Mr. Seyfarth, superintendant at Lieben-Werda. This author having said, that in our quality of Christians, we should believe, on the fact of Divinity, only what the scripture clearly tells us; the critic exclaims: '*What, and are we also to appeal to the Old Testament ?*" Now, what do you think of such an exclamation? Do you imagine, that the writer of this periodical paper, believes in the divine authority of the Old Testament, and that he considers it as a source of religious instruction ?

Edward. Your observation is but too true, and it fully confirms what you have previously said of the maxims of certain writers on the sacred books of the Old Testament.

Odilon. This is not all. Seyfarth having said, "That Jesus Christ had acquired for us, by his merits, and had ren dered possible the remission of the pains incurred by our sins," the critic observes, "That Scripture does not clearly say it, and that reason cannot approve such doctrine." Not content with this assertion, the periodical writer, entering abruptly on another question, ventures to say : "It is the same with the dogma of the divinity of Jesus Christ, and several other doctrines which Mr. Seyfarth has preserved and defended in his work. It is not probable, that a man so enlightened, of such a strong mind, could believe them, and it is likely, that on this occasion, he was led by considerations, that are owing to certain connexions with the church." Now tell me, Sir, if it be possible to profess anti-christianism, more formally, even though we pass over the downright notorious falsehood of the silence of Scripture, on the remission of our sins, by the merit of the sufferings and death of Jesus Christ our Lord?

Edward. I confess that such an assertion is shocking in the highest degree.

Odilon. The periodical writer also uses the following expressions, while speaking of the fundamental truths of Christianity, that he has just proscribed in such a horrible manner: "Far from recommending religion, they hinder it from becoming a general religion; they raise a new barrier between the Christians, Jews, and Pagans, which however the founder of our religion had overturned, according to the words of the apostle, 2 Ephes." Thus Christianity has no claim to the qualities of an universal religion, while it preaches to the whole world the sublime doctrine of the pardon granted by the merit of Christ, to the whole human race, lost and reprobate !

Edward. How could this writer overlook such a palpable absurdity ?

Odilon. You may be convinced, moreover, of the inextricable plan, or rather, of the entire bad faith of these biblical commentators, if you read yourself the passages 11, 14, 15, Ephes. in which the Apostle speaks clearly of the re-union of the Jews and Pagans, without any distinction or privilege, into one body, of which Jesus Christ is the head. But, it is evident, that these modern *enlighteners* among the Protestants only falsify religion in this manner, in order to effect an amalgamation of Christianity with Judaism and Paganism.

Ulric. Such an attempt seems to me the height of folly, as it supposes an impossibility, that is, that each religion will give up what constitutes it essentially and fundamentally. I see nothing but the word of Mahomet, that could clear the ground in this way, and fit it for the implantation of this new Islamism.

Odilon. Nobody could reason more justly, and what follows will prove it still better. Seyfarth having said in his work, " That the Father, the Son, and the Holy Ghost are only one Divine Being;" the critic first exclaims : *Credat Judæus Apella!* and adds, on the christian dogma of the Trinity : " That the passage of St. John, iv, 7, the falsity of which had long ago been asserted, is the only one favorable to it; that this doctrine of the Trinity affords no material for any *thought,* and that in general it could not be fashioned into any reasonable idea," &c. Where shall we find expressions to expose such audacious attacks on all that Christendom venerates and respects for the space of eighteen centuries !

Edward. What horrible extravagance !

Odilon. One should not be astonished if some obscure antichristian fanatic had published it in one of those papers which are born and die the same day; for such audacious excesses are but too frequent. But here, they are allowed in a production, which has created itself into a supreme literary tribunal, and *authentic interpreter;*[*] in a production generally read, as it deserves to be on many accounts; in a country, the sovereigns of which are considered as martyrs of the evangelical doctrine, their attachment to Protestantism having made them lose their electoral dignity. What then must be your religious situation, after so public a profession of antichristianism, and what is become of the faith of your fathers ?

Edward. Let us hope that prudent reflections will at length put a stop to such disorders.

Odilon. I cannot share this hope, and it appears to me very difficult to stop, after having launched out in this manner. One of your own divines thinks the same, and expresses himself very judiciously when he says: "One cannot stop in evil, any more than in good; as soon as one object is attained, the eye perceives another placed higher or lower; but, as in ascending towards one, we think we are nearer heaven, so he who descends towards the other, will also find hell open before him." (Thiess. a. a. o. p. 46, note 25). And I have actually perceived, that those same divines, among you, who have placed the essence of religion so entirely in morality, as to forget, or eliminate by little and little

* Interpres authenticus.

all the fundamental truths of faith, now attack morality itself, and attempt to shake it in every way.

Ulric. I will admit that, with respect to these dogmatic truths, a false exposition may lead, and really has led, to a multitude of errors; but far from conceiving any bad intentions with respect to morality, I can assure you, on the contrary, that nothing with us is more esteemed and respected.

Odilon. When the divinity of the Scripture, and the necessity of a belief in its truths, are denied, it is impossible but that the morality deduced from it must also suffer. What esteem can be had for the maxims of a religion, the founder of which, according to the notions of modern Protestants, was nothing but a magician and an enthusiast, giving himself a name and qualities that he did not possess, suffering his actions to be transformed into miracles, and consequently, adding falsehood to fanaticism? What regard could be had for the maxims of a religion preached by men full of prejudices, who did not even understand their Master, and whose writings known under their names are falsely attributed to them? Read the 1st and 3d No. of the second part of the Magazine of the late Henke of Helmstadt, and the 2d No. of the first part of his Eusebia, and you will there find, "that monogamy, and the prohibition of extra-matrimonial connexions, must be reckoned among the remains of monachism, and that this doctrine rests on a blind faith." Is it possible to give greater facility to every species of disorder; and that one of your journalist theologians, Scherer, has not hesitated to declare in the 1st No. p. 6, of the preface to his "Biblical Investigator." "That religion had nothing at all to do with duties." What dreadful consequences may be drawn from such a maxim?

Ulric. It is possible that this passage may not have dropped from the pen of Henke himself, but from that of some fanatical anonymous *enligthteners.*

Odilon. Even this supposition would still leave Henke the merit of the publication. But hear what the superintendant Cannabrich says, in his *Criticism of Practical Christian Doctrine,* p. 185: "A moderate sensual enjoyment of love, out of marriage, is no more immoral than in marriage." He adds, "it is to be avoided merely because it shocks the customs of persons with whom we live, and that the excesses committed in it are often punished by the loss of reputation and health." Does this morality appear sufficiently indulgent?

Ulric. I blush for the authors of it.

Odilon. After this fine outset of your divines, who had however pushed their zeal for morality, so far as entirely to forget doctrine, we may suppose they will not be long before they plead for the *morality* of a more abominable vice still; that vice, which Horace's father allowed his son, provided he used it moderately: for you have just seen, that the divine law is counted for nothing; and the superintendant cannot consider the Bible as a rule of morals, or he must entirely have forgot the following passages of St. Paul. " Let not fornication nor any other uncleanness be even named among you!"—"God will judge fornicators and adulterers."*

Ulric. I must allow you to be right on this point; for nothing can be objected against these passages, nor all those that condemn immodesty.

Odilon. I am only astonished at one thing, which I should never have expected from the Protestants, though it had been often foretold by Catholics.

Ulric. What do you mean?

Odilon. That nobody had remarked that your dogmatic and moral maxims would have the same fate as many other important objects among you.

Ulric. Explain yourself more clearly.

Odilon. Originally your *enlighteners* preached toleration with so much zeal and ardor, that it soon became the general war-cry, without any body suspecting what they meant by it. But when they had once obtained this toleration for *themselves*, they became very intolerant to others, decrying and persecuting all those whom they had reduced to silence by stunning them with this war-cry.

Ulric. But what is the meaning and object of all this?

Odilon. Your innovators at first affected to speak only of morality; representing it as the sole and supreme object of all religion, they extolled Jesus Christ as the most perfect of all moralists, and placed this morality so far above doctrine, that all the maxims of the latter, that were not a source of it, might be considered as null, as I have shown you above. They kept this line till they had attained their end, which, however, might and ought to have been easily guessed, because

* Fornicatio et omnis immunditia nec nominetur in vobis. Ephes. v, 3. Fornicatores et adulteros judicabit Deus. Heb. xiii, 4.

morality flows from doctrine, and receives all its sanction from it.

Ulric. But what could their project be?

Odilon. The chief thing was to destroy every thing belonging to dogma and to a positive doctrine. This grand step, once made, morality was left insulated, deprived of the divine sanction, the source of all truth, of all purity, and then every one was at liberty to act as he pleased. Delivered from the obligation of invoking the divine authority in support of morality, it could then be submitted to all the uncertainty of private interpretation, and the example of Cannaprich might be allowed, who pretends that concubinage is not immoral, provided it be carried on *without risking one's reputation and health.*

Ulric. This is unfortunately too true!

Odilon. I cannot tell you how much I am grieved in this respect. For, after having read several of those fine church hymns, composed by your Gerhards, your Gellerts, and so many others, those hymns which have been inserted in several of our modern books of piety, as precious remains of true Catholicity, I cannot help thinking of what the illustrious Bacon said of Jesuits: "Being such would you were ours!"[*]

Edward. My affliction is not less than yours, and is the more founded, as they are ecclesiastics, bound by their profession to preserve faith and morals, who are guilty of such excesses.

Odilon. St. Paul says: "It is time that the judgment of the house of the Lord should begin."[*] Your first reformers, carried away by the violence of their passions, had the injustice to give the Pope the title of antichrist; but, after all I have laid before you, tell me frankly, where is now that antichrist, and who deserves that title at present. But, after all, all this does not surprise me in the least, and I am persuaded the evil would be much greater still, if it were possible it could be.

Edward. Why do you entertain this opinion?

Odilon. If, according to the almost general opinion at present among Protestants, human reason has the right to bring before its tribunal the *truths* and *facts* contained in Holy

[*] Talis cum sis, utinam noster esses!
[*] Tempus est, ut incipiat judicium à domo Dei.

Scripture, to interpret, receive, or reject them as it likes, why should not this same reason enjoy the privilege of prescribing its *maxims*, when they are not conformable to her views, or are beyond the reach of her intelligence? Again, notwithstanding the ancient doctrine of Protestants, who considered Scripture as the sole rule of faith and of moral religious conduct, why should not reason have the right to reject wholly, or in part, those books of the Bible, which she disapproves, though indeed this reason be acknowledged incompetent to know and determine every thing, even in the sphere of merely physical and natural objects? One of your old divines, one of those who are no longer read but disdained, has expressed himself with great judgment on this subject.

Edward. Who is that?

Odilon. Weidner. In his work, entitled, *Schediasma de scientiâ falso si? nominatâ,* he says, "Philosophy is dangerous, especially for a Christian, when it begins to inspire pride, and pretends to measure the articles of faith by the rule of philosophical motives. Would you know how deceitful these are, and how frail is their foundation? Examine the multiplicity of sects that have resulted from them, and see in particular how their principles clash and destroy each other." In fact, what other result could be produced by such a way of proceeding, but the decline and total ruin of religion? On this account, since I have ascertained the truth of all I have now laid before you, I have felt myself obliged to admit the truth of an observation, which you know undoubtedly, that was made by some Protestants themselves to the Abbé Grégoire.

Edward. No, I do not know it.

Odilon. A Protestant of the academy of Berlin, told him, that with Protestantism one is half way towards incredulity; and Strapfer accuses the new exposition of modern divines as being good for nothing but to trick the people out of their religion.*

Edward. It is impossible to deny the great decline of religion among us, and the rapid progress of naturalism; but, be assured, Sir, we still reckon many persons who have preserved all the purity of sound and good doctrine.

Odilon. Nobody, certainly, will dispute it. When the Jews became idolators, God vouchsafed to preserve some who did

* Grégoire Hist. des Sectes relig. tom. ii, p. 242.

not bend the knee before Baal. And, on this account, one of your most distinguished clergymen† has made a proposition, if I am not mistaken, to separate those who are still Christians among you, from those who have embraced naturalism. But I fear, if the project were realized, their number would be very small, if we may judge at least by the emptiness of your churches. However, this is not our present subject; my object was to make you sensible of the great distance which separates you from primitive Protestants; and after all I have said on the prevailing opinion among you, respecting faith and morals, I have every reason to think you will not find Trembley's opinion in this respect too severe.

Edward. What, Trembley, who is himself a Protestant!

Odilon. Yes. "The new reformers (and among them are some of your principal divines)," says that writer, "hold an opinion which contradicts that of all Christians. They have not the same religion as they, and consequently cannot be offended if other Christians separate from them. A Musulman, who admits the miracles of Jesus Christ, is, in this respect, nearer the Christians than those innovators. Did not Luther and his collaborators believe that Jesus Christ performed miracles? and do not these gentlemen deny them? Did not Luther consider this belief as essential to Christianity? These, then, are not Christians, according to Luther. Their religion, therefore, is not that, which from the time of the apostles down to us, has been generally admitted and received."[*] . . . .

Ulric. All that you have hitherto advanced is perfectly true; but you are much deceived in thinking that by proceeding in this manner we have so much deviated from the *principles* of the first reformers: on the contrary, we conform to them with great exactness.

Odilon. This is what I do not understand.

Ulric. Merely with respect to the rejection of some books of Scripture, that you have just mentioned, I will observe one thing which you undoubtedly know; which is, that Luther himself rejected the Epistle of St. James, representing it as *totally devoid of the evangelical style, and consequently not the production of that apostle. He even called it an Epistle of straw.*

[*] Religion oppressed; 1801, by the Superintendant-general of Collin.

† Trembley, Present State of Christianity, p. 13, 17, 19.

Odilon. I know this too well! I know that he also called the book of Job *a collection of fables;* and said of Ecclesiastes, *that he neither had boots nor spurs, and rode in slippers;* he accuses the Epistle to the Hebrews of containing *errors contrary to all the Epistles of St. Paul;* in short, he asserts that it is *impossible to find in it an apostolical or divine spirit.*

Ulric. You see then that Luther himself rejected some books of Scripture. Why should not modern Protestants, therefore, still more enlightened, have also the right to proscribe others? In general, our ideas on Protestantism are much more luminous at present. We admit many things now which the first reformers would never have admitted, and *vice versâ,* as you may judge by what you have said before concerning the doctrines of divine inspiration and satisfaction; nevertheless, far from ceasing to be a Protestant by this method, it seems to me one becomes more so.

Odilon. I do not see how this is possible; it is only by the profession of faith of a church or of a religious society that it can be known. If it departs from it, it ceases to be the thing of which it bears the name.

Ulric. We think very differently in this respect. The Confession of Augsburg could never be considered as obligatory for all times; in the *Formulary of Concordances,* it is called the *symbol of its time,** and Melanchton himself writes: "Articles of faith must be often changed, and be calculated for times and circumstances."† You will allow that this overturns at once what you have advanced: what do you think of it?

Odilon. I cannot recover my surprise. I might first observe, that it was by this confession, delivered at Augsburg, that the Protestants obtained their rights and the freedom of their religion in Germany; but I will merely state, that I was far from having such an idea of the instability and uncertainty of your position.

Ulric. What do you mean by that?

Odilon. Why, that after what you have said, there is nothing to hinder you from rejecting *to-morrow* the Divinity of Jesus Christ and of the Holy Ghost, and the expiatory death of Christ, and the Bible altogether, which you believe in *to-day,* and admitting in their place the Koran, without ceasing

* Sui temporis symbolum.
† Vide Epistolas & Peucero editas.

at the same to be a good Protestant; for, according to the expression of Melanchton, *articles of faith must be often changed, and be calculated for times and circumstances.*

Ulric. Allow me to explain how this should be understood. Protestantism is, in fact, if I may be allowed the expression, a species of perfectibilism.

Odilon. As your most *enlightened* writers have the kindness to represent us Catholics, as endowed with rather a dull understanding in matters of religion, and as my head, in addition, is loaded with a monk's hood, I must beg a little indulgence, and request you to explain more clearly what you understand by this *perfectibilism.*

Ulric. It means, that it is the essence of Protestantism to be a religion susceptible of continual amelioration, and of constantly becoming more enlightened and more perfect.

Odilon. In this case the first Protestants were much to be pitied, and the last will be not less so.

Ulric. Why?

Odilon. It seems to me that the first of all must have been very confined in their knowledge, and wavering in their faith, and often exposed to the misfortune of admitting what was false; as to the latter, if, by always mending and perfecting, they go beyond the mark, as is possible, and as, no doubt, has already happened, they must have a very bad chance. But supposing what you pretend, I do not really understand how you can have tormented yourselves for three centuries with symbolic books, with confessions of faith, and that you have even confined yourselves to only one of the latter kind. "If variations," says Grégoire, "are an integral part of Protestantism, it was wrong to draw up formulas, symbolic acts, confessions," &c. In fact, what you swear to observe to-day, will have no longer any force to-morrow.

Ulric. It is in this way notwithstanding that our most enlightened writers understand Protestantism.

Odilon. I know it, and that Mr. Blessing, of Strasbourg, in particular, has attempted, in his *Notes on Reinhard,* to justify in this way the changes that have taken place in the Protestant doctrine, changes against which your reformers themselves opposed their symbols, by which they swore. This writer pretends, that a body of doctrine which forbade such changes would make no *progress* whatever; and it is this which induced Grégoire to make the observation I have just quoted.

Ulric. This continual improvement is even conformable to the precept of St. Paul, who says, " that we should constantly become more perfect, and increase in knowledge."

Odilon. Yes, St. Paul says, " Increase in the knowledge of God."* And St. Peter says, " Increase in the knowledge of our Lord and Saviour Jesus Christ."† I need not bring proofs to convince you, that this increase in the knowledge of God by no means supposes a right to *change* religion itself, and to reject its truths at pleasure; but it merely enjoins us to learn better, and more perfectly, every day, the truths revealed by God, which are as unchangeable as God himself.

Ulric. I flatter myself that such were the views of our modern reformers.

Odilon. Judge for yourself of the improved knowledge which your innovators have given to Protestants, how they have made them *increase in the learning and knowledge of God*, now that they have first shaken and afterwards destroyed their faith in divine revelation and in Jesus Christ, by denying what he is, and what he has done for us. Judge, in short, with what success they have perfected religion, by substituting a cold and desponding naturalism to the eternal and sublime word of God. I have had occasion too often to give you proofs of these cruel attempts; and Grégoire, in his History of Sects, part ii, p. 216, has likewise amply proved, that these changes, produced in Protestantism by modern divines, have only ended in subverting all Christianity, by annihilating the fundamental doctrines on which it rests.

Edward. This is unfortunately but too true, and is a very melancholy omen for religion.

Odilon. I remember to have read, on this subject, a very honest avowal of Mr. Müller, a Protestant writer, and professor at Schaffhousen: " Even divines themselves," says he, "endeavor to drown in a vain deism the fundamental principles of pure Christianity. All of them together, knowingly, or without suspecting it, act in the same way, and hold the following language: *Let us rend and throw away those ties which bound our ignorant and unenlightened ancestors to their faith and duty.* They give the name of theological pre-

---

* Crescentes in scientiâ Dei.
† Crescite in cognitione Domini nostri et Salvatoris Jesu Christi.

judices to the fundamental doctrines themselves. By hacking perpetually at the edifice of religion, they have brought it at last to a miserable hut, hardly capable of preserving us from the storm. In the midst of these uncertain waverings, between doubt, hypothesis, and some glimpses of certitude, among persons who turn religion into a mere literary job, when one can seldom say, I know in what and what I believe, in this vague state; when, in short, presumed certitude is itself only an opinion, the period is arrived of cool indifference, both in the master and the disciple, in the sovereign and the subject, while attempts are still continued to bring it below the point of congelation."

Edward. Melancholy and true description!

Odilon. There is another just as afflicting and still more circumstantial, by the learned Schrockh, of Wittenberg. In his Ecclesiastical History since the Reformation, part viii, p. 408, where he examines the latter times down to 1806, and we know, that since that time the evil has only grown worse, he says: "In the midst of its innumerable researches on faith, the Protestant church has lost its religious feeling, and has never been able, as yet, to find even a suitable and sufficient resource in its external signs. Its ecclesiastical teachers have lost the esteem and influence which they enjoyed, in a remarkable degree, and without any prospect of recovering them. The freedom of examination, and that of accumulating new opinions, and new hypotheses, have increased long since to a degree, which is very embarrassing to that church. In the nomination to professorships, that wise circumspection and severity of choice, which such an important matter requires, are far from being every where observed; and most of the heads only attempt to correct or improve what is immediately under their hands. A great mischief, especially, has resulted to the good cause, from that multitude of reformers without vocation, who, by accumulating dictatorial opinions, insults, sarcasms, and the grossest expressions, attempt to weigh down their adversaries under the yoke of their opinions and discoveries." What say you to this picture? What can be the duration of a religious society thus constituted, and what means can be efficacious enough to restore and maintain it? See, where this boasted perfectibilism, which is the essence of Protestantism, has conducted you!

Ulric. But the expressions of Melanchton, quoted above, prove, however, that perfectibilism, or the continual improvement of religion, is the spirit of Protestantism.

Odilon. One of your most judicious divines, Mr. Staudlin, thinks very differently in this respect, when he says, from page 190 to 221, of the third part of his Supplements to religion and morality : " The truths of religion can never make any progress : they cannot be subject to any change, nor attain the age of maturity, for they never had either childhood or youth. Always immutable, they had at first and entirely all the perfection suitable to them. He who speaks of the perfectibility of the dogmas of a revealed religion, absolutely mistakes the character of revelation."

Ulric. Yes, but Melancthon!

Odilon. Staudlin has experience in his favor. Time has proved that perfectibilism saps and ruins the foundations of your religion.

Edward. All this is very alarming, and very ominous for the future.

Odilon. The Holy Scripture, the basis of all religion, and considered by your ancestors as the corner-stone of the whole building, having lost its ancient consideration among you, insomuch that your own divines no longer consider it as an infallible rule of doctrine and morals; it is clear that your moral laws want *the divine sanction*, and it is easy to conceive all the melancholy consequences that must result from such a state of things. Locke, in the first part of his reasonable Christianity, has said some excellent things on the necessity of this divine sanction.

Edward. Certainly, protestantism was never in such a dangerous crisis as at present. On one side, naturalism is sapping it and threatening to swallow it up; on the other, Catholicity, still erect, notwithstanding all the attacks made upon it, seems to be aiming at a realization of the public proposals that have been made of a re-union between it and Protestants.

Odilon. As to the latter point, I think you may be quite at your ease. Thanks to the efforts of its *enlightened* divines, modern Protestantism is so well cleared of the principal truths of Christianity, that you can no longer doubt of the immense distance which separates it from its primitive doctrine and from that of the Catholic Church. How then think seriously of the union of two things so discordant!

Edward. I recollect, however, that in the beginning of this discussion, you represented this re-union as possible, and even as easier now than ever.

Odilon was preparing to answer this question; but perceiving it was very late, he thought it better to break up the meeting. Theodulus, who had been much interested in our conversation, invited him to resume it the next evening. We all agreed to this, and the Abbé, yielding to our intreaties, put off his departure to another day, and accepted the invitation.

In walking home, our conversation naturally fell on the principal persons of the party, and Edward could not help observing to me, that he would rather Ulric was not there the next day. "The Abbé," said he, "is a genteel man, with great urbanity, and much more information than I thought, and seems to have much mildness in his manners and character. But Ulric almost always governed by the tenacity of his opinions, frequently interrupts and diverts the thread of the conversation."

"That is of no consequence," said I, "his interruptions brought on several important discussions; and, besides, I am aware these little oddities will be easily overlooked by such a moderate man as the Abbé."

"But," continued Edward, "what do you think now of this projected re-union of religions, and of those especially who propose it?"

"I suspect," said I, "that your first alarms are now entirely dispelled; those projectors, as ignorant of Protestantism as of Catholicism, understood nothing of the matter; and as there is such a distance between the principles of modern Protestants and those of Catholics, I consider a re-union as absolutely impossible."

"My alarms," answered Edward, "are not the less on that account; have we not seen things brought about in our days that were before considered as impossible? And I confess I was very much struck, when I heard the Abbé declare, that after all a re-union was more possible and more easy than ever."

"Our conversation to-morrow," I replied, "will give us more insight into this business. I am not however of your opinion; the parties are too far off ever to come together."

"But what do you say of this separation itself?" continued Edward. I was silent. "What think you of the enormous distance, that has been proved to exist, between our modern opinions, and those of primitive Prorestantism ?" I remained silent. "Our first reformers were more than half Catholic, and modern Protestants have thrown themselves more than half way into naturalism. What think you of this? do answer me!"

"Since you positively insist on it, I must. All this is only a commentary on what I told you yesterday during our walk; truth can only be one and unchangeable. As our modern reformers have, in a manner, thrown Protestantism out of Protestantism; as they have so much shaken the authority of Scripture, whose inviolability notwithstanding was decreed by Luther, that their new commentaries allow none of the fundamental truths of Christianity to remain; as they even begin already to expatiate on a pretended Christian mythology which, if admitted, would throw all that relates to the history of religion, all that concerns the life and actions of Jesus Christ and his apostles, into the region of chimeras and fables, I have composed an *extract* or a *quintessence* for myself, to which I keep, allowing every body else to compose their own as they like, and as they understand it.

END OF THE FIRST EVENING.

SECOND EVENING.

THE following evening we all met at the house of Theodulus. The conversation naturally fell on the great political events of the times, which it was impossible to keep out of one's mind. Every one talked of the news he had heard, and reasoned about it according to his own way of thinking. At last Ulric of Stetten took up the conversation, and said: "What we have seen so far is of the greatest importance, but I believe that what we have still to witness will not be less so; for the revolutions which the states of Europe have just gone through, are quite of a nature to make us look for others. However, these probable conjectures ought not to make us forget the principal object of our meeting this evening. If a religious re-union," said he, turning towards the Abbé, "is more possible and more easy than ever, as you have advanced, and if the appeals made on this subject are listened to, we must expect still greater changes than those that have astonished us hitherto."

Odilon. I persist in my first opinion.

Edward. I hope it is not because Beaufort and others have summoned the despotism which now overrules us, to effect the re-union of the different religious parties by a dictatorial sentence.

Odilon. God forbid! minds are not flexible like bodies.

Ulric. Nevertheless, a very taking and seducing argument has been employed, that Catholicity alone was suitable to a monarch, and that Protestantism was favorable to a republican form of government.

Odilon. Not only does this assertion appear to me unfounded, but it also shows, that great ignorance of our projectors, of which I gave you several proofs yesterday. I allow, however, that Calvinism has always shown republican sentiments in France, and according to the work of the Abbé Tabaraud, which I have mentioned already, St. Lambert, Thomas, and Voltaire said some very remarkable things on the great disposition of Calvinists towards republicanism and democracy : Villers himself, the enthusiastic apologist of the Reformation, considers it as the source from which the Dutch, Americans, and revolutionary French drew their republican spirit. Grotius also did not hesitate to say, "wherever the disciples of Calvin have had the ascendant, they have troubled empires."* But Protestants, properly so called, that is, Lutherans, are as good monarchists in monarchies, as they are good republicans in republics; and it is the same with Catholics.

Edward. Supposing, however, this argument became popular?

Odilon. Do not be afraid of it. Our misfortunes would only increase, and without any good whatever; for minds are not to be controlled. I think I demonstrated to you, yesterday, that God alone can dispose them to a union; and it seems to me he has prepared and smoothed the ways, when I consider the actual situation of Protestantism.

Ulric. Your expectations may possibly be deceived; Protestants will never renounce their old principles.

Odilon. You saw more than enough, yesterday, to what a degree they have deviated from those of the first reformers. What then should hinder the same thing from happening in other respects? Extremes meet.

Edward. You have just said that the actual situation of Protestantism seems to prove that Providence has smoothed the ways towards a re-union: how do you understand this? From its *interior* situation, I should be inclined to think that a re-union with Catholicity presents more difficulties than ever.

Odilon. From my own peculiar way of considering Protestantism, I find the seed of its decay and ruin in its very primitive constitution.

Edward. How so?

Odilon. Examine all religions, Paganism, Judaism, Christianity; every where you will find an object of religious wor-

* Calvini discipuli, ubicumque invaluere, imperia turbaverunt. Grot. Animad. Rivet. Op. tom. iv. p. 649.

ship, which assembles men necessarily and periodically in certain places, where things are done, which no other person can perform, than those appointed by the religion. But this is entirely wanting in Protestantism. The public Sunday worship consists entirely in singing, preaching, and reciting certain prayers; it is therefore quite natural, that with such an establishment, the divine worship should naturally fall into decay, and at length cease entirely.

Edward. I do not see this consequence; it seems to me, on the contrary, that by these continual instructions, which are the essence of our religious worship, Protestantism acquires daily more vigor, and more preservatives against that total ruin you have supposed.

Odilon. Would you like to hear the opinion of a very judicious Protestant divine, on these preachings, which have so much become the principal part of your worship, that you have thrown off all other holy exterior practises?

Ulric. You would oblige me greatly.

Odilon. The learned author of the little work entitled, *The Holy Supper, a dogmatico historical Investigation,* says, p. 79, "We are as little able, by our eternal preachings, to communicate religion itself to man, as we are to bring back again the external worship of religion."

Ulric. Ah! since we have fewer holidays, these sermons have become much less frequent among us. But, how can you say, that we want holy customs and rites? Have we not still Baptism and the Lord's Supper?

Odilon. I admit it; but this same writer, whom I just quoted, will tell us plainly, what state those rites are in among you. "How cold and empty of symbols proper to elevate the mind is all that external worship, especially among modern Protestants!"

Edward. But as we should *increase in knowledge,* and as preaching serves for the instruction of adults, it would be very wrong to blame Protestants for having made this the principal object of their worship; it is, on the contrary, very well calculated to preserve religion, and guard it against decay.

Odilon. Permit me to abstain from expressing my opinion on this point.

Edward. You would, however, do me a great pleasure, by telling me your ideas fully and fairly on this subject.

9

Odilon. Very well : tell me then what are the maxims of the masters of this establishment of instruction ? Where is their uniformity ? Have the best of them the same religion, and the same dogmatical principles ? As it is evident that it is not so, must not confusion and disorder necessarily increase daily ? Who, besides, are the persons who often mount your pulpits ? Are they not such as the same author speaks of ? "Far from finding doctors in the churches, we see but too often only common schoolmasters."

Edward. This unfortunately is but too true ; but continue, I beg of you.

Odilon. Speaking only of those who have not yet rejected all religious ideas, how many of the faithful are there not among you, who think and say, "It is much easier for me to be confined at home, than in the church ; I can choose at will a much better sermon, than what I shall hear from the pastor or his assistant ; what is to hinder me from singing hymns at home, and better, perhaps, than those of the church ? Instead of their gothic and supernatural prayers, which are so little edifying to the greatest part of the audience, I can say others much more suitable to myself."

"It is thus, Sir, that the public worship is neglected, and that religion falls daily into decay. But if you have still any doubt of the truth and exactness of my opinion in this respect, enter your churches, and see how empty they are ? Plaintive lamentations on this subject are heard on every side. I read lately a very remarkable observation relative to this, by a protestant writer, and which contained at the same time a very singular, but not improbable prognostic."

Ulric. Be so good as to communicate it to us.

Odilon. Wagner, in his work entitled, *Return from abroad into my country,* part i. p. 318, says as follows : "Christians, and you especially, Lutherans and Calvinists, restore, I beseech you, to religion and to the sanctuaries of the Church, that dignity and ancient majesty which you profane and weaken every day more and more. Where are those millions which the abolition of holidays was to procure to the country? Do the poor eat their bread at the low price which your preachers announced ? Ah ! how these easy men endeavor to curtail the divine service more and more every day ! Every year a hymn less, and the sermon shorter. In what temple does the peasant still hear, during the morning service, those beautiful sacerdotal hymns, and that sublime *Gloria,* which the whole choir of the faithful accompained with so much majesty? They despise this art, at once so sublime and pleasing; they banish from their studies and exercises that music, which their Luther and their Melanchton, however, prized so highly. Really, if *enlightening* goes in the same progression, as for the last twenty years, it is probable that in a century hence, every man may smoke his pipe very comfortably in the Protestant churches. The women, sitting by their wheels, may listen with attention to the new waltz which the organist will play instead of the ancient psalmody. The schoolmaster may then mount the pulpit, and read some dissertations on the education of bees, and on other subjects useful to the citizen and peasant; for it is well known that, even now, there are only a few old pedants that know how to preach. On great feasts, I do not despair hearing of some drinking song, with a little dancing. Wretches that you are! answer me, I beg you, a single question; in what, at last, will the public exercise of your religion consist?" What do you say of this picture, and this fine prognostic?

Ulric. It is as hideous as true.

Odilon. I only find one fault with it, which is, that Wagner puts off the term too long. Unless some miraculous event happens, the epoch of this total ruin of all religous worship will long precede the period fixed by this writer. But whence proceeds this distressing decay? Is not the cause to be sought in the defective disposition of your divine worship? Without this, your antichristian *enlighteners* would have attacked it with so much fury in vain. Is not the divine worship daily neglected among you, and do not your churches become more empty from year to year?

Edward. I admit this melancholy truth; but, at the same time, it is perhaps impiety, which is increasing every day, that is the principal cause of this disorder.

Odilon. I am far from meaning to deny that this false philosophy has had a very great share in it.

"One of your most esteemed ecclesiastics, and who belongs himself to this doctrine of *enlighteners,* has recently declared in the 6th No. of the General Gazette, for 1808, *that the cause of the indifference for worship and religion, must be sought for principally in the universality of this philosophy.* But this truth does not destroy the other which I have established. On the contrary, it is confirmed by the numerous efforts of several of your religious teachers to improve the Liturgy. But all these plans of improvement for propping an edifice more tottering every day, sufficiently show that all its defects are known, and the evil is increased to such a degree, that in order to give some attraction to the divine service, some persons have proposed that the newspapers should be read from the pulpit. A still more extraordinary and extravagant proposition has been made in a public paper, which is very widely circulated."

Edward. What is that?

Odilon. To suppress entirely all these attempts to improve a worship that is no longer suitable to such enlightened men as our contemporaries ; and as religious instruction is no longer fit for any but the populace, to diminish the number of days consecrated to divine worship, as well as that of the clergy.

Edward. This is indeed an heroic remedy, taken in a fit of despair.

Odilon. Yes, and a remedy which shows that they are on the road to naturalism, *without worship and without clergy ;* this remedy proves likewise that the whole arrangement of your divine service is considered as irreparably defective.

Edward. I think however you are deceived in this point. You are acquainted, no doubt, with the proclamation of the King of Prussia, which appeared in September, 1814. In the preamble of this proclamation, it is said, that it was generally felt, " that the form of divine worship, in the most modern Protestant churches, had not that edifying solemnity and majesty, which seizes on the mind, and raises it to pious thoughts and religious sentiments." You see then that the defects in the modern form of worship are perfectly known.

Odilon. What does the proclamation say besides ?

Edward. It complains that preaching, though otherwise of the greatest importance, is considered as the principal part of divine worship, while it should be properly an exhortation to practise that worship, according to its real spirit; it says that the liturgies are partly so incomplete, and partly so unequal and imperfect, that several essential points in them are abandoned to the arbitrary disposition of clergymen ; and, in short, that the uniformity of sacred rites and customs, which is one of the principal conditions of their salutary effects, hardly exists at all.

Odilon. Thus to acknowledge the defects of the Protestant worship, is, I confess, making a great step; but, after all, what dispositions have been made?

Edward. Every one is invited to propose a *plan* for the improvement of divine worship, and to send it to the ecclesiastical authorities, who will make their report to the sovereign, that a decision may be made *concerning the best form of liturgy to be adopted.*

Odilon. If you wish me to tell you honestly my opinion, I must say, I expect very little from this attempt.

Edward. And why? It seems to me to be done quite in earnest.

Odilon. It is not the good will, but its success that I doubt. You will probably see from this improvement, an amalgamation of Protestantism and Calvinism, which will certainly not turn to the advantage of religion. New ceremonies will be introduced, with music, and even perhaps some theatrical effects; the clergy are even already stripped of their dress, for another, which, it is said, is to resemble that at the beginning of the Reformation; all this may take for a time, but will have no consistency. You will have new liturgies, a little *modernized*, though they are already numberless, and this new present will soon have the fate of the old. That is all. External worship, my dear Sir, must have its basis in the dogmas, and in the truths of religion; and instead of these precarious objects, naturalism has invaded your church. This is the real cause of the decay of your worship. One may foresee, besides, what is to be hoped from this new experiment, by the following words of the proclamation itself,—*as to symbols, there are but few of them.* Do you think that a worship so defective can subsist long?

Edward. But notwithstanding these pretended defects, Protestantism has already lasted near 300 years.

Odilon. I might very well take off forty years from this number; but, even reckoning them, you would not be much more advanced. But, however this may be, pray tell me to what you ascribe this long preservation of Protestantism?

Edward. To the profound sentiment we all feel, that this religion has, above all others, good and reasonable institutions.

Odilon. It seems to me that this feeling could neither have been very lively, nor very profound, since it has disappeared so quickly. Your opinions must be very different at present, for all those advantages are supposed to exist in deism and naturalism; your churches are empty, and your pastors preach in the desert.

Edward. But to what then do you yourself attribute this long duration of Protestantism?

Odilon. You will pardon me for speaking according to my real conviction, which is, that the same causes which procured it so many warm partisans in the beginning, also contributed, in the early periods, to preserve it.

Edward. But, as I have said that every one felt the great advantages which Protestantism affords by its good and reasonable institutions, you seem to allow that they also contributed to its preservation. This advantage was also felt in the beginning, and brought a great many partisans to Protestantism.

Odilon. I by no means agree to your maxim yet. A modern writer, who, from several of his opinions, is not suspected of having deviated from the spirit of the times, gives an opinion on this matter very different from yours.

Edward. Who is this writer?

Odilon. The author of the work entitled, *On the Spirit and Consequences of the Reformation.*

Edward. And to what cause does this author attribute the great number of partisans which Protestantism had from the beginning?

Odilon. To the cupidity of princes, to their desire of augmenting their territories by the spoils of the church, to the hopes of the high clergy of being freed from those burdensome *annates*, and from the retributions exacted for the *pallium*, and various other objects; to the expectations conceived by the lower clergy, of obtaining more liberty; to the wish of the imperial towns to terminate their long discussions with the bishops concerning their reciprocal rights, and to be delivered from the oppression of the neighboring princes. To these motives, and others more base, which I shall pass over in silence, I shall add the favorable dispositions of many curates and monks tired of celibacy and of the cloister. Such were the united causes, which according to this writer, procured so many partisans for the first reformers; and all who know the history of those times, will allow this sentence to be important. The opinion of Frederick the Great also agrees perfectly with it.

Edward. How can you invoke the authority of a man who was a declared enemy to all religion?

Odilon. What does that signify, if what he asserts be true. In his Memoirs of Brandenburg, he says, " If we wish to reduce the causes of the progress of the Reformation to simple priciples, we shall find that in Germany, it was the work of interest, in England of love, and in France of novelty !" This is perfectly conformable to history.

Edward. And, admitting all this, what would be the consequence?

Odilon. That each would endeavor to preserve what he had gained in this way, and that all were interested to employ all their efforts to maintain a religious society, which had procured them the satisfaction of all their desires.

Edward. But consider that Protestantism has already lasted three centuries ; and, even supposing that the motives you have mentioned, procured it many partisans *at first*, and *originally*, to its preservation, this fact is not applicable to subsequent periods, when no one had to fear respecting the property he had thus acquired ; it must be, therefore, that more perfect institutions, and a more suitable religious instruction, have essentially contributed to the long duration of Protestantism.

Odilon. If you wish me to give my opinion with perfect freedom, and if I am capable of judging this matter, I would say that this duration is to be attributed to a sort of exaltation and obstinacy ; and, in saying this, I think I use the most moderate expression.

Edward. I beg of you to explain yourself in a more clear and precise manner.

Odilon. I might admit, that, in Germany, in the early part of the Reformation, religious instruction was more popular, than with us ; and I know that Cardinal Julian expressed himself in a most energetic manner, on the profound decline of the German clergy in those unfortunate times.*

Edward. You admit then that better institutions have con tributed to the preservation of Protestantism?

Odilon. I have not finished yet. It is very possible, that

* Epist. Juliani Card. ad Eugen. iv, in Op. Ænes Silvii, p. 66.

in the beginning, novelty, a form of instruction accommodated to circumstances, and many other motives, may have procured more than one proselyte to Protestantism; but it is to *exaltation* alone, that it owes its long duration. All the efforts of zeal were employed to strengthen the party: for a long time they fought with desperation, and with all the arms of controversy against the Catholics, from whom they had separated, and even at times against the Calvinists, Anabaptists, and other sects, which had sprung out of the bosom of the Reformation. In the origin of these quarrels, the pulpit was the theatre of the fight, and the people, who had been carefully drawn into the same interests, took a part in them, and were kept in a continual fermentation: all this contributed essentially to the preservation of Protestantism, notwithstanding the defective organization of its worship. Read the writings of your divines, and the sermons of your preachers of that period, and you will find that my picture is exact, and that the colors are not overcharged.

Ulric. You do not pretend, however, to hope, that this long preservation is owing to fanaticism and the spirit of sects.

Odilon. I confine myself to the term *exaltation;* but still you cannot deny, that there was a great deal of reciprocal animosity, for a long time; and I could easily cite you numerous and not very edifying examples of this, all drawn from authentic histories of those times, and even much later.

Ulric. But are you not afraid of giving me arms against yourself in citing these *later* times? I see exactly what you are aiming at.

Odilon. I am not the least afraid of compromising myself; for I am only speaking of zealous Protestants, and not of those decided deists, who after having trampled under foot their ancient brethren, marched forward against the Catholics, to attack them with all the rage of the most furious fanaticism.

Edward. We will not interrupt you; pray have the kindness to continue.

Odilon. During the last forty years especially of the last century, French philosophism, finding support and many partisans in the states of Brandenburg, *tolerantism* sprung up, and spread rapidly over all Germany. I have no need, I hope, to point out to you the small distance there is between this tolerantism, and the most complete indifferentism.

Ulric. I think, I may assure you, that, as to the Protestant churches, their respective toleration is long anterior to the epoch of the birth of French philosophism.

Odilon. You are much better able than I to determine exactly, if the Anabaptists or Herrnhuters, who must however be classed among Protestants, have had reason to extol this toleration, and at the advanced period you have just mentioned. But, it is the essence of all religious societies, which have no prop in any authority whatever, to be very tolerant towards each other; for long-protracted battles would soon cause their mutual ruin. I forget however that I wished to speak of quite another thing.

Ulric. What is that, Sir?

Odilon. Of tolerantism; that is, of that false toleration, which I carefully distinguished yesterday from the true one; that toleration, in short, to which every thing is or may be soon quite indifferent, and which the great Bacon called one of the gates of atheism. But, there is no doubt that this dates chiefly from the epoch of French philosophism.

Ulric. This is very possible.

Odilon. The ancient heat soon cooled, and gave place to indifference; the churches became emptier every day, and Protestantism advanced with rapid strides towards its entire dissolution.

Edward. What you have just said is novel and true in several respects; but it seems to me, nevertheless, to return to the preceding discussion, that you are mistaken, in attributing the decay of Protestantism to the vicious organization of its worship. Do you not know that assistance at divine service on Sundays and holidays is of obligation with us?

Odilon. I know that the third commandment is still to be found at least in your catechism; but who superintends the exact observance of it? This puts me in mind of another very important circumstance, which would be sufficient to put an end to Protestantism, even if this defective organization did not exist.

Edward. What do you understand by that?

Odilon. No human society can exist without laws, nor without an exact superintendance over their observation. Melanchton himself said on this subject, " We shall soon see what kind of a church we shall have, if the ecclesiastical police be suppressed."[*] It is the entire suppression of this police among you, which must incontestably bring on the ruin of your religious community.

Edward. What! you suppose we are entirely without any ecclesiastical police? All the Protestant kings and princes, are they not the *supreme bishops* in their states? Have they not ecclesiastical counsellors and consistories?

Odilon. Whence then this enormous decay of Christianity, especially in Protestant countries? To what must these furious attacks against religion be attributed? What are the causes of this profound corruption of morals, and this desertion of public worship, which draw such bitter complaints even from your clergy themselves?

Edward. You must blame the spirit of the times.

Odilon. And cannot you find any exorcist to drive away this wicked demon? Let us speak honestly, my dear Sir. I honor and respect your princes, as sovereigns and rulers of the state; but their horizon is much too extensive for them to employ themselves with all the details of ecclesiastical administration, even if it were not under the influence of the spirit of the times. When a great political economy is to be governed, the finances to be looked after, justice kept up, war and foreign affairs to be directed, things all of the highest importance, and which must take up all the time of *the supreme bishop*, I think he can hardly find the leisure which is absolutely necessary for the exact superintendance of the affairs of religion and the church.

Edward. For these affairs, princes have counsellors and consistories, as they have also particular administrative colleges for the affairs of state.

Odilon. You see however that this establishment does not prevent religion and public worship from falling into a very visible decline among you. And yet I am sure you will not accuse these ecclesiastical counsellors and consistories of being more relaxed, in the exercise of their functions, than the other colleges. Excessive care is taken that no ill-made man becomes a soldier or officer, and nevertheless, you have not forgot that I gave you examples, yesterday, of a number of *ill-made* divines of Christian clergymen, who attack the fundamental truths of Christianity with rancorous animosity. Great care is taken that every soldier and officer mount guard

* Videbimus qualem habituri sumus ecclesiam, sublatâ politiâ ecclesiasticâ.

on the appointed days; but nobody minds whether the faithful serve the Lord Almighty on the great day destined to glorify him. The police exerts all its efforts to put a stop to contagious diseases; but who troubles himself to arrest the moral evil which attacks the conduct of the subject, and deprives him of the consolations of religion? Explain me this cruel difference.

Edward. Alas! it is still the spirit of the times!

Odilon. If it be so, I really do not know a worse spirit than that, and it would be well *to banish it into the desert* .... Or may it not be, perhaps, like that of the Gospel, which only flew off by force of prayer and fasting?

Edward. One cannot always do what one would wish.

Odilon. Let us speak plainly: your ecclesiastical constitution is as defective as your religious worship. I have certainly great esteem and consideration for your ecclesiastical counsellors and consistories, which are honored with the confidence of the sovereign; but tell me yourself, what think you of the members who compose them?

Edward. I consider them to be as able and as upright as those of the other administrative colleges.

Odilon. I am far from wishing to contest it; but, if you except two or three churchmen, all those councils and consistories, to begin by the director in chief, are laymen. Would it not be as ridiculous as injurious to the army, if an archdeacon were named chief of a council of war, composed also in great part of pastors and ministers of the Gospel? What, in a few years, would be the fate of the army and of military discipline?

Edward. This observation is perfectly just: pray continue.

Odilon. The legal knowledge and moral qualities of your lay directors and counsellors may be very great; but it is not less true, that they are, in general, little acquainted with canonical matters and ecclesiastical affairs, and that very often even they know nothing of religion but what they learnt at school. How many have been struck with the contagion of the new *light*, who would cry out fanaticism, and sound the alarm against any clergyman who dared raise his voice against the daily attacks that are made on religion? What would they not say of ecclesiastical despotism, if a clergyman attempted to draw the attention of the magistrates to the decay of morality or public worship, and call on them to take suitable measures for that purpose?

Edward. Have you been much in Protestant countries?

Odilon. The melancholy fate of my abbey, which, like so many others, was carried away by the revolutionary hurricane, has forced me unfortunately to remain a long time in countries where Protestantism prevails; and from all that I was able to observe, I drew the consequence after mature reflection, that a religion with such a defective worship, and a religious society without discipline and ecclesiastical police, could only have a very precarious existence. The numerous and bitter complaints of those among your clergymen, who have preserved any good intentions, prove too well how real and general this decay has become.

Edward. The stronger and more frequent these complaints are, the more we must hope that our *supreme bishops* and their plenipotentiaries will unite all their efforts to oppose the torrent, and to preserve our religion and morals from the inevitable shipwreck which threatens them.

Odilon. I am afraid you flatter yourself with false hopes. To attain the end you desire, your whole ecclesiastical constitution must be changed, and I see no appearance of it; a complete metamorphosis must take place in your clergy, a subject on which I shall have a word or two to say to you by and by.

Ulric. I have been on my guard not to interrupt you, for you have really said many fine and good things. However, I think I could make a pretty important objection.

Odilon. I will thank you for it; I am ready to hear you.

Ulric. You said that a proximate cause of dissolution of Protestantism may be found in its very organization; because, different in this from Catholicism, Judaism, and even Paganism, it wants an essential object in its worship. On this subject, you have forgot to mention Mahometism, which also wants this object, and which nevertheless has lasted 1200 years.

Odilon. You cannot be ignorant, that the Koran is, to Musulmen, not only the fundamental book of their religion, but that it seems at the same time as a code of civil law; thus the maxims of that religion are at the same time those of civil society; this is so true, that every Musulman, who neglects the hours of prayer, or does not visit the mosque, incurs very severe punishment. Consequently, it may be said that it is the bastinado which has preserved Islamism so long; and, notwithstanding the severity of that remedy, the edifice of that religion becomes weaker every day.

Ulric. And what do you say of our modern Jews and their divine synagogical worship, which seems to have been the model of the Protestant worship? What do you say of the Menonites, and other small sects, which, though also without this object of religious worship that you have so much at heart, subsist nevertheless for such a long time past?

Odilon. A party kept under the yoke, or oppressed, commonly draws closer the bonds of its union; its zeal becomes extreme, and the greatest exactness is observed. Give them the same liberty as Protestants, and you will soon see them degenerate. See how little the Jews of Brandenburg resembled those of other countries, on account of this liberty! Independently of this, it is certain that the Jews, the Menonites, and other small sects of this kind, have a sort of ecclesiastical discipline, which preserves them, in some sort, from total dissolution.

Ulric. But the Calvinists?

Odilon. I do not conceive how you can make an exception in their favor, as all that has been said of Lutherans may be applied to them. But, allowing that the synodal constitution of the Calvinists has contributed to stop the entire fall of their church, it is not less true, that, like the Protestants, they have made an enormous stride towards naturalism.

Ulric. How is that?

Odilon. Voltaire, who surely knew those among whom he lived, wrote in 1766, to D'Alembert, that in Calvin's town, that is Geneva, there were only a few wretches who believed in the *consubstantial*, and that from Bern to Geneva, a single Christian was not really to be found. In 1773, the same author wrote to the King of Prussia, that Swisserland was full of people, who had as much hatred and contempt for Christianity as the Emperor Julian.

Ulric. This is one of those exaggerations and falsehoods which characterize so exactly that old father of all species of lies.

Odilon. Do you know his opinion of the profession of faith of the minister Vernes? He said—"I sign your profession of faith—carissime frater in Deo et Serveto!"

Ulric. Can you possibly give any credit to the testimony of such a man?

Odilon. I am much inclined to think that Voltaire represented matters more as he wished them to be, than as they were in reality; nevertheless, it is incontestable that the profound degradation of modern Lutheranism has also extended to Calvinism. "Lutheranism," says a writer of our days, "has already ceased to exist, with respect to the eternal essence of its constitution, and Calvinism will soon follow the destinies of her mother."

Ulric. Being ignorant who this writer is, I cannot pronounce on the exactness of his judgment, and the truth of this prognostic respecting Calvinism; all I can say is, that Voltaire formed a very erroneous opinion of it.

Odilon. Well, I will name you a man to whom that religion and Switzerland were perfectly well known—Rousseau.

Ulric. Rousseau! That is absolutely impossible!

Odilon. I am very sorry to give you any vexation on this matter, and I know it is unpleasant to find people, whom one esteemed, different from the favorable idea one had formed of them; but Rousseau, in his Letters from the Mountain, says, "One cannot tell what they believe, or what they do not believe. Their only way of establishing their faith is, by attacking that of others." This portrait is hardly more flattering than that of Voltaire, and consequently, the Calvinists cannot, in this respect, be distinguished from the Lutherans.

Ulric. I confess this opinion of Rousseau surprises me; but many objections may be made against it.

Odilon. I will cite you one now then, still more important than the preceding. In the Memoir, already quoted, of the Calvinists in France, which appeared in 1775, the following plain passage occurs : " We are at present very far from the road, which our ancestors opened to us in the beginning of the 16th century. Luther and Calvin have few followers among us; our sect, hacked into a thousand different troops, is no longer distinguishable: Quakers, Puritans, Anabaptists, Arminians, Gomarists, Unitarians, Rationals, Supralapsarians, Nonconformists; in a word, a crowd of sects, come out of our bosom, has thrown such confusion among us that the very multitude of heads renders us acephalous. We no longer know to whom we belong, nor under what banner we march. To-day, Theists, to-morrow Christians : we are sometimes for natural religion, and sometimes for revelation. To the spirit of party, which animated us formerly, has succeeded such an indifference for all parties, that I should rather think Pyrrhonism was the dominant sect : our ministers themselves, shaken in their belief, talk to us much less of dogmas than of morality."

Edward. I am perfectly convinced you are quite right; and it is certain, that, independently of the progress of incredulity among us, the cause of all this melancholy decline must be sought in the first arrangement and very establishment of Protestantism.

Odilon. We must add other articles still, not less important than those we have spoken of now.

Edward. You will oblige me much by specifying them.

Odilon. They are three articles so essential, that the existence of Protestantism, down to this day, seems to me quite a wonder. The first serious defect in the establishment of your divine worship is, that it is too much forgotten that man is a creature endowed with senses; that he receives every thing through them; that it is sensual objects which make the greatest impression on him, and, so much so, that they preserve a great command over his soul, even when he is merely occupied with what is intellectual.

Edward. But is that not a fault, a weakness of human nature?

Odilon. Yes; for so far from being angels, we are only creatures endowed with senses. Do we not make use of external things and means, in all circumstances where simple reasoning is not sufficient? Why then should we reject from religion a means so proper for exciting religious sentiments? Examine those Protestant countries which have preserved in the divine worship some ancient customs which affect the senses, and you will most certainly find there much more respect and attachment to religion and worship, than in those countries where the worship has been wholly simplified.

Ulric. I hope you will not be displeased if I tell you, that these external forms and ceremonies of worship, in which you see so many advantages, have often scandalized me very much. Have I not sometimes seen a Virgin holding the infant Jesus with a doll in her arms, placed here by the pious simplicity of the faithful.

Odilon. Without discussing the present objection, I grant that there may have been local abuses, introduced occasionally by mistaken devotion, and strongly opposed by the church; but instead of being scandalized, we must follow, in this respect, the maxim of St. Paul; " We who are strong, must bear the weaknesses of the infirm."*

Edward. You will allow, however, that the primitive church, as it came out of the hands of the Lord, knew nothing at all of this worship so stuffed with ceremonies.

Odilon. An exact study of Christian antiquities will soon convince you of the ancient origin of the mass, and of many other ceremonies of divine worship among Catholics ; several Protestant writers, among whom I shall only quote Bingham, have not been able to deny entirely this truth.

Ulric. Allow me to call in question this high antiquity of the sacrifice of the mass. I am of opinion, that all this worship, which is the principal thing among you, is only a subsequent invention of the Popes.

Odilon. In this supposition, we must reject the clearest testimonies of all Christian antiquity. I have already demonstrated what Luther himself thought on this article, and that he considered this worship as having subsisted *from the beginning, in the whole* Christian church. It would be very extraordinary, moreover, if the Popes had invented and formed this establishment, as, with the single exception of modern Protestants, it is adopted and considered as an essential article of divine Christian worship, in all the other Christian communities, even those which are not re-united with the Roman church. With respect to the Greeks, it is a thing generally known. Among the Cophts, there is also a mass which they call *korbano,* that is to say, the offering of the sacrifice: they admit also, like the Catholic church, the real presence or transubstantiation, and they observe the adoration, after consecration, like the Catholics.* In the ritual of ordination of the Armenian church, it is said that the priest has received the power of consecrating and offering the holy sacrifice, for the dead as well as the living.† I defy you, Sir, to quote me a single epoch in which the Popes invented or proposed this worship to the whole Christian

* Rom. xv, 1.   † New Memoirs of the Missions, tom. ii, p. 57.
‡ Ibid, tom. ii, ɔ. 180.

church. Considering, therefore, its generality and high antiquity, it must have been instituted by Jesus Christ himself and his apostles.

Ulric. I do not believe it is possible to find any trace of the latter fact.

Odilon. As our Lord, after his resurrection, gave the apostles a rule of conduct concerning the establishment of his church, it is at least very probable, that he prescribed, at the same time, all the arrangements on which the whole of an external worship rests, in which all the churches of christendom agree, from the most remote ages.

Edward. The Scripture preserves a complete silence on the ceremonies of divine worship, and it is merely said that *we should adore God in spirit and in truth.*

Odilon. And it is thus that we adore him in the midst of the pomp of a majestic external worship. Joseph Mede, an English writer, has proved, if I am not mistaken, that the passage of Scripture you have just quoted cannot justify a divine worship deprived of all that affects the senses, and may produce a useful impression on them. Moreover, if you will only admit what is strictly ordered in Scripture, I do not see why you solemnize Sundays and holidays. Why have you not introduced the washing of feet? why are new-married couples blessed in your churches? why was confirmation introduced? why do you not celebrate the feasts of *Christian love*, which ought to be followed by the Supper, during the night, rather than by day?

Edward. I admit these facts, but persist in thinking, that divine worship, celebrated in silence, contributes more than all this ceremonial show, to the devotion of the heart, the principal object of divine worship.

Odilon. I might answer, that nothing in general can be determined on a subject which belongs to taste and feeling. But hear what Mirabeau the economist says on this subject, in his *Ami des Hommes:* "Every religion that is confined to a worship purely spiritual and without ceremonies, will soon be banished into the moon."

Edward. You forget that Mirabeau was a Catholic, or, at least, had been one.

Odilon. I see you are difficult about authorities, and I shall therefore now quote you one, which you certainly will not reject. If you wish to know the favorable opinion that Me-

lanchton had of religious ceremonies, read the following
passage of a letter he wrote to Carlowitz, respecting the book
which the Emperor had published in the *Interim:* "I willingly admit the ceremonies which that book prescribes; for
I think they form a part of ecclesiastical discipline, and I
imagine my whole life has shown my love for discipline and
order; my writings also testify in favor of the efforts I have
constantly made to instil this into youth. While still a child,
I felt a singular pleasure in observing all the church ceremonies, and my nature is very far from that life of the cyclops,
who admit no order, and hate customs as a violence done to
the understanding. I do not confine myself to my own
satisfaction in these reflections, but I endeavor to inspire
others with the same."

Ulric. Well, this passage proves certainly that Melanchton had a liking for ceremonies, but at the same time we see
that the prejudices of education had a great share in it.

Odilon. I think you must at last be of the same opinion as
Feller, when, guided by nature and experience, he says, that
men must be struck by senses; that they would conceive a
mean idea of the being proposed to their adoration, if he had
less external honor than an earthly sovereign, and that
wherever churches are gloomy and stripped of their ornaments, we may be sure that the people are either extremely
poor, or have very little religion.

Ulric. This opinion of Feller was evidently dictated by
the prejudices of education and habit.

Odilon. Let us have recourse then to testimonies that you
will think more conclusive. Beger, a learned Protestant,
says: "It is incontestable that the absence of ceremonies,
among Protestants, has cooled their piety." Salmasius, also
disapproving the total rejection of all external objects of worship, by the puritans, says: "Our friends have cut religion
to the quick." Every body knows that Misson, the traveller, is any thing but favorable to Catholicity; nevertheless,
speaking of the benediction given by the Pope from the bal-
cony of St. Peter's church, he exclaims; "I confess that for
that moment I am a Catholic." Brydone, in his travels in
Sicily, says he was an eye witness of the impression produced on the people by religious ceremonies; and adds, that
sincerely envying the feelings of these good people, he could
not help cursing philosophical pride, and its forbidding cold-
ness. Some Protestants even have been perfectly convinced

of the necessity of an external worship; as, for example, Lindemann, the superintendant at Danneberg. In his Essay on a new Liturgy, he proposes adorning the church with flowers, on certain festivals, placing a fine painting over the altar, with vessels full of incense, and thinks very good effects would be produced by it. It is true, the editors of the General Literary Gazette of Jena, criticising this work, exclaims: "In the name of God, no Pagan ceremonies, no pompous parade in our Christian churches." So great is the difference of taste and feeling, as I have already observed. This is so true, that that same Gazette, concluding a review of a work entitled, "System of Christian Morality," openly defends the practice of fasts in the Catholic church, and even religious orders. The experience of what is most useful can alone decide this point, and it is entirely in our favor.

Ulric. It seems to me, that the first Christian church of all, had not such a pompous external worship; and it is by that church we ought to regulate our customs: it was, no doubt, according to that, that Protestants endeavored to settle theirs.

Odilon. Why do you not wear the same dress as you had in your childhood and youth? I think you were wrong to make any change in it.

Ulric. How! I should make a pretty figure. A grown up man cannot be dressed like a child.

Odilon. It was this confession I wished you to make. But I can tell you that Erasmus made it before you; for he said, it was as extravagant to think of bringing back the church to its primitive state, as to replace a man in his cradle.* The church, in its first origin, persecuted violently for two centuries, can hardly be a model for the external forms of a church, which has attained all the development of mature age, and the full independence of perfect liberty. Besides, I have already observed that even, its worship was then not so bare of all external ceremonies as you seem to imagine. But, supposing you did not agree with me on that point, and persisted in taking the form of the first ages of the church, as a model for our times, why have you not resumed that *discipline of the secret,* which existed in the primitive church? Why have you not preserved the *vigils,* and so many other customs of those early times?

* Epist. de 1520, edit. Colon. 1541.   † Disciplina arcani.

Edward. Your observation is just, and well-informed Protestants are also of opinion, that an external worship with more pomp and ceremonies, would be beneficial to religion; they think you have gone beyond the mark, and that we have not hit it. But you meant to speak of another point.

Odilon. I leave it to yourself to decide whether *too much* can be done to honor Almighty God. Merz has said such judicious and beautiful things on this subject, in his sermon on Pentecost, that you could not help approving them. However, as I have perceived that this name is not in great favor with you, I will give you the opinion of a very modern learned Protestant, who is a real philosophical thinker.

Edward. What does he say?

Odilon. After having expressed himself very much in favor of ceremonies and external practices, he says: "Man should every where implore the Most High, in a sensible form; and in this way, a theocracy very easily becomes the country of the fine Arts. The sensible nature of man must never be entirely forgotten; for it is precisely from the propensity to contemplation, and from the want of reflection, with regard to oneself, that it follows that man separates less his sensible nature from the intellectual; that he subjects, if one may say so, without knowing it, all human affections to the Divinity; that he sanctifies them by its presence, and that he constantly requires, for all human nature, that harmonic satisfaction which the theocratical state should afford, if it be meant to have a durable existence."*

Edward. This observation is perfectly just.

Odilon. One of your most judicious divines has expressed the same opinion.

Edward. What is his name?

Odilon. The author of the work entitled, *The Holy Supper*, already quoted. He says, p. 81, "In these latter times of *illumination*, they have *cleansed* so effectually, to use an expression consecrated by the party, that our worship and our churches are as empty and as devoid of ideas and life, as death itself." In a note on another passage, he says, "Has the Lord's Supper, for example, been celebrated by greater numbers, or more frequently or piously, by our contemporaries, since the partisans of this bare and simple worship have suc-

---

* Welker's Essays.

ceeded in banishing all that was solemn and symbolic?" It is thus, Sir, that men return to ancient opinions, when the incontestable inconveniences of such a bare form of worship have been experienced.

Edward. But the point you wish to speak on.

Odilon. As to that, I believe we shall agree perfectly, or at least the discussion will not be long.

Edward. And what is it?

Odilon. The great dependance which the Protestant clergy is in with respect to its princes and communities, in all ecclesiastical matters, a dependance which occasions their degradation.

Edward. I admit it; the consideration which they formerly enjoyed is terribly diminished.

Ulric. It is the same in all countries where this dependance exists. In Russia they give *padoggs* to the popes; and, after having kissed their hand, they repeat the dose if necessary.

Odilon. Religion is, however, in a very brilliant state in that country, and they would be very cautious of *padogging* a monk or a bishop. In reality, in the early periods of the Reformation, the consideration which the clergy enjoyed, was not excessively great; for in some places, they hired their evangelical pastors, like servants, for one or more years. The individuals, chosen for this purpose, had therefore no right to look for much respect. Gallus, in his History of Brandenburg, relates, that during the visitation of the churches, ordered in 1541, by the elector Joachim II. they found several pastors, who were properly only tailors, blacksmiths, masons, tanners, and such-like persons. Luther himself gave ordination to some journeymen printers, and sent them into parishes which wanted pastors, to read his printed sermons. What examples of good morals could be expected, when the models of the flock were chosen in this way? You are acquainted, no doubt, with the letters of Erasmus to Bucer and Melanchton; read over the 3d, 72d, and 113th, on the morals, life, and monstrous doctrines of the reformers in his time; their excesses were so great, that Wicelius of Falda, who had at first taken part with them, was forced to leave them. Yet those were the men whom Luther defended as the pillars of the Gospel.

Ulric. The Calvinists of those times were very different.

Odilon. I shall not stop to examine this, and shall only say, "Trojanos muros intrà peccatur et extrà."

Ulric. Say without any restraint all that you know on this subject. I remember to have read somewhere, that a little before the Reformation, Eneas Sylvius (Pius II). made bitter complaints on the corruption of morals among the Catholic clergy.

Odilon. He had too much reason. But since you desire it, hear what the synod, held in 1533, after the death of Zuingle, thought of the Calvinist clergy of that age.—" Leon Juda must apply to preaching with more diligence. Nicholas Steiner is a quarrelsome fellow, with a very bad tongue. Felix Deck does not study to make himself respectable in the pulpit, and he is quite vulgar when he has drunk a little. Othmar also minds his bottle much more than his books. Matthias Bothmer is an idler, and moreover has not proper respect for his old father and his mother-in-law ; he is entirely governed by his wife, who is much given to drinking. Henry of Landenberg, is a poor simpleton, who passes his time in drinking to such a degree, that he is known by no other name than that of the Landenberg hog; besides he is a broker, loves quarrels, and is apt to break his word. The dean, Laurence Meyer, is a man of gross brutal manners; he drags a long sword after him, and dresses like a dragoon. The pastor and vicar of Ossingen, have had a scandalous hatred against each other for these thirteen years past; their wives are excessively ill tempered; the pastor's wife is always insulting her husband ; and the vicar's wife does not frequent the holy table: she has not even seen a church these six months."

Ulric. Where did you discover all these fine things? probably in the works of some father Wetslinger?

Odilon. No, indeed. I found them in the works of a very worthy Calvinist clergyman, called Hess, author of " Collections destined for the History of the Churches, and of the Reformation in Switzerland." I now hope you are convinced I was sincere when I hesitated to touch that string ; and that you will allow that these models of pastors were quite on a footing with Luther's tailors, tanners, blacksmiths, and journeymen printers!

Edward. Certainly.

Odilon. Now what consideration do you think religious instructors of this kind could enjoy among the people?

Edward. None at all; and as a hierarchical constitution was wanting to obviate the mischief, it was necessary the temporal authority should interfere.

Odilon. By and by, however, the Protestant clergy assumed more form and consistency; but, in our days, their decline has become greater than ever, and thus has been verified the maxim of a very learned writer, and well informed of the state of things. " All those," says he, " who separated from the great body of the church and its head, have always fallen under a profane and arbitrary authority."[*]

Ulric. This is another effect of the spirit of the times, without reckoning the faults of the clergy themselves. Depend upon it, a virtuous ecclesiastic and a good preacher will always be respected.

Edward. I do not deny it, but at the same time it must be admitted, that the Protestant clergy is in a state of great dependance, and has lost a great deal of the credit it formerly possessed.

Odilon. I believe I have already shown that this inconvenience was felt in the first periods of the Reformation. Melanchton complained, that instead of the old papal yoke which was of wood, they had got one of iron, namely, that of statesmen or laymen, who had assumed an authority much more terrible than that of the Pope. The centuriators of Magdebourg, in their introduction to the 7th century, complain bitterly of the same evil.

Edward. This is very unfortunate, I confess, but what can be done?

Odilon. The clergy was hardly better treated even by its founders. I will not mention Luther, but will quote what Rousseau, in his Letters from the Mountain, says of Calvin : "What man was ever more outrageous, more imperious, more decisive, more divinely infallible than Calvin, to whom the least opposition that any one dared to make, was a work of satan, a crime that deserved burning." This, it must be allowed, was a yoke much heavier than the one that had been shaken off, together with all ecclesiastical authority.

Ulric. The severity and warmth of the two reformers, was only a defect in their character.

Odilon. This is is no excuse. But the oppression must

* Feller, Diction. Hist. tom vii. p. 262

have appeared very hard to the partisans of the Reformation, subjected, as Melanchton complains, to statesmen, in order to remedy the disorders that had crept into their church. Time has not softened their situation. Now judge yourself, with how little energy an ecclesiastic must fulfil his duty, with respect to men on whom he depends, and to whose benevolence, favor, or pity, he owes his comforts, and even often all that he has. Who will be inclined to listen to the advice, the remonstrances, or reprimands of a man, who exercises a profession despised in society, and which is only retained, because it already exists and cannot well be suppressed? Would you like to hear what a modern writer has said on this subject from his own melancholy experience?

Edward. What is his name?

Odilon. Beaulieu. In his Historical Essays on the French Revolution, tom. i. p. 4, of the introduction, he says: "When a people has ceased to honor their ministers of religion, they begin also to be prejudiced against the doctrines which those ministers explain; the principles of virtue and of vice become a problem: egotism, ferocity, and every vice follow, and the state is soon overturned."

Edward. This is but too true; and we have seen public worship, religion, and morals, decline from day to day, since clergymen, metamorphosed into mere servants of the state, and instructors of the people, or givers of advice, an office which every one may perform himself, have much less authority over those who are entrusted to them, than all the other servants of the state have over those who belong to the class which they govern: especially too, since the ties, which ought to unite closely the clergy and people for the support of religion and morals, become looser every day.

Odilon. Do you think that a religious society so constituted can last long? It seems to me, that if it does not die of apoplexy, it will end in a consumption. I am not therefore at all astonished that some of your most distinguished divines have laid down principles, from which we may conjecture, that they are convinced of the end of their church, and that in consequence of this conviction, they only defend its nonexistence,

Edward. I confess I did not suspect this.

Odilon. A learned Protestant divine has expressly said, "that though Jesus Christ foresaw that a church would arise in the course of time, and from the dominion of circumstances, and though he most probably might wish it should be so, nevertheless it was never his intention, that the disciples of his doctrine should appear in the world as a visible society, or united by any external tie, in order to form a church in that sense; but he wishes them to confine themselves to the sentiment of being united and connected by the moral ties of unity of mind, harmony of affections and inclinations, and equality of intentions and hopes; that Baptism and the Eucharist are not essential articles of external worship, nor a necessary condition for forming an intimate external connexion."[*] I leave it to your own judgment to appreciate the vast results of such a maxim.

Edward. You would oblige me by drawing the consequences yourself.

Odilon. Te late Mr. Schneider, superintendant at Eisenach, a man as learned as judicious, says, in his Library of Ecclesiastical History, "that the modern Protestant *enlighteners,* do not wish for a unity of faith, but a moral unity of the heart, and reciprocal inclinations." This is the same doctrine as Plank has adopted in the passage I have just quoted; and this is what induced Grégoire to say with great truth, "According to this theory, I do not see how Mahometans or even Pagans can be excluded from the Church." See, my dear Sir, into what fine company you are introduced? what do you think now of this explanation of your tolerant Church-doctors?

Edward. I am thoroughly grieved at it.

Odilon. Though it has likewise afflicted me very much, yet I could not help smiling a little afterwards.

Edward. How is it possible?

Odilon. Why I recollected the fine summons made by the learned author of the *Words of Peace,* in the preface to that work; a summons, which contrasts prodigiously with the explanation we have just been considering.

Edward. Have the kindness to explain yourself more clearly.

Odilon. In that preface, the learned author summons each of his readers, *to help to stop the progress of the car of the spirit of the times, which is rushing too rapidly from the top of the mountain.* This summons, expressed in rather strange and

---

[*] See Plank, on Separation and Re-union, p. 10, to 13

11

ambiguous terms, calls for assistance which is nearly useless, as the author adds that the car *is rushing down, and all that is to be done, is to hinder its entire destruction, by making it arrive at the bottom, as little out of order and as little broken as possible.*

Edward. Well!

Odilon. Instead of giving the example, by putting his hand to the business to stop the car, your learned divine, on the contrary, seems to me to push it on, by means of his singular explanation, and gives it such a vigorous and energetic impulse, that nothing can any longer suspend its course.

Edward. I do not see that.

Odilon. Judge for yourself. Is it possible to deserve the reproach I have made against Plank, in a more decided way, than by maintaining, against the unanimous testimony of the apostles and of all Christian antiquity, " that Jesus Christ never intended that the disciples of his doctrine should form themselves into an external society or church, but merely wished them to feel themselves united and connected by a sort of Platonic union of the mind, in a harmony of reciprocal affections and hopes?" It is clear, that if such an union were possible, there would be no reason for refusing admittance to Jews and Pagans; Baptism and the Eucharist would no longer be essential articles of external worship, nor a necessary indication for forming an intimate and external society; and, nevertheless, these two sacraments are considered so indispensable even by those, who have otherwise deprived them of all their divine efficacy, that they have been preserved as the signs of admission into the Christian society, and as a public profession of faith of the maxims and doctrine of that church. Yes, I am justified in saying, from all the observations I have just made, that you daily make a frightful progress in this way of fraternizing with the Jews, Mahometans, Pagans, and all the partizans of the most absurd opinions.

Edward. How do you mean? I have no precise idea on this subject.

Odilon. The learned author of a work entitled, The Holy Supper, which we are already acquainted with by the preceding discussions, says, " Things are come to such a pitch, that allusions more or less clear are made towards the entire suppression of the Eucharist, *as a rite become absolutely useless.* What is more, one of the co-operators in the Literary Review

of Wagenitz, has dared to say, that most probably there will
soon be no further question of Baptism and Eucharist." See,
how after having labored to destroy all ideas of a Christian
church, what pains are taken among you, to suppress also
all the sacraments, in order to effect that fine union of the
mind, that harmony of affections, and that equality of hopes,
which will connect us at the same time with all infidels, and
is so strongly recommended by Dr. Plank.

Ulric. Yes, I see too clearly, that the progress of the car
of the spirit of the times is so rapid, that it carries away the
church itself and all the sacraments. We have only now to
take leave of St. Paul and his ecclesiastical institutions, which
he says he founded by the order of Jesus Christ. We shall
soon be quite at our ease, and nothing will hinder us from
suppressing henceforward the entire article of *the Church*
from our dogmatical books. It seems to me, that the synod
of Dordrecht and the catechism of Heidelberg are not so com-
plaisant as Dr. Plank.

Odilon. St. Irenæus, in opposition to this writer, maintained, even in his time, the existence of the church from the
time of the apostles, and especially that of Rome, as the necessary model of all the others.

Ulric. What! Irenæus, who was bishop of Lyons, in the
year of Christ 157? you will never persuade me that.

Odilon. You must, however, make up your mind to it, for
nothing is more true than the testimony of that bishop, who
was almost contemporary with St. John the Evangelist; but,
supposing even that Irenæus did not personally know that
Evangelist, who, according to the testimony of most Christian writers, only died under Trajan, it is still certain, that
Polycarp was his master, a disciple of St. John.

Edward. This is, undoubtedly, an authority of high antiquity and of great importance.

Ulric. What is this testimony of Irenæus?

Odilon. After having said, in the third chapter of the third
book against heresies, that the Roman church was founded
by the apostles Peter and Paul, he adds these remarkable
words: "The whole church, that is the faithful in every
part, should agree with this church, on account of its more
powerful principality, in which the tradition of the apostles
has always been preserved. The blessed apostles, therefore,
having founded and established this church, gave the bishopric and administration of it to Linus. Paul makes mention

of this Linus in his Epistles to Timothy. To him succeded
Anacletus; after whom, the third who obtained the bishopric
from the apostles was Clemens, who saw the apostles themselves, and conferred with them , while their preaching was
still sounding in his ears, and their tradition before his eyes;
and not he alone, for many others still remained who had
been taught by the apostles."* Here then is an authentic
testimony, which formally contradicts an assertion near 1800
years younger than it; it is of such weight, that I may leave
it to you entirely to draw your own consequences from it,
without mentioning the learned observations which Feuar-
dent has made upon it. St. Cyprian, also, who had sometimes discussions with the bishops of Rome, nevertheless
calls the church of that city the *mother*, the *procreatrix*, and
the *root of the Catholic church.*† Calvin himself, agreeing in
this point with Holy Scripture and ecclesiastical history,
thinks very differently from Dr. Plank.

Ulric. Calvin, do you say?

Odilon. Yes, in the book iv, chap. 1, paragraph iv, he
says what follows : "As we do not wish to dispute on the
visible church, it will be sufficient to state in one word the
praise of this our common mother, which will show how
useful and even necessary the knowledge of her is to us,
since there is no other entrance into life but through her, by
being conceived in her own womb, by being born, and
nourished with her milk, and by living under her protection
and direction, till, delivered from this mortal flesh, we become like unto angels. . . . Out of her bosom neither pardon
of sin nor salvation is to be hoped for." Yes, if there be no
visible church of God here below; if it was not even the intention of Jesus Christ that there should be one; if Baptism
and the Eucharist are not essential parts of external worship,
and a necessary indication of an external union, nothing bet-

---

* Ad hanc ecclesiam necesse est, propter potentiorem principali-
tatem, omnem convenire ecclesiam, hoc est, qui sunt undique fideles,
in quâ, semper ab his qui sunt undique, conservata est ea quæ est ab
apostolis traditio. Fundantes igitur et instruentes beati apostoli ecclesiam, Lino episcopatum administrandæ ecclesiæ tradiderunt. Hujus Lini Paulus, in his quæ sunt ad Timotheum epistolis, meminit.
Succedit autem ei Anacletus; post eum tertio loco ab apostolis episcopatum sortitur Clemens, qui et vidit apostolos ipsos, et contulit
cum eis, cum adhuc insonantem prædicationem apostolorum et tra-
ditionem ante oculos haberet: non solus, nam adhuc multi supere-
rant tunc ab apostolis docti.

† Matrem et matricem radicem catholicæ Ecclesiæ. (Epist. 1, ad
Cornel. lib. iv, epist. viii, et epist. lv, ad Cornel. papam).

ter can be done than to dismiss directly all the servants of the church, and all the distributors of the sacraments; for, the fine harmony of sentiments of Dr. Plank, can very well be formed without them, the Jews and Pagans may be called in, and all find themselves connected together in an equality of hopes.

Edward. You are perfectly right. Formerly, we used still to sing, "If Jesus Christ protects his church," &c. But we must now take up a very different tone.—But did not you wish to speak of another very important article?

Odilon. Yes, and I flatter myself you will easily admit the first and fundamental principles of it; but I am not so certain of your flexibility respecting the consequences that flow from it.

Ulric. We do not consider divinity among us like logic; when once we grant the premises, we dispute no further the consequence.

Odilon. Very well; you allow that no human society, monarchical or republican, can subsist without a head?

Edward. Most certainly.

Ulric. I see what you are at—you wish to demonstrate the necessity of a Pope.

Odilon. I am still far from that article. You admit, besides, that no human society can be preserved without a reciprocal union of the members among each other, and in connexion with their head?

Edward. Perfectly just, and every edifice that has not this quality, must necessarily give way.

Odilon. In short, you will admit that no human society can be of long duration without an authentic interpreter of its laws?

Ulric. I see clearly that you wish to bring us insensibly to admit the infallibility of a supreme ecclesiastical head.

Odilon. I repeat, that I am still very far from that article. But if you like it better, answer me honestly the following question: can a society of men subsist, when each of its members has a right to interpret the laws in his own way?

Edward. No, certainly not; the most dreadful confusion would follow, and it would be better to have no laws at all. But what is your object with all these questions?

Odilon. To show what some eminent men allowed, even among the first reformers themselves.

Edward. Among the first reformers themselves?

Odilon. Hear what Capito, a divine of Luther's party, and moreover, an intimate friend of Bucer and of other Calvinists, wrote to Farel: "As the clergy have been deprived of all consideration, it is natural that every thing should go topsy-turvy. There is no longer the least order in the communities. I acknowledge the great mischief we have done the church, by rejecting the authority of the Pope, with so much impudence and precipitation. The people are now without rein and curb; they despise all authority, as if, by the abolition of the papacy, we had, at the same time, suppressed all the power of the servants of the church, and all the force of the sacraments. Every one cries out now, ' I know enough to guide myself; as I have the Gospel, in which to find Jesus Christ and his doctrine, why do I want your help ?' "*

Edward. This is indeed a very remarkable testimony of the disorders of those times.

Odilon. Melanchton, who was a man of a mild character and a feeling heart, also complains of this matter, and in a most affecting way : " The whole Elbe," says he, " could not give me tears enough, to bewail the misfortunes of the Reformation, at war with itself. The people will not resume the yoke, which the love of liberty made them throw off. The imperial towns, especially, which prize religion less than their liberty, are the most restive. Our partisans do not fight for the Gospel, but for dominion. Ecclesiastical discipline is annihilated. Doubts are formed on the most important points. The evil is incurable."†

Edward. Such a situation deserved such lamentations.

Odilon. You may find the counterpart in the picture which the famous Dudith drew of the state of the religious reformation, in one of his letters to Beza : " Our people are pushed here and there by every wind of doctrine. To-day, perhaps, you might learn what they think of religion, but nobody is capable of answering for to-morrow. On what dogmatic point do the characters, that have declared war against the Pope, agree amongst themselves ? If you take the trouble

---

* Epist. ad Farell. inter. Calv. p. 5.
† Melanch. epist. lib. iv, epist. 100—129.

to look over all the articles, from the first to the last, you will not find one that is not admitted by some, and condemned by others." I could produce you a multitude of similar passages.

Edward. But what has all this to do with our times?

Odilon. It should convince you, that this defective organization of Protestantism, would be sufficient to destroy it, even if it existed in reality, and not merely by name, as is the case at present.

Edward. I do not see this consequence at all.

Odilon. You see I was not wrong in fearing that you would admit the premises without granting the consequence.

Edward. Explain yourself more clearly.

Odilon. Tell me, then, where is the head of this great religious society, called Protestantism? You will answer, perhaps, that like republics, it has several heads, or *supreme bishops,* in the person of its sovereigns, and in the most distinguished divines of all Protestant countries; and that, in fine, it possesses a federative constitution. Where then is the general agreement, the common operation, the united cares of these different heads, " to prevent the constitutional commonwealth from receiving any detriment?" (Ne quid detrimenti capiat respublica ecclesiastica). What part have those sovereigns and divines taken in what concerns religion, and the ecclesiastical constitution in any *other* Protestant country but their own?

" It would even seem that these rulers trouble themselves very little about the state of religion in their own country, since persons, calling themselves ecclesiastics, attack it with impunity, and with such obstinate rage as I have proved by numerous examples."

Edward. You are right. Formerly, when a Protestant clergyman fell into any error, or attempted the slightest innovation, all the divines, even of the most distant countries, rose up against him, as the history of the modern church sufficiently proves. But things have mightily changed since the progress of toleration. Nobody troubles himself any more about the maxims and opinions of others.

Odilon. Where is the union and connexion among the members who compose the great religious body of Protestantism? I will not say that the Swedes, the Danes, and other more distant Protestants do not concern themselves at all about those in Germany ; but shall only observe that the latter have the same indifference for their countrymen ; all intimate connexion has ceased long since.

Edward. I allow that in this respect times are wonderfully changed. England and Sweden formerly took a lively interest in the fate of their brethren in Germany. In our days, on the contrary, tolerantism has produced a cold indifference, and the interest of the state has entirely absorbed the interest of religion.

Odilon. It was soon perceived, after the beginning of the Reformation, that it would be giving birth to all sorts of errors and absurdities, if every one were allowed to interpret Holy Scripture in his own way. Nevertheless, they had separated themselves from the supreme tribunal and authentic interpreter of the law. To obviate therefore the mischievous consequences that would result from this, it was decreed that Holy Scripture should be understood and explained, according to the analogy of the doctrine, and of the profession of faith, adopted by Protestantism ; for experience soon showed the consequences that would necessarily flow from the principle originally established by Luther.

Edward. What is that principle? I know nothing of it.

Odilon. It is much the same as what Protestants now acknowledge by the name of *reason ;* formerly it was called *the spiritual man,* or every one's own *internal sense.*

Edward. I protest I have no idea of what you have advanced.

Odilon. Well, then, read the eleventh discourse of Luther on the words of Jesus Christ: *take heed of false prophets :* read also the 115th article among the 500 of that name ; you will there see that *the spiritual man* alone, or each one's interior sense, might decide on the truth or falsehood of a doctrine. As in our days the greatest confusion and highest absurdities would spring from the exclusive liberty, granted to each man's individual reason, in judging religious disputes ; in like manner, the greatest disorder would have resulted from the prerogative given by Luther to the spiritual man, or the interior sense to decide the same questions ; each one would have been justified in saying: "My spiritual man has decided, that my opinion is the only true one, and that yours is false." It was on this account that prudence inspired the resource I have just mentioned ; but I will not decide whether it be otherwise conformable to the spirit of Protestantism.

Edward. Why not, if it be necessary, as you allow yourself? the universality and long duration of this mode of precaution prove completely that it was conformable to the spirit of Protestantism.

Odilon. A modern writer of my acquaintance could tell you many truths on this subject.

Edward. It appears so clear to me, that it wants no commentary.

Odilon. The author of the work, " On the Spirit and Consequences of the Reformation," says that Luther soon made his individual way of seeing religious questions obligatory on others ; and that for the infallibility of the church, he only substituted the infallibility of the Confession of Augsburg.

Edward. Never was that confession considered among us as infallible ; we oblige ourselves to teach conformably to its doctrines, as far as they agree with Holy Scripture.

Odilon. However mild the name given to this method, it is not less true, that it was contrary to the free spirit of Protestantism, to throw off *one* authority, in order to adopt *another*, which had much less motives in its favor.

Edward. Without these measures, Protestantism would soon have become the prey of all parties, and the number of sects might have been counted by that of interpreters of the Holy Scripture ; all the heresies condemned by the first article of the Confession of Augsburg would have been revived, and have become more audacious than ever.

Odilon. This is precisely the case of modern Protestantism, which, in this point, and perhaps in this alone, still agrees with Luther ; and, if you will allow me to say it, with the Quakers likewise.

Edward. With the Quakers ?

Odilon. Yes, as Luther and the Quakers established their *spiritual man*, and their *interior light*, as judges of Holy Scripture ; so, the *enlightened* divines of modern Protestantism submit it to their *reason*: " We shall easily agree about words, provided we undertand the things."[*]

Edward. And what consequence do you draw from all this ?

Odilon. What you yourself will undoubtedly draw, for it

[*] In verbis sumus faciles, dummodo convenimus in re.

is pointed out by evidence. How can we be astonished, that without an authentic interpreter of the law, without an ecclesiastical head, and without respect for the symbolic books,* each one should comment the Bible at his pleasure, and that the most absurd and dreadful interpretations of the most sacred truths of Christianity should be introduced among Protestants? Things are come to such a pitch, that an Arian, or a Macedonian, provided he be not entirely given to naturalism, has still a right to boast of being a Christian. But some modern Protestants themselves, Casaubon for example, were perfectly sensible of the inconvenience of not having an authentic interpreter of the law.

Ulric. Casaubon, the declared antagonist of Baronius! how can we believe such a thing of such an enlightened critic?

Odilon. Still, I cannot help attributing such an opinion to him: for he says in one of his letters, that though he acknowledges no other foundation of true religion than Holy Scripture, yet he thinks nevertheless that the dogmatic doctrines, which flow from it, were transmitted through the canal of antiquity, and that this is the opinion of Melanchton and of the church of England; and that if this maxim were rejected, there would be no end to innovations in the interpretation of Scripture. Casaubon adds, that from having rejected tradition, it became impossible for Luther, Calvin and Zuingle to agree about the sacrament, and other essential points.†

Ulric. My surprise is extreme.

Odilon. It will not be diminished when you hear that he

In one of the duchies of Saxony, the law which obliged clergymen to maintain the symbolic books, has already been abrogated; and a work entitled, *Free Thoughts,* which appeared at Berlin in 1774, proved, that even at that period, those same books and the whole confession of Augsburg had no longer any credit among Protestants. It must even be allowed that they were merely consistent in the abrogation of this law, and that the cessation of the ancient obligation is become beneficial to morals. For it is absurd to make an oath to be taken on a book, in which not the least faith is put. And moreover, is not he, who has taken it, exposed to the temptation of breaking it, or to the necessity of openly dissembling a belief which his heart has long since rejected? But, on the other hand, the suppression of this law has broken the last tie which still kept the Protestants together, and has given up their society to all the caprices and all the whimsical ideas of the doctors and masters of its doctrine. What monstrous consequences are we not to expect hereafter, and how can the duration of a society so organized be expected?

† Epist. præst. vir, p. 247— 9; in Tabaraud, a. a. o. p. 323, 324.

thought in the same way on many other articles. He was indeed very much prejudiced against some doctrines of the Catholic church; but he formerly confessed, that most of those, from which the Protestants thought proper to divide, were exactly conformable to the most ancient maxims of the Christian church, and that the opinions of Catholics in this respect were much sounder than those of the reformers.* You will not deny that Casaubon was a competent judge in this matter.

Ulric. I repeat it, his opinion on the necessity of an authentic interpreter of the law, gives me the greatest surprise.

Odilon. What will you say then, if I assure you that some very late Protestant divines, and even *enlighteners*, have expressed the same opinion?

Edward. This opinion, nevertheless, would be very contrary to the principles of the day.

Odilon. In a dissertation on the Schütes and the Samnites, among the Mahometans, in the "Magazine of the History of Religion," by Staudlin, the author, after having said that these two sects have a complete resemblance with the Catholics and Protestants, adds, that if in religion we set out from a *supernatural principle* (as a written revelation, the Bible, for example, or the Coran) *we must necessarily admit that the Divinity, who gave the revelation, must also have appointed the means of preventing that revelation from being abandoned to the fluctuations of human judgment.* It is the non-admission of this principle, which the author of the dissertation very justly considers as an absurdity.

Edward. Very right; but would your author then admit a sort of permanent miracle, or an established authentic interpreter, like the Pope?

Odilon. Neither the one nor the other. He asserts this absurdity, while at the same time he endeavors to justify it, in the following way: "This absurdity has had very advantageous effects for mankind, who, without it, would never have attained the high degree of illumination in which we are placed."

Edward. Wonderful indeed!

Odilon. Draw yourself the consequence of this singular maxim.

Edward. I will thank you to do it.

* Tarbaraad, a. a. o. p. 219, 220.

Odilon. The author, as you have seen, felt the necessity of an authentic interpreter, the omission of which, after the benefit of revelation, would have been, on the part of God, a great absurdity. But as his Protestant principles would not allow him to admit the establishment of such an interpreter, he preferred asserting that God had acted *absurdly*, maintaining all the time that this absurdity has had the most advantageous results.

Edward. An *advantageous* absurdity is such a new and extraordinary thing to me, that I beg you to put me in the way of comprehending the author's meaning.

Odilon. Yes, I will explain these pretended advantages. It is to the absurdity committed by God, in giving the world a revelation, which he left at the same time to the arbitrary interpretation of human caprice, that Protestants are indebted for the loss of all belief in that same revelation, for having renounced its most holy and consoling truths, and, in fine, for having been precipitated into the abyss of naturalism. According to this advantageous absurdity, it is also said, in the same work, speaking of the morality of the Bramins, "that the Gospel of John is incontestably the production of some sages of the school of Alexandria; that the *Logos,* that is to say, the Word, of which St. John speaks, is nothing but a spark of the Divine Spirit, which shines in the intelligence of every reasonable being in a word, that spirit of Brama, which penetrates the whole creation: that the reveries of divines, concerning a hypostatic union and the eternal generation of the Son, as they are announced in the Athanasian creed, would soon go into smoke; and that the envious host of divines had dared to accuse the partizans of Brama of idolatry, without reflecting that they themselves had made an idol of that beneficent sage Jesus Christ."

Edward. I am so confounded with what I have just heard, that I can make no answer whatever.

Odilon. In consequence of this beneficent absurdity, the author makes no difficulty of deriding the incarnation of the Son of God, from the doctrine of the Bramins, on the pretended incorporation of Brama, Vischnu, &c.; and antichristianity is consummated. However, I shall observe, by the bye, that in thus combining the doctrine of the Bramins with that of Christianity, the author has given a proof of very great ignorance.

Ulric. In what way?

Odilon. Because Brama, Vischnu, and Schiwa, are merely the personified *properties* of the Supreme Being, according to which he is the creator, preserver, and destroyer. How then can the *corporification* of Bramu, Vischnu, &c., be compared in this way with the incarnation of the Son of God? The Hindoos name that Supreme Being *Ixchur*, supreme will, and sometimes *Bren*, or supreme being. He has no image, and his worship only consists in prayers and religious songs. I beg you to read the interesting particulars on this subject, in Sprengel's Library, 39th part, pp. 33–35, where he gives an account of Hafner's travels to the coast of Coromandel. You may also compare the relations of the celebrated traveller and missionary, Fra Paolino da San Bartolomeo, one of the most learned and best informed persons in every thing that regards the East Indies. He assures us that the Hindoos call the Supreme Being *Parabara*, that is, the most excellent and sublime Being of all; and they give the name of *Svayambhu* to the being who exists by himself. See the "Magazine of New Travels," 15th part, p. 326, Berlin, 1798.

Edward. And what consequences do you draw from all this?

Odilon. Allow me to quote, on this subject, the opinion of one of our divines, at the time of the Reformation; an opinion which experience has unfortunately too much confirmed.

Edward. You will oblige me very much.

Odilon. It is what the celebrated Melchior Canus says against the famous Cajetan, (Loc. Theol. lib. vii. cap. iii. No. 17.) "If each one be allowed the right of explaining the Holy Scriptures in his own way, I tremble already at the dangers which threaten the whole existence of religion. For, if a single parcel of the Scriptures be given up to the human will, it will soon seize on the second, the third—in short, on all, in the usual way of mankind, who form a habit of every thing. If every man be permitted to comment Scripture according to his genius and caprice, nothing stable will remain; and instead of the sanctuary of holy and pure truth, we shall see a shameful den of errors, as Vincent of Lerins long ago observed with equal elegance and truth." You will observe, that this Vincent of Lerins lived in the fifth century, and the passage to which Canus alludes is in the chapter of his *Commonitory.* Do you find this authority ancient and great enough?

Edward. Certainly; but what do you mean to deduce from it?

Odilon. That Protestantism, deprived of a head, without any intimate connexion between its members, and without an authentic interpreter of its laws, cannot have a long existence. Tertullian said in his time—"What was allowed to Valentin, will be allowed to the Valentinians, and what to Marcion also to the Marcionites; that is, they may all change their belief at pleasure." What was free to Luther must be equally so to his successors. Without a fixed authority, each one may cut out a religion according to his fancies; and I should not be surprised to see as many different religions in Protestantism, as there are now *masters of the people*, to use a modern denomination of all these gentlemen : should it be otherwise, Protestantism would be a singular exception in human society.

Ulric. This exception is completely established; for Protestantism has still continued to exist.

Odilon. Nominatively, it is true, but not really.

Ulric. I see you are absolutely determined to deprive us of our qualification of Protestants.

Odilon. Our conversation of yesterday proved the distance which separates you from your ancestors; and you will admit, that no society whatever can any longer assume the name of the essential quality it has lost, and which distinguished it from all other societies.

Ulric. That is an indisputable rule of logic.

Odilon. Apply it to the religious society of the Protestants. It is clear that its particular doctrines distinguish it essentially from all other religions. If then, after having rejected these doctrines, Protestantism adopts others, it ceases to merit that name, to take *in reality* the character and qualification of the new doctrine it has adopted.

Edward. But what is, after all, the end of all this? I find no connexion in it with your first position, on the facility, now greater than ever, of effecting a re-union between the Christian societies.

Odilon. If Protestants still adhered firmly to their ancient religious system; if they had such a worship as every religion must have that pretends to duration, if they had an ecclesiastical police in the midst of them, to watch over the preservation of religion generally and particularly ; if the individuals, who preside over the exercise of that religion, enjoyed a proper degree of consideration, and had moreover a common head, to preserve the intimate connexion of all the parts of that religion, it is very probable that its re-union with Catholicity would be exposed to great difficulties.

Edward. I understand from this why all the attempts to unite the Greek church with the Latin have hitherto proved ineffectual.

Odilon. You know that none of the advantages I have just mentioned exist among you. The decay of your religious society increases from day to day, and it may even be said, that, considered as an ecclesiastical body, it has ceased to exist; it is only an aggregation of men with different opinions, and even diametrically opposite, without order, harmony, and connexion. Would it then be an insurmountable difficulty to bring back such persons under the beneficent yoke of a religious society ?

Ulric. You will not be offended at my observing that there is a great harshness in such an accusation as this, against so distinguished a religious society as that of the Protestants. To refuse it the title of a church, to call it an aggregation of men, divided among each other by the most opposite opinions, to consider it, in a word, as a misshapen chaos, is rather too severe.

Odilon. I should be extremely sorry to have said any thing disagreeable or disobliging ; but this opinion, of which you think you have reason to complain, has been given by very well informed persons, as I have already proved to you ; and very recently, the author of *Confidential Letters,* to Biester, has said, " Properly speaking, there is no longer any church among Protestants, if by that word is understood a society of Christians united by the same faith, by the same religious principles, and the same means of salvation ; they are only a mass of men, of whom those in the polished and best informed classes have ceased, for the most part, to have any connexion with Luther, Calvin, &c. The multitude, on the contrary, only follow their own opinions, however false and erroneous ; they consider the Holy Scripture merely as a vehicle, in which morality must be conveyed for the sake of some pious unenlightened souls, who are *bigotted* to the Bible ; finally, the greatest part reject the whole of Scripture, all revelation, and all the dogmas of Christianity, in order to sacrifice to Deism, the half-brother of Atheism."

Edward. Dreadful, but incontestible truths!

Ulric. This is, perhaps, nothing but the opinion of one of those Catholics, who, at all times, have endeavored to prove that we do not form a church.

Odilon. Examine the validity and justness of the opinion, and not the condition of him who pronounces it. I can tell you, moreover, that the author alleges the testimony of Protestant men of letters. Their opinion, perfectly conformable to that of the question, will probably have more weight in your eyes.

Ulric. Will you have the goodness to produce these testimonies ?

Odilon. They are from the celebrated authors of the Universal Literary Gazette. Here is what they say very drily, after having examined the passage of the author in question : " The signs and marks of an almost entire dissolution and disorganization of the society called *church* are now perceptible ; the greatest number consider Christianity a mere human invention, mixed with all sorts of fables and illusions ; they are ashamed of a closer connexion with that church, above which they feel themselves greatly elevated ; in a word, this church, being capable of nothing further towards the regulation and amelioration of mankind, is insensibly decaying of itself!" From this, you will easily understand how the distinguished Protestant divine I mentioned above, could say *that Jesus Christ never meant that the followers of his doctrine should form themselves into a visible and external society;* or, what is equivalent, they should found a church. Consequently, there exists no longer any Protestant church.

Edward. But what could you say, if our sovereigns, in their quality of *supreme bishops,* obviated these causes henceforward : in a word, if they gave us a new religious society, better organized and connected in all its parts ?

Odilon. To effect this, it would be necessary, above all, that they should have have one mind, and one and the same interest ; but political affairs have unfortunately too well shown us how impossible such harmony would be in a much more delicate affair, since it affects conscience. It would be much easier to enter a religious society already existing.

Edward. But you know very well what an enormous distance now separates the two parties, and how great is the indifferentism for every thing which bears the name of religion?

Odilon. This is precisely what makes the union more easy at present than formerly ; and your *enlighteners*, without suspecting it, and wishing it, have themselves labored exceedingly for the Catholic religion.* Let any external circumstance whatever presents itself, and you will see the indifferents approach Catholicity more readily and more easily than would the partisans of any religious system still subsisting.

Ulric. This would be, truly, a fine acquisition!

Odilon. That may be, but our gain would not be less indisputable.

Ulric. How?

Odilon. We should gain all their posterity.

Ulric. Do you not think that those indifferent parents, though bound by circumstances to your communion, will inculcate their principles to their children, and thus deceive all your future hopes?

Odilon. I imagine that proper means will not be wanting then, any more than now, for preserving youth from the influence of these bad principles. But where there are no principles at all, as with the indifferents, none can be inculcated.

Edward. Do not forget that Protestants, though not indifferents, are still very far from the principles of the Catholics.

Odilon. This is very true ; but it is likewise certain, that those who have not yet entirely embraced naturalism, would have less difficulty to form a re-union with the Catholics, than is commonly supposed, if they were only better acquainted with the principles of our church.

Edward. It seems to me, however, that your maxims, explained in such a number of works, may very easily be learnt.

* The author of the *Confidential Letters* to Biester says: "The most zealous proselytes the Catholic church can have, are now among the Protestants, whether philosophers or divines, who make every effort to destroy Christianity." In fact, they who know what Christianity is become in their hands, and that individuals, as well as society, cannot subsist without a positive religion, must feel how true this assertion is.

Odilon. Your divines not having sufficiently studied even the writings of the first reformers and ancient masters of their doctrine, it is hardly to be presumed that they have examined more closely the writings of the Catholic divines, or that they know the maxims of our church, and the great and important proofs on which it is founded.

Edward. I doubt this, however; if the maxims of Protestants and Catholics were not so opposite, nor the points of this opposition so serious, it is not probable that our ancestors would ever have abandoned you.

Odilon. I showed you yesterday what was the opinion of Luther on the Catholic church and its dogmas; and that of Melanchton was the same. He assured Theopulus, that he and his partisans were faithfully attached to the Catholic religion and its dogmas, and that it was the defending them with so much zeal, which had got him so many enemies; that with the help of God, they would prove this their faith to Jesus Christ, and the Roman church; and that in general, it was only a slight difference of rites which prevented their union.

Edward. Nevertheless, Luther afterwards opposed the Catholic church and its dogmas very violently, and Melanchton was of opinion that the latter ought to be often changed.

Odilon. One fault of this kind commonly brings on another. However, Protestants were not so generally separated from the Catholics, in their doctrines, as is commonly believed. Erasmus was also of my opinion, in this respect, and nobody certainly will accuse him of not having known both the maxims of the Catholic church, and those of the first reformers.

Ulric. I must tell you, that I value the opinion of Erasmus, much more as a scholar, than as a divine.

Odilon. Well, let us return then to Dr. Plank, who is both a divine and a Protestant. In his *Words of Peace to the Catholic church,* he says, "The way in which they separated, and the circumstances which occasioned it, were the principal obstacles towards the reconciliation of the two parties." The motives of separation, therefore, could not have been serious and important enough, at least in the beginning, to render it irrevocable.

Ulric. I doubt whether the consequence you draw from this assertion, will be granted. For my part, I am much surprised at it.

Odilon. I could cite you a modern testimony, much more important still, and which would surprise you the more, as it is from a Protestant, a philosopher, and a writer of the first rank.

Edward. Who is this?

Odilon. The great Leibnitz. You know, of course, that he not only defended the dogma of the most Holy Trinity against the Socinian Wissowatius; but proved, moreover, that this doctrine was very reconcileable with sound philosophy. Leibnitz did not confine himself to this; in the manuscripts which he left, and which are preserved in the library at Hanover, he also defends the maxims of the Catholic church, and especially those, from which the Protestants have deviated. It is truly lamentable, that this part of Leibnitz's works has never been printed.

Ulric. I am not able to refute what you assert concerning the religious opinions of Leibnitz; but, it is astonishing, that with such sentiments, he should have broken off so abruptly his correspondence with Bossuet on a religious re-union.

Odilon. You will be much more surprised to hear, that Bossuet, on his side, had agreed with him on several important points; namely, respecting the council of Trent, the use of the cup, the vulgar tongue, Luther's translation of the Bible, the Divine worship, and the marriage of such priests as had already contracted that sacrament.

Ulric. You had reason to say I should be surprised; but, I ask you again, why did Leibnitz break off these conferences?

Odilon. You may hear it from himself, in the following words, which he wrote to Fabricius: "You know that the whole right of our sovereign to the crown of England is founded on the hatred and proscription of the Roman church in that kingdom." Thus, it was not the opinions of Leibnitz on the Catholic religion, but mere political considerations, which caused the rupture of those conferences.

Edward. I should never have expected such a thing from Leibnitz: however, the philosopher and the divine have very different ways of thinking, and the one often adopts what the other rejects; the opinion of a divine should be fixed, I think, by the Holy Scripture alone.

Odilon. But as Protestant divines admit the authority of the primitive church, when there is question of determining the canonical authenticity of the sacred books, they cannot, without inconsequence, reject the same authority, when there is question of explaining the Scripture, and treating of doctrines, believed and adopted at all times, as I have already shown. It was also by the study of Christian antiquity, and consequently of primitive Christianity, that the learned Hugo Grotius was at length decided to declare entirely in favor of the Catholic church.

Edward. Grotius! that is impossible.

Odilon. If his friend Pétau had not been convinced of his having these sentiments, he would never have said a mass for the repose of his soul.

Edward. However, he died in the arms of Dr. Quistorp, a Protestant divine, at Rostock.

Odilon. But are you sure he died a Lutheran? One may accept words of consolation and piety from any one.

Ulric. The opinions of Grotius, in this respect, deserve no regard; for his writings testify that he was a Calvinist, Arminian, and Socinian, each in their turn.

Odilon. Yes, but at length one comes back to the right way. Read, in the mean time, his book on the powers of sovereigns, respecting sacred things, his notes on the consultations of George Cassander, and the work entitled *Discuss. Rivetani Apologetici,* and you will have no doubt of his predilection in favor of the Roman church: this feeling is also visible in his letters to his brother, which I have already mentioned. But, to confine myself to the question; I say— if, when there is question of fixing the canonical authenticity of Scripture, we may appeal to the authority of the ancient church, that same authority cannot be rejected without inconsistency, when there is question of the tradition of doctrines, as I have already proved.

Edward. Granting this, what would be the result?

Odilon. Without reckoning several other important objects, all parties would gain by it, from this circumstance alone, that fewer obstacles towards a re-union would occur, than was imagined.

Edward. I will thank you to enter into further details on this point.

Odilon. Most willingly. Allow me only to ask you, whether you know for certain what were the sentiments of

Luther, Melanchton, Calvin, and Zuingle, on religion? We
have seen already that they were not always consistent with
themselves; and a letter from Calvin to Melanchton proves
that they were sometimes in opposition with each other. "It
is of great importance," says he, "that posterity should not
be sensible of our dissensions; for it would be very ridiculous,
if we, who attack the whole world, should be so disunited
among ourselves, and even at the beginning of the Reformation." But supposing they agreed perfectly in their opinions,
do we know exactly what they were?

Edward. Why should we not know them? Their writings
are in the hands of all the world; and even if these writings
were lost, have we not those of their contemporaries, and
their disciples, and of the divines, their immediate successors? All these may teach us the real opinions of the reformers and founders of our church, on such and such articles of faith.

Odilon. What you have just said, and which I wished to
hear from you very much, is extremely just. But, pray
observe, that we have also undeniable witnesses, since they
are classed even by Protestants in the primitive church;
such are, Clement of Rome, who was still living in the first
century, and was a disciple and companion of the holy
apostles, Peter and Paul; Ignatius and Polycarp, who
having lived at the end of the first and the beginning of the
second century, had intercourse with the apostles; a Justin,
an Irenæus, a Meliton, and several others of a little later
period, and who are all in our favor.

Ulric. It seems to me, however, that among these witnesses, some might with good reason be rejected; for example, you know that the letters of Ignatius and Polycarp
are partly forged and falsified.

Odilon. I do not trouble myself with those that are forged
or interpolated; I keep strictly to those which are acknowledged to be authentic by the Protestants themselves.

Edward. And what consequence do you draw from them?

Odilon. A very simple one. As the writings of the disciples of Luther, and the divines, his immediate successors,
are competent testimonies of the principles of that reformer,
in like manner, the writings of the most ancient fathers of the
church, are valid testimonies of the faith of Christians in the
very first ages. But, this faith is still ours at this day, and

if we have any shadow of respect for what Jesus Christ and his apostles themselves taught, a respect which we cannot consistently refuse, it is evident that all the advantage is on our side, and a re-union will not then present so many impediments.

Ulric. But this does not destroy what I have already observed, namely, that the principles of Catholics, which we know much better than you seem to think, are at such a distance from ours, that this re-union would, on the contrary, be very difficult.

Odilon. I have known many Protestants, who, after having read the *Exposition of the Catholic Doctrine* by Bossuet, freely confessed, that before they had quite a different idea of our doctrine.

Ulric. It is impossible to allege that work in your favor; for the doctrine contained in it is commonly called *Protestantized* Catholicity.

Odilon. If this were the case, it is impossible that Pope Innocent XI., and so many bishops and prelates, could have given their approbation to this work. If you read Tabaraud's work on the re-union, you will find in it a complete refutation of what Rabaut dared to assert, in maintaining that Bossuet's *Exposition* was the consequence of his conferences with Leibnitz, and that the learned Bishop of Meaux had been even much alarmed for fear of being reproved for it by the Court of Rome. You will find, especially, that in this business, Rabaut made an anachronism of twenty years.

Edward. Excuse these frequent interruptions; I recollect you meant to speak of some other very important points.

Odilon. Protestantism, with respect to its external form, was, perhaps, never in a more critical, and more dangerous position, than at this moment. All its ancient buttresses are not only worm-eaten, but entirely overthrown. Add to this, its internal constitution, the defects of which I have already sufficiently pointed out to you, and you will find that nothing can be more frail.

Edward. Unfold your idea entirely.

Odilon. Your profession of faith, according to which you obtained your religious liberty, and equality of rights with the Catholics, has been abandoned and annihilated by yourselves, and even in several countries has been already suppressed. The peace of Westphalia, which confirmed all these advantages for you, is no longer in vigor. *The body of the Evangelicals*, the great bulwark of Protestantism, which preserved it against all attacks, has ceased to exist, as well as the Imperial Diet, and nobody can now have recourse to it.

Edward. This is but too true; but what do you conclude from it?

Odilon. That if any power, foreign or indigenous, had any motive whatever for re-uniting the Protestants with the Catholics, the actual situation of Protestantism would render this operation easier than formerly, and that *externally* also, there would no longer be any obstacles.

Edward. The princes, who are now all *sovereigns*, will effectually prevent it, and will no more permit Protestantism to be Catholized, than Catholicity to be Protestantized.

Odilon. That same sovereignty, when it thought proper, formerly surmounted all obstacles; and if a prince now thought proper to effect such a re-union in his country, no *State*, like those formerly of Cassel and Wirtemberg, would oppose it, no body of *Evangelicals* could occasion any impediment; for nothing of that kind is now in existence.

Edward. But what motives could the princes have in this respect?

Odilon. Luther once said : " Many are good evangelicals, because the monasteries have still lands and sacred vessels."

Edward. I know that motive, and lament it; but what do you wish to deduce from it?

Odilon. If *such* reasons could suffice formerly to effect a schism with the church, *others*, though different, may also suffice to effect a re-union now. I will even give you the liberty of classing among these motives, those which I cited yesterday, after Tabaraud and Beaufort, namely, uniformity, monarchism, and so many other things so calculated to operate powerfully, particularly in our times.

Edward. I will not deny the *possibility* of it; for, for some time past, we have been accustomed to impossibilities; but I still believe the event is not very near.

Odilon. But supposing it to be necessary, must we not believe that it will take place?

Edward. What motives, I beseech you, have you for thinking it? Have the prognostics and alarms expressed on this subject any foundation?

Odilon. This event is only the result of the actual *interior* organization of Protestantism. It is natural, that the fall of a body from a height should be more accelerated as it approaches the ground.

Edward. Give us, if you please, a more precise explanation.

Odilon. I have proved, that in the ten years that have just elapsed, the progress of Protestantism towards naturalism has been more enormous and rapid, than in all the preceding years; and I conclude that its future progress will be still more rapid and frightful.

Edward. I cannot contest this melancholy and cruel truth, the unhappy causes of which we know but too well, and there is nothing, I confess, to remove our fears for the future.

Odilon. I conceive I have proved that Protestantism has experienced violent shocks and revolutions. You were obliged to admit it, and I showed that one of your distinguished divines was so much struck with the greatness of the danger, that he proposed to make an entire separation of the old and new Christians; that is, he wished, in order to save his religion, that the Protestants who are still Christians should be separated from those belonging to naturalism. I really cannot see how one could go further, unless it were to abolish Christianity by a formal act, and substitute naturalism or atheism in its place.

Ulric. I allow it; but explain yourself still more clearly.

Odilon. As the attacks directed by your *enlightened* writers and divines against revelation, are scattered through a heap of pamphlets and reviews, the full extent of the evil which afflicts you cannot easily be known; but put them all together into a body, and what will you find? That the divine and immediate revelation of the Holy Scripture is a chimera; that the Old and New Testament can no longer be considered as an infallible rule of life and manners, that all belief in the doctrines of the Holy Trinity, of the Divinity of Jesus Christ and the Holy Ghost is at an end; that there is no more question of original sin, propitiatory satisfaction, and the expiatory death of Jesus Christ; that the miracles and predictions of the prophets, of Jesus Christ, and the apostles deserve no credit, being sometimes the effect of natural causes, at other times the illusion of an exalted imagination, or even impostures; that the same may be said of the resurrection and ascension of Jesus Christ, although St. Paul considers our whole faith as vain, without the admission of the first of those two miracles; that baptism and the eucharist can no longer be considered as essential parts of Christian worship; that in general, all that is essentially and exclusively proper to Christianity, should disappear, to give place to human reason, the supreme arbiter, which alone should decide every thing; that, in short, teachers of religion, and divines themselves, have dared, in order to crown the work, to attack and shake all the foundations of morality. Such are the monstrous opinions that are met with, when the scattered assertions of the new Protestant writers and divines, the *enlighteners*, are collected and compared. What then remains of Christianity? has not pure naturalism taken its place, although its formal establishment is not yet declared?

Edward. Your observations are but too true.

Odilon. They have come to such a pitch as to give Paganism the preference over Christianity.

Edward. Stop, Sir, I cannot believe it. True, the most abominable incredulity is professed; but to prefer the shameful and absurd superstition of idolators to Christianity, is an excess which my nature entirely abhors and rejects.

Odilon. Hear what the anonymous author of a Dissertation on the Christianity of St. Paul says: "Since the abolition of that *good* Paganism, nothing so absurd as Christianity has been seen. But the first of these two religions was abolished merely because the proselytes of Christianity were men unacquainted with Paganism, and who did not properly know themselves what they should put in its place: however, something new now was wanting, for the decay of Paganism was visible." In another place, the author asks whether the reestablishment of the religion of the Greeks and Romans would not be the best step that could be taken.

Ulric. You know I have no regard for anonymous authors.

Odilon. *Your masters of the people* have not hesitated neither to grant this priority to Paganism, as you may be convinced by the 72d note in the work of Thiess. The French philosophists, of whom the German *enlighteners* are the miserable imitators, were also the apologists of idolatry; and Raynal, among others, in his Philosophical History, has mournfully complained that the cross of Jesus Christ has replaced the amiling divinities of Greece and Rome."

Edward. This is pitiful! And can you pretend that a re-union of the Protestants with the Catholic church must necessarily come out of all this abominable rubbish?

Odilon. Most certainly; as it is impossible to drag Protestantism from under its ruins, as I have already proved, what remains for those, who having preserved any attachment for Christianity, and wishing to preserve their children from the insipid worship of the *Goddess of Reason*, what remains for them, but to re-unite with the Catholic church, which, according to the confession of Protestants themselves, is the guardian of the principal and fundamental truths of Christianity? In a word, this Christianity being entirely destroyed among Protestants, those who cherish it, and wish to preserve it henceforward, are absolutely obliged to seek it in the only asylum where they are sure of finding it. The Protestant princes, far from opposing this, ought even to co-operate towards it.

Edward. The sovereigns themselves, do you say? But I think I heard you confess, that the great ones of the earth trouble themselves very little now with religion and religious constitutions; and this is so true, that in all the treaties of peace concluded in our times, no mention has been made as formerly, of this important matter. And you would expect our princes to co-operate towards the re-union in question?

Odilon. Yes; for if they have not yet had sufficient experience, they will not be long in learning that a state cannot subsist without a positive religion. Paganism itself pleads in favor of this truth; for we know that the Greeks and Romans, who wanted a positive religion, invented one. Plato, in his tenth book of Laws, says: "Ignorance of the true God is the greatest of misfortunes for any state; and he who shakes religion, shakes at the same time the foundations of all human society." This consoling truth is found in all the works of that great genius. As to Plutarch, he has even said, "that it would be easier to build a town in the air than to found a state without religious worship." Machiavel also, in his twelfth section on the first decad of Livy, says: "Monarchs and republics, anxious for their preservation, should, above all, contrive that religion be constantly honored and preserved inviolate; nothing so much proves the decay of a country, as a contempt for divine worship." Yes, no state can exist with naturalism; and Voltaire himself, in the lucid moments which his passions and self-love left him, felt so thoroughly the necessity of this maxim, that he said: "I would not have any concern with an atheistical prince, whose interest it might be to have me pounded in a mortar; for I should be sure to be pounded. If I were a sovereign, I would have no atheistical courtiers, whose interest it might be to poison me; I should be forced to be taking antidotes every day. It is therefore absolutely necessary, for prince and people, that the idea of a Supreme Being, the creator, governor, remunerator, and avenger, should be deeply engraved on the mind." I have therefore reason to maintain, that after the entire destruction of Christianity among Protestants, their sovereigns would be obliged to contribute efficaciously towards a re-union with Catholicity, as the only harbor where Christianity is still to be found.

Edward. I am more inclined to think they will convoke a general council, in which all the Protestant divines will assemble, re-establish Protestantism, and form it into one common body, more perfectly and more vigorously organized than before.

Odilon. Even supposing, what I am far from thinking possible, that these divines could be assembled, what, I pray you, would be the aspect of a council composed of Protestants properly so called, of Arians, Socinians, Calvinists, Deists, Naturalists, Herrnhuters, Pietists, and I do not know how many other sects?

Ulric. I confess, I have no great opinion of such a council; nevertheless, I should not be sorry to see such a sight, though, according to all appearances, they would come to acts of violence, without reckoning the insults of *Heretics, Fanatics, Obscurants, Ultra-orthodox,* and all the other fine titles to be found in Bahrdt's Almanac of Heretics. If, from the beginning, the Lutherans had been prudent enough to form a synodical constitution, like us, they would not be reduced to this extremity. A council would then have no obstacles, and all would happen to the satisfaction of the contracting parties. Are you not of this opinion?

Odilon. I doubt it very much. For, do me the favor to tell me which of the two *Protestantisms* this council would re-establish? That of Luther, and the first reformers, or that of the epochs which immediately followed his death, or, in short, that of the first half of the 18th century. Who will preside over this council? Who will decide the contested points?

Edward. Probably the majority; perhaps also the most learned of the divines would unite to decide on the maxims and form of the new church.

Odilon. On this supposition I shall pity you very much, for you would run a great risk of seeing naturalism, or christo-deism, as those gentlemen call it, both sanctioned and established. These fears are certainly not imaginary; for we know positively that the most celebrated of those divines already belong to that party. The General German Library can afford you details, quite unequivocal on that subject, (part 69, p. 238). As to that production itself, you will find in Trembley's excellent work on the present state of Christianity, that its principal tendency always has been, and still is, to destroy all the truths of Christianity from top to bottom. But, I only say this by the way.

Edward. I think those Protestants who are still attached to Christianity, would rather unite with the Moravian brothers than with the Catholic Church.

Odilon. As to them, my opinion is very different from what you probably imagine; I consider them as the hermits of our regions, and to be those principally who have preserved religious conviction and the soul of Christianity; that is, a lively faith in the crucified Saviour. Yes, I have had the consolation to find in that community of *brothers*, men truly Christian, and really good and pious. But if Christian Protestants had really the intention of joining that community, I doubt very much whether they could come to an agreement. Observe, also, that this community itself has experienced very considerable changes, though to its advantage, since the death of its founder Zinzindorf, while other Protestant societies have insensibly fallen off. Moreover, this society of brothers is only made for a very narrow circle, and would be soon entirely metamorphosed, if it were turned into a great religious society. The church of Herrnhut, is perfectly convinced of this truth, and shows no wish for aggrandizement.

Ulric. I was unwilling to interrupt you, but I have still more than one important objection to make against the necessity, possibility, and facility, now greater than ever, of a re-union of Protestants with the Catholics.

Odilon. I will thank you to mention all these objections.

Ulric. You will surely agree with me, that those Protestants whom the love of Christianity might induce to form a union with the Catholic religion, ought, above all, to be well convinced that they would find more advantages in that church than in their own; for otherwise they would fall from Scylla to Charybdis.

Odilon. This is certainly a necessary condition; and, of course, I am fully convinced that, with respect to religion, all the advantage is indubitably on our side.

Ulric. From what I have heard you say, I perceive you are very well informed of the progress of naturalism among us. But can you be totally ignorant of the situation of your own church in this particular, or have you purposely concealed it? I have found in many of your Catholic writers principles very worthy of our *enlighteners;* and without mentioning the innumerable pamphlets produced by the Josephian reformation, I will confine myself to a work which appeared a few years ago, at Munich, entitled *Cogitata quædam pro Ecclesiâ.* It is most probable that the author is a divine, and nevertheless the mass is there styled a heap of monkey tricks, *congeries actuum simialium.*

Odilon. It is very true that the quack doctors, sellers of *reformation and illumination,* who have caused such evils to Protestantism, are also beginning to distribute their drugs very liberally among Catholics. Divines, who formerly would have rejected the profane eulogiums of a Protestant, now seek them, are often corrupt enough to sacrifice their religious principles to the approbation of newspaper writers and reviewers among the Protestants, who, in return, honor them with the title of *enlighteners.* Yes, I know that not only the Voltairian philosophism, which has plunged France into an abyss of evils, troubles and distracts us, but that that also of the new German school, which has overturned all our ideas, begins to exert its fatal empire over our minds. The church has been also attacked in its external organization, and has experienced oppressions or persecutions that have no example in history.

Ulric. As this is the case, according to your own confession, how then can you suppose that our Protestant Christians can safely unite with the Catholic church? have they not reason to fear that this same naturalism, having attacked it also, may overwhelm them along with it? What then is the difference between you and us?

Odilon. Immense. You have just mentioned the perverse principles that were disseminated during the epoch of the Josephian reformation. Well, where are now those principles and their authors? What is become of all that mass of libels and pamphlets, in which the new doctrine was hawked about? What attacks were made against religion, in every way, by revolutionary France? Never was there a like oppression and proscription in any known part of the world, and still religion, you see, is erect as before.

Ulric. Yes, every thing changes, and such a state of things must have been foreseen; but how has your church risen from the midst of its ruins? Has it not since experienced shocks as violent as the first? The suppression of four great archbishoprics, of so many abbeys, monasteries, and foundations; the destruction of your churches, the spoliation of their property, their ornaments, and sacred vessels; acts of violence performed not by Protestants, but by the faithful themselves; the most considerable Catholic countries given to Protestant princes, who can now put all kinds of limitations on the worship of their Catholic subjects, insomuch, that it may be affirmed that Catholicity, properly speaking, has taken refuge in the Austrian States. What say you to this picture?

Odilon. Do you think then that what happens in our days in other countries, will always remain the same, and never change? It is well known that exaggerations, and all violent means, cannot be of long duration; they resemble hot-house plants, which grow and die rapidly.

Ulric. The same events took place at the Reformation, and yet, notwithstanding all these reverses, Protestantism subsists, while Catholicity has not yet been able to recover from the blows it has received.

Odilon. How is it possible, you can compare those old events with what is passing in our days? Then, a religious society was formed at the same time, entirely separated from the Catholics, and which strongly supported the new establishments. Nevertheless, the end proposed was not generally attained, and even in those countries where religion was the worst treated, it recovered sooner than elsewhere.

Ulric. This is quite new to me.

Odilon. Have you ever read the "History of the War of the Peasants," by Sartorius? This learned historian is obliged to admit that the *preachers* of the Reformation contributed greatly to propagate this insurrection of the country people; that they were the leaders and speakers in it, and that after having drawn up their manifestoes, they took care to spread them through all parts of Germany. In Swabia, Austria, Carinthia, Hungary, the archbishopric of Saltzburg, Franconia, Wurtzburg especially, and Bamberg, in the archbishopric of Mentz, all along the Rhine as far as Cologne, in the bishopric of Spire, in the Palatinate, in Alsace, along the Sarre, &c., the churches and monasteries were destroyed and burnt; all the clergymen who could not escape were cruelly used; the images and crucifixes were broken; the church ornaments were pillaged, and the sacred cups and chalices were often employed for the most sacrilegious purposes: in short, all the horrors were committed of our own disastrous times. But how long did the effect of these abominations last? did they produce the irrevocable destruction of the Catholic religion in all those countries? Was it not seen, on the contrary, in a few years, even a few months after, to rise more glorious than ever, and take root again down to our days?

Ulric. Very true; but it was not the same, however, in other countries; in Saxony, especially, which may be considered as the cradle of Protestantism.

Odilon. You are right; but as the facts, taken from the History of the War of the Peasants, destroy that unfortunate horoscope you have drawn for the Catholic church, so in like manner, what you have said of Saxony and other Protestant countries, is a proof of what I have asserted above, by maintaining, that from the beginning, a religious society had been established, separated from the Catholic church, and which had left nothing undone to preserve itself.

Ulric. Do you think then there is no longer a similar society, in our days, with the disposition and direction of all the enterprises that may be prejudicial to the Catholic church?

Odilon. I shall not examine whether such a society, with intentions so directly destructive, ever existed; but supposing it did, I would ask you, what will be its duration? The reign of the Jacobins, was it not all-powerful? did it not threaten to swallow up every thing? and what is it now?

It is the very essence of error to undermine and destroy itself.

Ulric. But do you not fear, however, that these disorganizing principles, spread about every where by Catholic writers, and even by clergymen, will not at length get the upper hand, and precipitate us all, without distinction, into the gulph of naturalism?

Odilon. We have maxims peculiar to our own church, which are these: *It is founded on a rock, and the gates of hell shall not prevail against it.*

Ulric. Certainly, nothing can be said against the *ground* of that divine promise. Nevertheless—

Odilon. If we had a constitution as defective as yours; if we wanted, in fine, for the preservation of our church, all that you would wish to have for the support of yours, we might, perhaps, abstracting the divine prom·se in question, run the same risks as you, by the propagation of these incendiary maxims. But we are in a position which places us in this respect above these fears.

Ulric. I admire your confidence.

Odilon. The Catholic church has a *head,* who keeps the whole church together; and all the parts of the religious body are in the closest correspondence with that head; in a word, we have a *hierarchy,* which must be broken to the last thread, before it is possible to extinguish the faith in the heart of all the faithful. Casaubon was very sensible of this truth.

Edward. What! the learned and able critic of Baronius's annals? This would surprise me very much.

Odilon. Speaking in his fifteenth *exercitation* of the efforts made by St. Leo, in the fifth century, to augment the credit and power of the See of Rome, he not only does justice to that pontiff, approves his intentions, and maintains that the bishop of Rome alone was in a situation to oppose heresies, but he adds, "That every man acquainted with ecclesiastical affairs knows, that during several ages God made use of the exertions of the bishops of Rome to preserve the doctrine of faith sound and entire." Such, according to Casaubon, was the salutary influence of the head of the church on the preservation of religion; but that head still has it, and as long as he preserves it, his position will be im·moveable.

Ulric. I am inclined to think so, too, as long as that *head* subsists, with his *influence,* and with a *hierarchy* so strongly connected in all its parts. But you know how much his power in the time of Joseph II. was limited in Austria, Parma, Naples, Tuscany, and other places. From the way they went on, it was very easy to foresee the total end of that authority, and consequently, the destruction of the hierarchy, from which you draw so much advantage. And what will you say to what has happened in our days, in the infamous treatment of that august and unfortunate prisoner, whose firmness and constancy have rendered him respectable even to Protestants? In a word, what can one augur of the duration of a church, whose head is reduced to such an extremity?

Odilon. I repeat my preceding maxim: *It is founded on an immoveable rock!* Run over the history of the church, and you will meet with epochs just as disastrous as those you have mentioned. But, you will likewise always meet with that legitimate chief, at the head of that hierarchy, founded by Jesus Christ; no, he will never cease to exert his influence over all the members of that church, though their number should be diminished as much as possible, and by all imaginable means. "They have often attacked me, even from my youth, but were not able to overthrow me."*

Ulric. I cannot but admire the firmness of your faith, and am tempted to say to you, "Thy faith is great, be it done unto thee according to thy desire." But you wished to speak to us of some other properties of your church.

Odilon. It possesses a worship which acts on the senses, to the great advantage of religion; and though many Protestants think, perhaps, that we do too much in this respect, nevertheless this pretended *exaggeration* would suit them much better than the *nullity* of the naturalizers. Thus Frederick the Great assisting one day, at Breslau, at a solemn office, celebrated by Cardinal Zinzendorf, could not help saying, "The Calvinists treat God as their servant, the Lutherans as their equal, but the Catholics treat him like a God." It is united with the constitution of the state by much more solid ties than Protestantism, and consequently, in every state where it is the established religion, it cannot be overturned without endangering the state itself. It has, in short, an ecclesiasti-

* Sæpe expugnaverunt me à juventute meâ, etenim non potuerunt mihi.

cal discipline, which embraces every object without distinction; and if, in our days, this discipline has been unfortunately relaxed, to the great disadvantage of religion, severe experience has taught us to draw closer the ties of this salutary institution, and take suitable measures to stop the attacks of impiety, and preserve religion and the state.

Ulric. I allow all this, and it is most probable that the want of an establishment like that of your church, is the cause of the great revolution which Protestantism has undergone. It is evident, also, that the throne of the kings of France would never have been overturned, or never so easily, at least, if the philosophers had not taken care to undermine the hierarchy and destroy religious feeling. But it is precisely these enemies which the Catholic church contains in her bosom, those writers whom I mentioned above.

Odilon. If, to save us and themselves from total ruin, governments themselves do not protect those mad fanatics, as was the case in France; and if a similar revolution does not assail us, I dread nothing from the attacks of some insulated madmen, who will never succeed in destroying the faith of the whole church. And even supposing this disastrous protection were granted to them, the faithful, who escaped the shipwreck, would be only more united among themselves, and more submissive to the common head of the church, as we find by a multitude of examples in ecclesiastical history, from the time of the apostles down to our days.

Ulric. I have just given you striking examples of such protection being given to the enemies of religion. But, pay attention to what is going on at present, and tell me whether you can conjecture from it the duration of your church.

Odilon. I recollect to have read in a very judicious writer the following opinion, which I think very just: " It is evident, that in the middle age, the supreme Pontiff of Christianity would necessarily become the independent sovereign of Rome, or some other country. Vassal or subject of a prince, he would have lost the confidence of all other sovereigns, and would only have been the blind instrument of the egotism and ambition of his own. Confined to one state, and one country, where the chains of the temporal power would have cramped the liberty of all his notions, no universal religion, no common church would have been possible; all Europe would have soon fallen into several caliphats, and have been inevitably and ignominiously subjected to an oriental government, oriental oppression, and oriental stupidity."[*]

Ulric. This quotation is certainly in my favor, and you will admit that the opinion of this writer, concerning the middle age, is quite applicable to the present time.

Odilon. You are perfectly right, and the history of the Greek church, as well as that of Protestantism, affords melancholy proof of it; for those two religions owe their decline to the dependence of their clergy, to the chains with which they are bound, and to the fall of their hierarchy.

Ulric. Well, if this be the case, where then is that immoveable fixity of your church, which baffles all attacks made against it? Do you not think that Protestants will soon be able to say of the Catholic church, *Adam is become one of us?* Who could be tempted then to take refuge in the bosom of this church, which has no better guarantee than Protestantism?

Odilon. I have already answered this objection, by observing that those who are really attached to religion would only be the more united among each other and with their common head; but I shall add, moreover, that he who promised an eternal duration to his church will be very able, should its independence be destroyed, to inspire into the head and all the members of the hierarchy, that unconquerable fortitude which makes one prefer death itself to the sacrifice of what one owes to religion and conscience; yes, with that spirit the church will remain unshaken in the midst of the most violent storms, and will be free even in irons.

Edward. I grant that those Protestants, who, to escape naturalism, are disposed to re-unite with the Catholic church,

---

[*] See the German work, entitled "On the Spirit and Consequences of the Reformation," p. 132; and Fleury, Eccles. Hist. tom. xvi. Disc. iv. No. 10.

Henaut also, whose opinions respecting the Church are not suspicious, uses these remarkable expressions in his "Chronological Abridgment of the History of France," edit. 1768: "The Pope is no longer, as in the beginning of the Church, a subject of the Emperor; since the Church has now spread through the world, he has to answer to all those who command in it. Religion is not a sufficient restraint for so many sovereigns; and God has justly permitted that the common father of the faithful should maintain the respect due to him by his independence. It is well, therefore, that the Pope has a *temporal* power, together with the exercise of the *spiritual*, but provided that the first be only in his own territory, and the other be exerted within the limits prescribed to him."

have no reason whatever to fear that it will soon experience
a degradation like that of Protestantism ; but there are other
points, and of such importance, that they alone, in my opinion, are sufficient to place insurmountable obstacles against
this re-union, which seems to you so easy, so possible, and
so necessary.

Odilon. I think I have sufficiently developed and discussed
all these points.

Edward. You are far from having said every thing; and I
would prove it to you, were I not afraid it would carry us
too far.

Odilon. These obstacles, however, cannot be so invincible
as you seem to think; for Woltmann, one of your most modern writers, expresses himself, in the preface to the second
part of his History of the Peace of Westphalia, in the following manner : " The ancient partisans of Protestantism show
here and there a liking for the Catholic church ; and, in the
main, this Protestantism is, and can only be, a fragment,
which, by its constant opposition, has itself contributed to
preserve the Catholic church from total ruin.   At all events,
the period of unity for the whole Christian church cannot be
very distant."   You see, Sir, that in this most remarkable
passage, there is no question whatever of points of doctrine
important enough to prove any obstacle against the re-union
in question.

Edward. I am acquainted with that passage, and it is very
striking in more respects than one.   But I still persist in
thinking, that the points which I meant to speak of, are of a
nature to give alarm to every well informed Christian.   As to
the Protestants who have preserved any zeal for Christianity,
I am persuaded they would show a decided repugnance to
those points.

Odilon. You will oblige me much by mentioning them ;
for really I cannot guess how they can be insurmountable
obstacles to a re-union.

Edward. Well, since you wish it, I will first mention your
idolatrous veneration of saints, images, and relics.   Certainly,
original Christianity knew nothing at all of them, and it is
not to be presumed that Jesus Christ our Lord, when he gave
to his disciples his maxims for the establishment of his church,
ordered them at the same time to form a religious worship
for future saints and martyrs, as well as to their images and

relics. He knew too well the little distance there is between such a worship and idolatry; and it is here, perhaps, we ought to seek for the source of Polytheism among the Pagans, which, most certainly, was originally nothing but a similar worship decreed to heroes and great men.

Odilon. I am going to grant you much more than you, perhaps, expected. I will grant that the idolatry of the Pagans was originally a grateful remembrance, bestowed on men who had deserved well of the commonwealth. I will go still further: I will suppose that Jesus Christ never spoke to his apostles of a worship for future saints or martyrs, for their images and relics.

Edward. If you allow this, I cannot see what answer you can make to my objection.

Odilon. I shall make an answer, not without weight, I conceive. I will say, above all, that even on the supposition of this silence of Jesus Christ, it is not less true that this worship is dated from such remote times, that they may be classed among those acknowledged by yourselves to belong to the primitive church.

Edward. To the primitive church!

Odilon. Yes, for you certainly place in this number the second and third centuries.

Edward. Undoubtedly.

Odilon. You know, of course, that in the second century, the *nativities* of the martyrs were celebrated; that is to say, the days on which they perished for the faith, and religious assemblies were held in the places which contained their remains. In the same century, the community of Smyrna wrote to that of Philomele that it had the intention of assembling annually, and of solemnizing the memory of St. Polycarp, their former bishop, who was martyred in the year 68, in the very spot where his bones were preserved.[*] And a multitude of analogous passages are also found in Tertullian and Cyprian, the first of whom lived at the end of the second century, and the other in the first half of the third. Tertullian thus expresses himself: "On the consecrated days, we sacrifice to the memory of their death." And Cyprian, in his Letters, exhorts "exactness in the precise inscription of the day the martyrs died, in order that it may be celebrated

* Euseb. lib iv. cap. xv.

by gifts and sacrifices."* I think you can make no objection to these examples and proofs, which I could multiply at pleasure; and, indeed, several very learned Protestants have thought, on this point, in a very different manner from the common opinion.

Ulric. I declare that their opinion is not at all mine.

Odilon. Even some English writers have held it.

Ulric. This I am still less inclined to believe; for who does not know the aversion of the English for every thing which they call *papistical?*

Odilon. Instead of a number of authors of less importance that I could cite, I will confine myself to the testimony of Richard Montague, bishop of Norwich. He maintains that it cannot be denied, that Christian antiquity believed that the saints in heaven pray for us; that, consequently, it is right to address them, in order to obtain their mediation, and that in this way Catholics did no injury to the mediation of Jesus Christ. The English bishop also declares himself in favor of images, as you may see in Tarbaraud's work.

Edward. I shall make no objection to this. The zeal of the first Christians for Christianity, and their respect for the martyrs and witnesses of their religion, soon introduced those anniversary festivals, as well as the preservation of relics; and in that, perhaps, there is nothing dangerous or blameable. But if I were not afraid of offending you, I would show in lively colors, how, in the lapse of time, these practices degenerated into real idolatry, and this veneration of the martyrs and saints became a worship perfectly similar to that which is due to the Divinity alone.

Odilon. Ah, how little you know us! Open all our missals, our books of liturgy, our breviaries, our diurnals, and you will find, that at the present day, those feasts of martyrs and saints are just what they were seventeen centuries ago; that is to say, solemnities consecrated to the recollection of their faith, their death, their zeal for religion, and the points of imitation in them, according to this maxim of St. Paul: "Remember your elders who preached to you the words of God, consider their end, and imitate their faith." Such a worship, therefore, is very improperly compared to that which is given to the Divinity.

* Tertull. de Coron. mil. 3.—Cyprian, Epist. xxxvii.

Edward. I know, that in order to justify the worship of saints, you make a difference between *veneration* and *adoration.*

Odilon. Yes; and this difference, I conceive, is very great and essential.

Edward. It may be; but the invocation of saints nevertheless is much more than simple veneration; and you know that Scripture orders us to invoke God alone, and also says, "Abraham knows nothing of us, and Israel is not acquainted with us."

Odilon. Our veneration for the saints has its foundation in their merits, and in our gratitude towards them; the prayers which we address to them, to obtain their intercession, are founded on the conviction that they know our wants, and do not cease to pray to God in favor of their brethren left here below, and that he certainly still favors them in heaven after having been so merciful to them on earth. In truth, I see nothing unreasonable in all this.

Edward. Even supposing the saints really knew our wants, still does not this religious invocation, addressed to them, appear to you to be like the worship offered to God, and due to him alone?

Odilon. How little you know our principles! Once more, I say, read all our missals, as well as our breviaries, and you will find that all our prayers, on the days consecrated to the saints and martyrs, are addressed only to God. When, in the litanies, the mother of our Lord and the saints and martyrs are invoked, it is always expressed that they are to pray to God for us, *orate pro nobis.* Scripture itself attests that the members of the church triumphant pray for those who live here below; and according to the symbol of the apostles, they are closely connected; for it is there said, *I believe in the communion of saints.*

Ulric. But is it not the Christian church that must be understood by that last expression?

Odilon. No; for there is question of this church immediately before, where it is said, "I believe in the Holy Catholic Church;" words, which Luther metamorphosed into these —"I believe in the Holy Christian Church." This alteration drew reproaches upon him, even in his life time, and he only permitted it after he had separated from the Catholic unity. In general, to destroy whatever had any connexion with our relations with the saints, explanations and commentaries have been admitted much stranger still than that of Luther, or those which some Protestants have chosen to understand by *the communion of saints.*

Ulric. And what are those commentaries?

Odilon. I remember reading, among others, in the Latin History of the Symbol of the Apostles, by King, a work, however, full of excellent information, that *the communion of saints* signified nothing but the union of Christians all over the earth, for the purpose of keeping up an *epistolary* correspondence, and exercising the rights of reciprocal *hospitality.*

Edward. I grant this idea does not belong exactly to the *Credo.* . . But you meant to add something else.

Odilon. Yes, I meant to say that such interpretations are precisely calculated to destroy one of the first thoughts, and one of the most delightful feelings of our nature.

Edward. Pray explain yourself more clearly.

Odilon. Do you know any thing more soothing and consoling than the persuasion, that we are not wholly separated by death from those who were dear to us? that in this life of trials and preparation, we are closely united with that celestial world, where we are destined one day to live? in short, that we have as mediators and dearest friends persons who, already in the bosom of God, enjoy that ineffable felicity reserved for us? The excellent work on *The Spirit and Consequences of the Reformation,* which I have frequently quoted before, contains, at page 143, a description full of feeling and truth on the salutary effects which the veneration of the saints, properly understood, may produce on the mind and heart.

Edward. Very right; but you cannot deny, however, that this veneration has been often so exaggerated as to become that worship due only to God.

Odilon. I grant that there may have been some abuse in this; and I know that Lewis Vives, in his notes on St. Augustin, says, that several may have erred in this matter, which is good in itself, by extravagantly honoring the saints like God himself, and acting in such a manner as almost to make one think their opinion of the saints was the same as that of the Pagans respecting their gods.

Edward. This is precisely what I have just said.

Odilon. We never have pretended to deny, that there may
be among us, some ignorant and stupid people, who confound
the veneration due to the saints, with the sentiments that are
only due to the Supreme Being; are not such people to be
found every where? But I go further—I frankly confess,
that in some places this worship has sometimes been exaggerated; it is even very possible that a passage susceptible of a
wrong interpretation may have crept into missals and breviaries: but the ecclesiastical authority has never failed to
obviate it; and the whole church has said, in the Catechism
of the Council of Trent, "We must take care not to grant to
another what is due to God alone."

Edward. But considering these abuses, which you allow
yourself, would it not be much better to proscribe entirely
such worship, instead of tolerating it, or even commanding it?

Odilon. I see you have still but little acquaintance with
us. "The church," says the learned author of the Philosophical Catechism, tom. iii, p. 239, "the church approves
and recommends the veneration of the saints; she even gives
an example of it in her liturgy; but she does not make it a
law, nor does she consider it as an essential part of Christianity." The same author points out the manner in which
those passages of our missals and breviaries might be corrected, which may give rise to false interpretations. But
what in the world should we have remaining, if all the useful and good things that can be abused were destroyed?
Have the goodness to think, that our people have right and
sound ideas, much more than you seem to imagine.

Ulric. Is not this owing to the Reformation?

Odilon. I beg your pardon; we possessed such ideas more
than a thousand years before your Reformation; for St.
Augustin then wrote as follows: "We do not honor our
holy martyrs as gods; we consecrate neither temples nor
altars to them, nor do we sacrifice to them. Far from us
such an idea! it is God alone whom we have in view, it is
ne alone whom we adore, and to him alone that sacrifice is
offered in those days of commemoration. Whom did you
ever hear say; I sacrifice to thee, O holy Paul, O holy Peter!
No, never; for that is not allowed. And if somebody asks
you; is it not to Peter that you offer religious worship?
Answer him immediately: No, it is not Peter that I honor,
but Him who is honored by Peter himself." St. Jerome also
enters into a holy wrath at the reproach which Vigilantius

had made to him in this respect: "Fool," he exclaims, "who ever had any intention to adore the martyrs? who ever thought of taking a man for a god? Did not Paul and Barnabas tear their garments, when the Lycaonians, taking them for Jupiter and Mercury, were preparing to sacrifice to them? not that those saints considered themselves below those false deities, but because a worship was offered to them which only belongs to the true God."

Edward. What you have said hitherto on this subject, is, in general, very satisfactory; however, the veneration of images and relics has many inconveniences, especially when one reflects that there are some to which you attribute miraculous virtues.

Odilon. You may as well be scandalized at reading in the Holy Scriptures, that a dead man, placed in the tomb of Eliseus, was raised to life, by touching the bones of that prophet. You will be offended at the Christians of Ephesus, for having put the garments of St. Paul on some sick persons, who were thereby healed. You will blame the Christians of Jerusalem for having placed the infirm in the shadow of St. Peter, which cured all their complaints. Was it the bones, garments, and shadow which performed those miracles?

Edward. No, certainly not; it was God alone, who, by those miraculous cures, meant to recompense the faith of those sick, and that of their friends.

Odilon. Believe me, there is not among us even any old woman, ignorant, foolish, or superstitious enough, to think that the relics of the saints contain any magical power, or that some powerful genius covers them with his wings; but we are convinced that God alone acts, that he alone can perform miracles, either to reward piety and the faith of those who recommend themselves to the mediation of the just, or to preserve among men sentiments of piety and religious truth.

Ulric. Do you not think that these salutary effects might be produced without those relics and images, which frequently lead to all sorts of superstitions?

Odilon. Upon my word, I do not see that heaven has granted more benediction and grace to you, who are without relics and images, than to us, who have preserved that veneration. Supposing even, as you do, that we are rather more superstitious than you, you will allow that you are much more incredulous than we, and I leave you to decide which side has the advantage in this business. If we ought to destroy every thing which a corrupt heart can make an abuse of, we ought, if possible, to annihilate the sun and moon. You remember the celebrated Montesquieu says : " If I should relate all the evils that have been produced in the world by civil laws, by monarchy, and by the republican government, I should say dreadful things." If all these things, therefore, must be destroyed on account of the abuse that may be made of them, men have nothing left but to go and live solitary in the woods. Besides, I could cite many examples of the efforts that have been and are still made, to destroy the abuses of superstition, and that cupidity which makes a shameful traffic of images and relics. You will be the more surprised to know the persons to whom we are obliged for these efforts, as they belong to a class of men of whom you have no very high opinion.

Edward. Have the kindness to satisfy my eager curiosity on this point.

Odilon. Read the Travels of Labat in Italy, part iv, p. 331 : you will there find, that the inquisition condemned a priest to the galleys for seven years, for having contrived a crucifix to nod with its head, to testify that it heard the prayers addressed to it ; you will there see that that inquisition exerts the greatest vigilance to hinder all frauds and cheats with images, which are carefully examined every where, and every pious fraud in this respect is punished severely. You may be sure the same caution is more or less exerted in every thing else.

Edward. I admit this, but am not less convinced, that, as it could be hindered, it would be as well not to allow a thing which can be so easily abused.

Odilon. Respect, love, and piety, introduced very early among us the preservation of relics, as well as the exposition of images. Unless you choose to deny that indecent statues and images are capable of exciting irregular thoughts and passions, you must allow, by the rule of contraries, that the images of persons distinguished by their piety and charity, are very proper to inspire sentiments worthy of such fine examples. Moreover, images, with us, do not belong at all to the essence of religion, as you perhaps think, but are ranged in class of *adiaphorous,* or indifferent things : and it depends

Urbain. ... I set aside all the legends and figured representations, which rational Catholics have long since discredited. But do you not still solemnize the feast of the Assumption of the Virgin: do you not place her on the altars crowned with a certain glory, and carried by angels towards the heavenly spheres? Do you find in the Holy Scripture a single word in favor of such a representation? On the contrary, does it not formally oppose it? for Jesus Christ says: "Nobody ascends to heaven but he who descended from heaven, that is to say, the Son of Man, who is in heaven." Do you not therefore make the Mother like the Lord, who never raised her to such a high degree of glory?

Odilon. I will ...
me, how you wi...

departing from this world, to spring into the mansions of eternal bliss?

Edward. But even though we would let this point aside, there are still several most important articles that are hostile to a re union.

Odilon. I will thank you to point them out, and will endeavor to destroy those obstacles you fear.

Ulric. Allow me to interrupt you an instant. Does the idolatrous adoration of the host also belong to the *adiaphorous* or indifferent things?

Odilon. I thought, that the quotation I gave you yesterday from Luther on this point, would have removed all your doubts. But I will add a testimony of still greater weight, and of the same period, namely, the famous Erasmus. Here is what he says in one of his letters: " I can never be persuaded, that Jesus Christ, who is truth and love itself, would allow his beloved spouse, the church, to be exposed for so long a time to the abominable error of adoring a piece of dough." " It is neither the body nor the soul of Jesus Christ," says he, in another letter, " that are divinely honored; what we adore is his divinity. But you will say, perhaps, that the people nevertheless are deceived. No, for nothing is so easy as to instruct the people, and make them sensible that no created being ought to be divinely adored."* But I could even mention some English divines, who have not hesitated to declare themselves in favor of the real presence of the body and blood of Christ in the Eucharist. Bilson, bishop of Worcester, expressing the opinions of the divines of his church, says: "Heaven preserve us from denying the real presence of the body and blood of our Saviour in the Holy Supper!" Forbes, Thorndyke, Parker, and Montague, alluding to the invariable doctrine of the Fathers of the church, go so far as to declare themselves decidedly for transubstantiation.† But, whe̶r̶e̶ ̶ ̶ ̶u̶s̶ Christ our Lord is present, as God and man, i̶t̶ ̶ ̶ ̶ ̶e̶ ought also to be adored. But you wished o̶t̶h̶er point?

f̶i̶r̶st observe, that the doctrine of your p̶u̶rgatory, so frightful and so contrary to P̶rotestants, concerning the future state

). Edit. Lugd. tom. ii.
.24, 425.

on the church and its head to let them subsist or not, according to the advantage the church may derive from them, for the supreme object of all our worship is that Jesus Christ be glorified. *Ut magnificetur Christus.*

Edward. I should not have thought so.

Odilon. You will find many most interesting things on this subject, in a work printed in 1574, and reprinted in 1771; the author is a divine of Louvain, called John Molanus.[*] But I will confine myself to an author, who certainly will not be accused of having lent himself to arrangements, in order to gain the Protestants. It is Petavius, who says: "Above all, it must be established, that images belong to the things called indifferent, that is, to those which, not being essential to religion, can be preserved or suppressed by the church."[*]

Edward. I consider this last point to be of great importance, and I now think, that if the thing were properly presented and explained, it would not have such difficulties towards a re-union, as I thought at first.

Ulric. All that you have said on this subject is very persuasive, as you express it; but I doubt whether the reality be equally correct.

Odilon. Put no restraint on yourself, I beg of you, and explain your opinion without reserve.

Ulric. I set aside all the legends and figured representations, which rational Catholics have long since discredited. But do you not still solemnize the feast of the Assumption of the Virgin; do you not place her on the altars crowned with a celestial glory, and carried by angels towards the heavenly spheres? Do you find in the Holy Scripture a single word in favor of such a representation? On the contrary, does it not formally oppose it? for Jesus Christ says: "Nobody ascends to heaven but he who descended from heaven, that is to say, the Son of Man, who is in heaven." Do you not therefore make the Mother like the Lord, who never raised her to such a high degree of glory?

Odilon. I will answer this question when you have told me, how you would contrive to represent a blessed spirit

* Historia SS. imaginum et picturarum, pro vero casuum usu et abusu.
† See Petav. dog. Theol. lib. xv, de incarn. c. xiii, No. 1.

departing from this world, to spring into the mansions of eternal bliss?

Edward. But even though we would let this point aside, there are still several most important articles that are hostile to a re union.

Odilon. I will thank you to point them out, and will endeavor to destroy those obstacles you fear.

Ulric. Allow me to interrupt you an instant. Does the idolatrous adoration of the host also belong to the *adiaphorous* or indifferent things?

Odilon. I thought, that the quotation I gave you yesterday from Luther on this point, would have removed all your doubts. But I will add a testimony of still greater weight, and of the same period, namely, the famous Erasmus. Here is what he says in one of his letters: " I can never be persuaded, that Jesus Christ, who is truth and love itself, would allow his beloved spouse, the church, to be exposed for so long a time to the abominable error of adoring a piece of dough." " It is neither the body nor the soul of Jesus Christ," says he, in another letter, " that are divinely honored; what we adore is his divinity. But you will say, perhaps, that the people nevertheless are deceived. No, for nothing is so easy as to instruct the people, and make them sensible that no created being ought to be divinely adored."[*] But I could even mention some English divines, who have not hesitated to declare themselves in favor of the real presence of the body and blood of Christ in the Eucharist. Bilson, bishop of Worcester, expressing the opinions of the divines of his church, says: " Heaven preserve us from denying the real presence of the body and blood of our Saviour in the Holy Supper!" Forbes, Thorndyke, Parker, and Montague, alluding to the invariable doctrine of the Fathers of the church, go so far as to declare themselves decidedly for transubstantiation.[†] But, wherever Jesus Christ our Lord is present, as God and man, it is clear that he ought also to be adored. But you wished still to speak of another point?

Edward. I will first observe, that the doctrine of your church, respecting purgatory, so frightful and so contrary to the mild opinion of Protestants, concerning the future state

[*] Erasm. epist. 1035. 1053. Edit. Lugd. tom. ii.
[†] Tabaraud, a. a. o. pp. 424, 425.

of man's existence, is not much calculated to procure you
many partizans.

Ulric. In truth, I cannot conceive how a Catholic can die
peaceably, however great his piety may have been, since, on
quitting this life, he knows beforehand that frightful torments
await him in the other, and that, like gold, souls must be
first purified by fire.

Odilon. In general, it is difficult to form exact ideas, at
present, of what happens in the other world. If you were
better acquainted with our principles, you would never have
made us such a reproach as this.

Edward. How do you mean?

Odilon. Neither the church nor Scripture have decdied
whether the fire of purgatory, be an elementary fire, though
we may have good reasons to believe it.

Ulric. Decided nothing, do you say? It is expressly called
a *purifying fire*, and all the figured representations that you
give of it, positively express the same thing.

Odilon. It is not our custom to form our decisions from
painters. It is enough that several of our divines are
entirely of my opinion, as you may be convinced by reading
the third part of Feller's Philosophical Catechism. The
Council of Trent also ordered, respecting purgatory, carefully
to avoid all subtleties, all that does not serve for edification,
and the increase of true piety; the same council forbids, in
the most rigorous manner, any uncertain theories on that
subject.

Edward. In fact, this passage of the council seems to strike
at the representation, by painters, of the purification of souls
by a material fire. But if this fire does not really exist, what
then is it? and why call it purgatory?

Odilon. Give it any name you like, that of purification
or expiation, the thing at bottom is the same, and Protestant
divines have, in some respects, considered it in the same
light.

Edward. Protestant divines!

Odilon. Montague and Gunning, among the English, were
for a state of purification; and Forbes, bishop of Edinburgh,
asserts, that prayers for the dead are derived from an ancient
practice, which can be traced to the time of the apostles, and
that a fine observation, on this subject, is to be found in the

English Ritual, for the year 1549. Sheldon, Blaudford, Barrow, and Thorndyke are also favorable to prayers for the dead.* But this, you will allow, would be perfectly useless, if our state in the next world were immediately and wholly decided.

Edward. Those are, undoubtedly, names of great authority: but, among the Germans, if you except those who have maintained the opinion of a sort of *restoration* of all things, I do not know one who has admitted such an intermediate state.

Odilon. Among the moderns, I will only cite one, Dr. Less, a divine of Gottingen: in his Theory of the Christian religion, he espouses this doctrine, which is certainly conformable both to nature and Scripture.

Edward. I do not see this at all.

Odilon. Nothing, Sir, nothing in all nature is done abruptly; and the same maxim is applicable to the human soul. But you will allow that nothing could be more abrupt, in the fullest sense of the word, than for some souls to be snatched from this terrestial life, and be transported directly into the bosom of celestial and eternal beatitude. Where are those souls so pure and perfect, as to be fit to be presented into the mansions of the eternal God? Does not revelation say, "Nothing defiled shall enter it?" And what must we say of those who are only converted on the bed of death? Certainly we do not mean to deny them the grace of the divine pardon; but we are not authorized to maintain, that during the few moments that have elapsed since their repentance, they have been able to expiate entirely habitual propensities that have become a second nature; have acquired virtuous dispositions, to which they were so long perfect strangers, and have acquitted all the debts they had to pay. Ought not such persons to be happy to find such an intermediate state of expiation, or purification, or whatever you may please to call it? For, in fine, the sentence is irrevocable: "Nothing defiled shall enter."

Ulric. It seems to me, however, that this opinion has been borrowed from Paganism; for Scripture and the ancient Fathers are silent upon it.

Odilon. As to the ancient Fathers, you may soon be con—

* Tabaraud, a. a. o. p. 358. 420, 421.

vinced of the contrary ; for you have only to read with attention the passages which Bingham, a Protestant writer, has
extracted from them on this subject.* But as to the Bible,
it is impossible you can be ignorant, that, in the second book
of Maccabees, prayers and expiatory sacrifices are ordered
for those who perished in the fight; a practice certainly not
borrowed from Paganism. One of your most modern writers
likewise, Young, in his "Theory of the Knowledge of
Spirits," stands up for this state of expiation, for the *limbo*
of the Fathers, and for the intercession of the saints in favor
of the dead. This opinion of his has even given him the
honor of being treated as an enthusiastic and a fanatic, qualifications that might as well have been given to Calvin, for
he makes this intercession for the dead go back to the earliest
epochs of Christianity.

Edward. Calvin, do you say?

Odilon. Yes, here is what he says in his Institutions, book
iii. chap. v. No. 10: "It has been a custom in the church,
for more than 1300 years, to pray for the dead." But he
did not trouble himself with this fact more than with many
others.

Edward. How do you mean?

Odilon. He cuts the Gordian knot, by maintaining that
this maxim belongs to those errors into which the ancients
fell. He gives the same opinion of celibacy, public ecclesiastical penance, and the quadragesimal fast. By acting in
this cavalier way, it seems to me that very few things would
remain that might not be taxed as errors into which the ancients had fallen.

Edward. That is very certain.

Odilon. As to that intermediate state, of which intercession for the dead is the natural consequence, I could cite another learned writer of your church, of great piety and high
reputation.

Edward. What is his name?

Odilon. Scheidt, the celebrated historian of the House of
Brunswick, and librarian to the King of Hanover. Here is
what he wrote to Büsching: "I have seriously thought, a
thousand times in my life time, whether there is not perhaps

' Bingham, orig. eccles. tom. vi. p. 330, sqq.

in the next world still another school of preparation. An innumerable multitude of men quit this terrestrial scene, before they have begun to love Jesus Christ, though at the same time they had no hatred against him. But they have never put themselves in a state of sanctification, and without that none can see the Lord. May there not be, in eternity, a place of instruction where this advantage may be obtained?"[*]

Edward. I admit, that all that you have said on this point, deserves at least the most serious reflections.

Odilon. Intermediate state, state of purification, school of preparation, name the thing as you like, it seems to me that nature and the knowledge of man lead us spontaneously to it. The Jews and Mahometans also even now admit a similar intermediate state, or one of purification. The former believe that by a prayer called *Kadish*, or commemoration of souls, they may procure them help and relief. As to the Musulmen, who hold the same opinion, they call the prayer *El-Kathme.*

Ulric. Every body knows that this opinion of the Jews belongs to the reveries of their rabbins and thalmudists, who communicated them to Mahomet and his followers. Consequently, it is not a proof in favor of your maxim, that this opinion is founded in nature and the knowledge of man.

Odilon. Notwithstanding the important observation I could make respecting the Jews and Mahometans, I am willing to admit the truth of your supposition. But tell me, Sir, was it from the rabbins, or from the imans of Mahometism, that the Pagans of Greece and Rome borrowed their opinion on an intermediate state, or of expiation for the souls of the departed?

Ulric. The Pagans of Greece and Rome! I never knew they had such opinion.

Odilon. I must be allowed to doubt this; for I am too well acquainted with your eruditon to believe you so easily. St. Clement of Alexandria assures us, that the stoical philosophers believed in a state of expiation after this life, and called it *empyrosin.* The doctrine of the Pythagoreans, on the metempsychosis of souls, has the same idea for its fundamental basis, since it admits that human souls ought first to be puri-

* Büsching's Supplement, or Remarkable Personages, part iii. page 313.

fied before they arrive at the perfect state of bliss, of which they are susceptible in the other world. To this, also, belongs what Zoroaster, according to Eusebius, held of the transmigration of souls through the twelve signs of the Zodiac before they attained celestial happiness.   Plato even taught the soul, till entirely purified, would remain in slime and darkness.   The sixth book of Virgil's Eneid, speaking of the descent of Eneas into hell, enters into great details on this doctrine of a state of expiation.   The Hindoos also maintain that the dead should be relieved by sacrifice and prayers, and that by this means they may obtain pardon of their faults.*

Ulric. Very well; but do not these quotations evidently prove that this doctrine came from Paganism to the Catholic church?

Odilon. I thought I had answered that objection before. But instead of considering a maxim so conformable to human nature and to reason as a fable of Paganism, would it not be more judicious to look upon it as a precious remnant of an original revelation, sanctioned by all nations, and preserved by the Christian religion?

Edward. We have still another very important point to discuss, on which I should like to hear your opinion; it is the communion in one kind *alone*, an article which I conceive cannot be passed over lightly.

Odilon. I do not think it will offer so many difficulties as you suppose.

Edward. I can hardly agree with you on this; for setting aside the doctrine, the discussion of which would carry us too far, I am convinced the Protestants will never give up the use of the chalice, as the privation of it would appear to them a mutilation of the sacrament, and in direct opposition to the establishment of Jesus Christ; therefore, this article alone would, in my opinion, occasion the greatest obstacles against our re-union with the Catholic church.

Odilon. The history of the church and of its dogmas affords innumerable proofs of her opinion on this subject, from the first ages down to the time of the Reformation.   In the learned Philosophical Catechism, above quoted, you will find a complete detail, in my opinion, of the objections that have

* See Hafner's Travels, part ii. page 39, in Sprengel's Library, part xxxix.

been made to it, and their refutation. In modern times, the learned Abbé de Lignac, in his work entitled "The Possibility of the Corporal Presence in several places, against Boullier," has shown that the doctrine of transubstantiation is by no means incompatible with sound philosophy. I earnestly exhort you to read those two works attentively. But since you have no intention to touch on the dogmas, I agree to set them aside, though, at the same time, I must draw your attention to another very important point.

Ulric. What is that?

Odilon. Run over all the writings of the Lutherans respecting the Calvinists, from Luther down to these times; compare with them the union already effected between the Calvinists and the Lutherans, showing they have no longer any difference of doctrine respecting the Eucharist; and you will be forced to subscribe to the justness of the following expressions of Tabaraud: "When a church fraternizes with those whom it had formerly condemned as heretics, we must think it has declined from its primitive orthodoxy."

Ulric. It is the Lutherans who must consider how they can preserve their orthodoxy.

Edward. But the privation of the chalice?

Odilon. Luther must have been very far from considering the communion in one kind to be a mutilation of the sacrament, as you have asserted, since, in his "Answer to Stolpe," he wrote as follows: "I like to hear it established and taught that Jesus Christ is not partially, but *wholly* and *entirely* under each kind. I condemn the Bohemians for not having followed the great number, for having refused to obey authority, and for not having been satisfied with one kind alone." Luther even thought that one or more bishops had not the power to establish the use of both kinds, but that a general council alone could authorize it.[*]

Edward. If it be so, how then could he think of establishing the practice of communion in both kinds, which is invariably followed in his church?

Odilon. Luther himself will answer this question: "If it should happen," says he, "that a council permitted communion in both kinds, we would decide, merely out of con-

[*] Op. Lutheri, p. vii. pp. 26, 27.

tempt for the council and its declaration, not to use them,
and rather to take only one kind, or rather no kind; we
would likewise curse all those who should conform to this
communion in two kinds, in consequence of the authority
and order of the same council."[*] But observe that Luther
had declared before, "We follow the word and order of
Jesus Christ!" Thus, if the council had made a decision
according to this *word* and *order* of Jesus Christ, Luther, notwithstanding his engagement, would have deviated from
them merely to vex the council.

Edward. I am equally afflicted and astonished at what you
have just said. Nevertheless, as Jesus Christ gave his disciples the communion under both kinds, why have you abandoned the primitive establishment, and only preserved one
kind ?

Odilon. In the very first ages of the church, this point was
classed among those of mere discipline. As to modern times,
I could quote you a very remarkable instance, which I am
far from approving, to show that the Greek church also considers it as belonging entirely to discipline. Their opinion
is, that provided the principal thing be preserved untouched,
its distribution may be regulated according to circumstances.

Ulric. I am the more curious to be acquainted with this
opinion of the Greek church, as I know it is punctiliously
exact in conforming to the primitive establishments of Christianity.

Odilon. On Maundy Thursday, the Greek priests in the
East cause a great loaf to be baked, which they consecrate
while it is still hot. This being done, they steep this loaf,
thus consecrated, in consecrated wine, and the whole is then
dried in the sun. When the exsiccation is complete, they
pulverize the bread in a little milk destined for that purpose;
the powder which comes from it is carefully preserved in a
leathern bag, and of this they give a spoonful to the sick.[†]
What do you think of this communion ? Is it in one or both
kinds ?

Ulric. This is very extraordinary indeed!

Edward. How remote from the primitive establishment!

Odilon. It was not my intention to speak of abuses like

* Op. Lutheri, part iii. p 338.
† New Memoirs of the Missions. Paris, 1724, tom. iv. p. 151

this, but merely to show you what, at all times, has been the doctrine of the church on this point. In the first ages, when it still groaned under the heaviest oppression, the holy sacrament was sent to the sick, and even to prisoners, as you may learn from all those who have written on Christian antiquities; and I trust your authors have been impartial enough not to conceal this truth. But as they might have attracted too much notice, by sending the chalice also, they merely gave the communion with the *single* species of bread. It was in this manner that St. Ambrose communicated immediately before his death. Children, on the contrary, who at this period went to communion very young, and could not easily have swallowed any hard substance, took only the wine. Those, in short, who were very much afraid of being discovered, and yet would not deprive themselves of the holy sacrament, carefully kept in their houses consecrated bread *alone*, and there took it very secretly. You may find a multitude of examples respecting all these practices in Tertullian, Cyprian, and almost all the writers of those remote times.

Edward. Very well; but nevertheless, you will admit that these practices only took place in cases of great necessity?

Odilon. I am willing to suppose so; but can you really believe, that in those exact times they would have risked the commission of a sort of sacrilege, by thus giving a *mutilated* sacrament to the sick, the dying, and the martyrs who were going to death for Christianity, unless it had been firmly and perfectly received in either kind, that is, the *living* body of Christ, or his flesh and blood united? for a body cannot be living without the blood.

Edward. It seems to me, notwithstanding, that wherever this necessity was not urgent, the primitive establishment should have been adhered to exactly.

Odilon. I believed I observed to you yesterday, that if we were absolutely obliged to keep strictly to the first establishment, we could not make use of hosts, as at present, but must use bread like the *azymous* cakes of the Jews, and only employ red wine in celebrating the Lord's Supper. But I will now prove to you, that if in certain circumstances the church was satisfied with *one* kind, she has, on the contrary, at other times positively ordered the communion in both kinds.

Edward. I am quite ignorant of any such order.

Odilon. Pope Gelasius I., who reigned from 492 to 496, gave a decree to this effect against the Manicheans, who began to creep into the church. Among the treasures of some ancient churches are still preserved chalices with pipes, for sucking up the consecrated wine, which evidently proves the use of the communion in both kinds. You see then that the church merely considered these practices as disciplinarian, applicable to the more or less important circumstances of the moment. In the Armenian church the consecrated bread alone is distributed into as many bits as there are communicants, after each bit has been dipped in consecrated wine. This way of dipping the host in wine also crept into the Latin church, in the beginning of the eleventh century ; but the Popes Pascal and Urban thought proper to forbid it. The first addressed a letter against this custom to Ponce, abbot of Cluni ; and the other condemned this *infusion* in the Council of Clermont, because Jesus Christ ordered his disciples to *drink* his blood. It was undoubtedly on the same principle, that, in the year 1053, Cardinal Humbert disapproved of the method of the Greeks and Russians of the church of Constantinople, who gave the communion in a spoon, containing a bit of consecrated bread, steeped in consecrated wine. Consequently, the communion of the *two* elements or kinds was not condemned, but only the irregular manner in which it was presented. We also see by the decrees of the Council of Clermont, held in 1095, that the communion had been given in both kinds, but with this restriction, " if no necessity or prudence obliges to act otherwise."

Edward. If this be the case, why then has the use of the chalice been so obstinately refused to the laity ? What torrents of blood would have been spared by this indulgence!

Odilon. In acting thus, the church followed the same principle, which determined the Council of Ephesus only to admit *one* kind, because Nestorius maintained, with others, that the body of Christ alone was in the bread, and his blood only in the wine. But when there was no fear of this practice leading to error or favoring it, they were far from being so obstinate as you seem to think.

Edward. Recollect what passed respecting the Hussites. What evils the use of the chalice would have prevented on that occasion!

Odilon. Allow me to tell you that you are under a great mistake ; for what you have just said of the Hussites, precisely confirms the doctrine I had established. The Council of Basil, in its thirtieth session, declared that he who communicates in *one* or *both* kinds would obtain a salutary effect, and that the whole body of Jesus Christ was undoubtedly received under *each* kind. Such, you have seen, was the opinion of the church in the most remote periods. Nevertheless, the same council permitted the Calixtins, headed by the famous Rokyzene, to communicate in both kinds, because they had subscribed to the doctrine of the church in this point. But ecclesiastical and profane history must have shown you pretty clearly how little influence this indulgence had on those people at a later period, who aimed at nothing less than to overturn the church and state. From all this it is evident that this article is merely of discipline, and that the church may decide the manner of it, as it thinks proper, in its wisdom. But pray observe that I am only speaking here of *the distribution of the sacrament;* for in the sacrifice of the mass the *chalice* is indispensably necessary, and is a practice which the church has never changed in the least.

Edward. In the event of a re-union, do you think the chalice would be allowed to those who desired it? I can hardly believe it.

Odilon. For my part, I am persuaded it would, provided the ancient and invariable maxim of the church were admitted, namely, that communion, in one kind *alone*, is not a *mutilated* sacrament, and that Jesus Christ is received wholly under either kind, though I may possibly be mistaken in this point. Allow me to observe by the bye, that your modern divines are far from being so decided on the ancient prejudice of the communion in one kind *alone* being insufficient.

Edward. I know no instance of such a change of opinion.

Odilon. I will give you one then in the person of Schlegel, superintendent at Griefswald.

Ulric. But recollect that that minister belongs to the class of our old sturdiest orthodox believers.

Odilon. So much the better; I will not take notice of another very singular opinion of that clergyman, who pretends that, in default of wine, any other liquor might be used for the Lord's Supper that is not inebriating, as beer or cider, as if these two liquors were not intoxicating also. I will merely quote the page 218 of his " Elements of Pastoral Theology," where he says: " those who cannot bear wine, or who cannot procure it, may be allowed to use the bread *alone.*" You see then that he does not consider communion in one kind only as a mutilation of the sacrament.

Edward. This is strange, I allow.

Odilon. How wavering are your divines! Abandoned to their own judgment, they argue successively for and against.

Edward. You think then that the chalice would be allowed to those who desired it?

Odilon. Yes, but on the strict conditions I have mentioned. The modern history of the church will also confirm my opinion; for, when the Emperor Charles V., in order to effect a re-union, demanded of Pope Paul III. the suppression of the celibacy of priests, and the chalice for the laity, the Pope sent two nuncios into Germany, with authority to grant these *two* demands, according to the exigency of cases. The same thing took place under the Emperor Ferdinand; and it is said, that after the famous conferences of Bossuet and Leibnitz, on the subject of a religious re-union, the Bishop of Meaux declared that the use of the chalice would be one of the points conceded. Assuredly, that celebrated and well informed man would never have made this assertion, had he not known that it *might* be conceded.

Edward. I confess that the concession of this important article would be one great obstacle less towards a re-union of those among us who have preserved any attachment for Christianity.

Ulric. Not so quick, gentlemen; the difficulties are far from being smoothed so much as you suppose. It is true, that in our days, people trouble themselves but little with points of doctrine; but I have many other difficulties to lay before you, which will be an everlasting subject of disgust and opposition with Protestants. These are those vagabond rambles of pilgrims, the cause of so many disorders; those frequent processions, that are any thing but edifying or pious; those endless paternosters, which make not the least impression on the mind; those litanies, so like the pagan *battologies,* which were forbidden by Jesus Christ; finally, those signs of the cross, which give one such an idea of narrow-minded superstition. I would mention the whimsical dresses of your priests during divine service, such as albs, tunics, stoles, &c. Yes, I repeat, these objects will never have any charms in our eyes and I must declare I have often been scandalized.

when, after having heard one of your sermons full of unction, I heard the preacher immediately after recite twenty or
thirty paters and aves, which could excite no reasonable idea,
either in the priest or his flock. When one prays, it should
be done with recollection and piety, as we perform it.

Odilon. The practice of the sign of the cross, which you
choose to call superstitious, is of the highest antiquity among
Christians. You will find in Tertullian and Cyprian, that
even in the second and third ages it was in use at the ceremonies of Baptism, at the Blessing of Catechumens, at the
Eucharist, and on many other solemnities. The father of
the Reformation even, Luther, wrote, that "on getting out
of bed, in the morning, one ought to sign oneself with the
holy cross." This custom still subsists in saxony, and other
countries of Lower Germany, where the Protestants make
use of it in Baptism, in the consecration of the Eucharist, in
giving benediction in the church, and probably in other ceremonies. I can also produce a testimony, on this subject,
which you will not think unimportant.

Edward. Do me the pleasure to mention it.

Odilon. The superintendent Schlegel, whom I have just
quoted, says in his "Pastoral Theology," p. 241, "that the
sign of the cross, in the consecration of the bread and wine,
is now suppressed, and that it might be omitted also in con-
ferring Baptism." But a critic of Gottingen, makes the
following judicious remark on this point: "In our days,
they have labored, on one hand, to give more dignity and
majesty to the acts of religious worship; but on the other
side, writers have used all their efforts to destroy all the
symbolic acts, consecrated by antiquity, and sanctioned in
every age by the love and piety of the faithful." What a
contradiction!

Edward. Perfectly just and true.

Odilon. The Lutherans therefore cannot consider the sign
of the cross as an effect of superstition, but for what it was
considered in all ages of Christianity down to ours; that is,
as an external mark of faith in Jesus Christ, and in the salvation he brought us.[*]

Ulric. But what answer do you make to the rest of my
observations?

_____
[*] Externa professionis tessera, et tacita Salvatoris invocatio. Tertull. See also St. Athanasius: De incarnatione Dei.

Odilon. I cannot see why you should be shocked at the particular dresses of our priests, during divine service, as this custom, of very great antiquity, is followed likewise in several of your own churches. According to this, you should make the same objection against the Spanish ruffs, or high collars of your clergymen, their flowing surplices, and bands that look like the tables of the law. I have every reason to think that you are scandalized, not at the thing itself, but by the false point of view under which you consider it.

Ulric. But those strange devotions, those processions, litanies, paternosters, &c. which I quoted before?

Odilon. I will not deny that abuses may sometimes be found, in certain respects, in the exercise of these practices; but the church has, at all times, endeavored to reform them; and you may be certain, that in all objects of pure discipline, which, far from being of the essence of religion, were only introduced to preserve and augment its dignity, all possible modifications will be readily made, especially if a sincere re-union should be the result.

Edward. But such abuses in the adiaphorous, or disciplinarians matters, might pass into the dogma itself; and, in fact, has it not been tainted by them?

Odilon. The dogma! how is that possible?

Edward. I shall perhaps explain myself more precisely, by saying, that these extravagant practices may give rise to false ideas in religion. It is thus, undoubtedly, that the invocation and veneration of saints, have given the idea to more Catholics than one, that the grace they obtained proceeded less from God, than from the saints themselves. I myself know perfectly well, that men notoriously wicked, think they have satisfied every thing, provided they have recited a certain number of beads, and walked in some processions : as to an amendment of their past life, or any reparation of the evil they have done, it is the least of their considerations; and it is well, if they do not imagine, that by a repetition of these practices, they obviate the evil they still wish to commit! You must allow, that for religious Protestants, this is a real and permanent obstacle against their re-union with the Catholic church.

Odilon. I think I have already given a sufficient answer to the first point. As to the second, I only see a fresh proof of your ignorance of religion. Read all the fifth chapter of the Catechism of Trent on the sacrament of penance, and you will find that our doctrine, on this important point, is very different from the idea you have of it. Like you, we rigorously exact the confession of sins, the detestation of them, a sincere repentance, a lively faith in the mercy of God, and in Jesus Christ, a real amendment of life, and, as much as possible, the most exact reparation of the evil committed. Yes, we are far from believing that the dead recitation of certain prayers can reconcile us with God, much less authorize us to commit new offences, as you have presumed to say.

Edward. How then are we so much shocked at you in this respect?

Odilon. What! and are you entirely free from those Pharisees, who, like ours, think they have satisfied all their duties, by frequenting the sacraments, and performing some religious practices, without any idea at the same time of sincerely making reparation for the scandal of their past life? Every thing, in this respect, with you, as with us, depends on better instruction; and the close intimacy which our pastors have with their parishioners, gives us good reason to hope for a speedy and effectual suppression of any abuse that may exist.

Ulric. But, after all, do you think the Protestants will give up the liberty they have purchased by the effusion of so much blood, in order to submit their consciences again to the oppressive yoke of the Pope?

Edward. That is right, you have anticipated me in the last objection which I intended to make.

Odilon. What you have just said, surprises me the more, as in our own times, you have submitted your consciences to a much more whimsical, capricious, and arbitrary despot, as you may have learnt from the whole of our conversation.

Ulric. This is an enigma to me; I do not know what despot you are talking of.

Odilon. This despot is philosophy, that proud reason which you have established, as the supreme arbiter of all your religious opinions.

Ulric. I did not think it was so whimsical, capricious, or despotic as you represent it.

Odilon. Look over all the philosophical systems, from the

Abus of Anaxagoras, down to the numberless absurdities
and extravagances of our modern sages, who anathematize
each other's systems, though they all invoke the same
philosophy and the same reason. You well know that it
was necessary to bend under each of these systems, on the
penalty of passing for a simpleton; and nevertheless, none
of these oracles could ever pronounce any thing really satisfactory, certain, or permanent, respecting God, nature, or a
future state. It was this that made Anthony Fussal say with
great judgment, after he had examined all the philosophical
sects: "I can find nothing better than the belief in Jesus
Christ." *Nil inveni melius quam credere Christo!* Nevertheless, it is to this reason, this variable tyrant, that you
submit every thing; faith, hope, life, morals, and a future
state!

Ulric. But this variable despot, as you choose to call it, is,
after all, the most divine part of man; it is the ray of light,
sent to us by the omnipotence of God. No, my dear abbot,
Protestants will never abandon this reason, which teaches
us to know every thing, to judge of every thing, and tells us
how we are to believe, think, and act: never will they give
this up to fall into the stupid creed of the multitude.

Odilon. Nobody requires of you a blind sacrifice of your
understanding; and I have reason to think you will not deny
that there have been, and are still, among our divines, many
individuals who unite the most profound erudition to the
most enlightened reason.

Ulric. Very true, but . . . .

Odilon. I know very well, that when there is question of
the authority and limits of human reason, the judgment of a
Catholic, zealous for his religion, and of a man of my profession especially, is of very little consequence in your eyes.
It seems to me, however, that St. Paul himself had not that
high and exclusive idea of worldly wisdom, and of the
authority of reason, in faith and morals; for, speaking of the
pagans, he says, that from having performed the will of the
flesh and of reason, they fell off from God.* This apostle
required that reason should be subjected to the obedience of
faith; a doctrine held by your own church.

Ulric. Allow me to observe, that those passages are susceptible of a quite different interpretation.

Odilon. Be it so; but Trembley, whom I have already

s
* Ephes. ii, 3; Col. i, 21; 2, Cor. x, 5.

quoted so often, will convince you, in the last chapter of his excellent work, that this reason, the idol of modern Protestants, is insufficient, vain, and tottering, in a multitude of things purely terrestrial, purely scientific, and in all that concerns the moral conduct of man, and consequently much more so in objects of a sphere above our human nature, and which concern our eternal destiny. Another of your divines also, a very learned man, and who certainly does not belong to the class of the *obscurants*, is perfectly in unison with Trembley on this point.

Ulric. Is it Jacobi, whom you mentioned yesterday?

Odilon. No; it is Staudlin, who says: "Reason has no voice to give in the explanation of the system of Divine truths, communicated to man by a supreme revelation."

Ulric. You must, however, admit, that the right of examining, of admitting, and rejecting, is an inherent and inviolable right of the human mind; but the conquest of this inestimable advantage is owing to the Reformation.

Odilon. This may be allowed; but you will admit, in your turn, that the human mind is never stationary: and do you think that no limits must be prescribed to it, even when it erects itself into the master and supreme arbiter of what is above our nature? For my part, I know that this glorious conquest, which you boast of so much, has led you to the privation of all positive religion, by plunging you into a cold and barren naturalism. Hear with what disdain Bayle speaks of this arbiter, for whom the Reformation conquered the right of pronouncing its definitive sentence on the doctrines of Divine Revelation.

Ulric. Bayle! that is absolutely impossible: he was an *esprit fort*, in the true signification of the word.

Odilon. Here are his own words, extracted from the fourth part of his Dictionary: "Reason is a principle of destruction, and not of edification; it is only fit for forming doubts, and for turning to right and left, to eternize a dispute; to make man know his darkness, and impotence, and the necessity of a revelation. There is nothing more foolish, than to reason against facts; and the tribunal of philosophy is incompetent to judge of the Christian religion." You see that Bayle reasons exactly like the learned Staudlin. Such is the uncertainty of this tribunal, to which Protestantism has endeavored to give supreme authority! This arbiter has proved what use it can make of its authority, by depriving you of the last regard for Christianity, and by precipitating you into the horrors of naturalism. But I perceive we have wandered from our first subject ; for we were speaking of the refusal which Protestants would certainly make, to submit their consciences to the oppressive yoke of the Pope.

Ulric. Yes, certainly; and you will forgive my asking you, whether a man who has any head, information, or heart, would willingly bend his judgment under that of a man, who would, perhaps, be infinitely below him, if he had not his tiara ? I know nothing more shocking than to give a man, subject to sin like all others, the title of Holiness, which belongs to God alone.

Odilon. I cannot get over my astonishment to hear you speak in that way seriously ; for you must know that even now the Greeks give their patriarch and their bishops the titles of *holy*, *most holy*, and *holiness:* the patriarch is called *panosiolatos ;* when the bishops are mentioned, they are called the *saint* of Heraclea, the *saint* of Chalcedony, &c. as you may see in Sprengel's work on *the Knowledge of foreign Countries and Nations.* Even the Pope Athanasius gives the name of your *holiness* to John, bishop of Jerusalem.* What is more, the Patriarch Jesaias, in a letter to the Emperor Andronicus, calls him *most holy Emperor*, as you will find in *Ameilhon's Histoire du Bas Empire*, tom. xxiv. p. 303. It seems to me, after all this, that you have little right to find fault with the Pope on this subject.

Ulric. Well, I will confine myself to that blind submission to the decisions of the Roman Pontiff.

Odilon. I observe, with fresh surprise, the false ideas you have formed of the supreme head of the church, and of his decision in matters of faith. Read, I beseech you, the work already quoted, *On the Spirit and Consequences of the Reformation*, and you will find that this establishment has not only nothing shocking in it, but it is even very wise and salutary. What would you say, if I quoted one of your most *enlightened* theologians, who has even made the apology of this pretended oppression of the popes, and of the hierarchy of the popes, and of the hierarchy of the Catholic church in the middle ages; an oppression, which, if it ever existed, is certainly not in the least to be dreaded at present.

Ulric. You will excuse me, for having strong doubts respecting this apology.

* In op. Hieronymi, tom. v. p. 260.

Odilon. You shall hear the very expressions of Herder: "The yoke of the Roman hierarchy was perhaps necessary to curb the gross people of the middle ages; without this indispensible curb, Europe would most probably have become the prey of despots, a theatre of eternal discord, that would have ended, by rendering it a Tartarian desert. This hierarchy, therefore, as a counterpoise, deserves your regard." It is true, that immediately after, Herder, in unison in this respect with the author of the *Spirit and Consequences of the Reformation,* adds, " that as a primary spring always in action, this hierarchical spirit would at length have metamorphosed Europe into an ecclesiastical state, like that of Thibet; but that *the beneficent spirit of time and of humanity* had fortunately prevented it." I confess, I cannot comprehend this variation of the two authors, even on the principles of the two philosophers.

Ulric. How so?

Odilon. Do you not see that they seem to dread a theocracy? I frankly confess, I am not of the number of those who would like to see the thurible and sword in the same hand, though Raynal considers this form of government as the best of all. But I merely meant to say, that a spiritual sovereign is not so oppressive a thing, as modern Protestants pretend.

Ulric. That is possible; but it seems to me, you have carefully eluded my preceding objection, as to the intolerable injustice of a man of superior intellect, being obliged to submit it to a person who has, perhaps, no other advantage over him, than that of his tiara.

Odilon. Pray explain yourself a little more clearly.

Ulric. What! do you not perceive that I have in view here the doctrine of your church, on the infallibility of the Pope?

Odilon. I am sorry to be obliged to say it, but this is a new proof of the little knowledge you have of the doctrine of our church. Infallibility is an attribute of God alone. Nevertheless, this right belongs also to the church, because Jesus Christ, who has promised it the assistance of his Holy Spirit, will not leave it till the end of the world. But, as supreme head of the church, in the most intimate connexion with her, in the midst of all its prelates, and doctors, and as organ of the judgments of the infallible church, the Pope cannot err. If he were alone, it would be quite anothe. thing.

Ulric. I am just as if I had fallen from the clouds. I should never have expected such an explanation.

Odilon. Before he was raised to the chair of St. Peter, Adrian VI. had written a Latin work, entitled, " Disputations on the Four Books of the Master of the Sentences," of which he had a new edition published, exactly conformable to the first, after he was named Pope. But, as he there established the maxim, that the Pope, *alone and without the church,* could err even in matters of faith, and as Jesus Christ himself said, " Who hears you hears me," I flatter myself that the infallibility of the head of the infallible church, will no longer appear so shocking to you as before. Permit me also, in confirmation of this, to quote the opinion of a modern Protestant, a very learned man, and whose way of thinking is very philosophical.

Edward. You will oblige me.

Odilon. It is Welker, who, in his *Essay on the Foundation of Right, of the State, and of Punishment,* says : " As long as faith remains pure, vigorous, and very active, the theocratical state is, without dispute, the finest and most energetic of all ; but without these qualities, it is soon attacked to the quick, and devoted to ruin as speedily as inevitably. A theocracy also absolutely requires a belief in a positive revelation, as well as a permanent communication with the Divinity. An interpretation merely human of a divine law constantly weakens that firmness which faith ought to have in its infallibility ; and the law can never give forms of sufficient extent for the government. For this reason, a governor chosen and inspired by God, in general, prophets, and frequent miracles of all kinds, and priests, the interpreters of the theocratic government, are its indispensable elements."

Ulric. This passage, I allow, is very striking.

Odilon. It is thus one finds again the true path, when, deaf to prejudice, we only listen to instruction and *true* philosophy.

Edward. I persist notwithstanding in thinking that Protestants will never cede a liberty so dearly bought, to resume a yoke, which they are in the habit of considering very hard.

Odilon. I really cannot conceive how people can talk so much of their dread of oppression and violence, while the are so ready to subscribe to what I consider a much more insupportable constraint.

Edward. I confess I am quite ignorant of this.

Odilon. What! you have not read Beaufort's project, repeated in a newspaper, respecting the re-union of the pontificate with the imperial dignity, *as was practised formerly.**

Ulric. What do you think of it? Does not this project seem to you very judicious?

Odilon. I might answer you, by Count Albon, whose good intentions nobody probably will contest : "That nothing is more absurd, and at the same time more dangerous for the state, than to strip all the world of their rights to heap them upon one individual." An author, we have already often quoted, says: "If the sword, thurible, imperial sceptre, and the keys of heaven are entrusted to the same hand, who can possibly foresee and calculate the effects which such a situation will infallibly produce?" But, leaving this matter to your own judgment, I shall only observe, in order to calm your fears respecting the despotism of the Pope, and the loss of your liberty, that that Pontiff has not half a million of soldiers to employ for that purpose.

Ulric. But seriously, what do you think of this project?

Odilon. Dr. Thiess shall answer you for me ; "It is wished that the temporal power, already carried to excess, should subject, without restriction, the remains of that spiritual authority, which it has already so much mutilated ; this power will no longer be satisfied with sending laws to thrones and nations from its central point, but will also command in the church and schools ; it will even prescribe dogmatically the forms of instruction ; it will give to certain usages all the sanction of acts of divine worship ; it will establish a particular liturgy, and a determined rule for establishments of education and instruction ; it will promulgate a code of literature, and a censorship as severe as arbitrary. It will dictate to masters themes for their thoughts, and to thinkers it will point out the sphere in which they should exert themselves. In a word, in order that in this machine of state, the head and hand may only move methodically, that not the man, but the subject alone may be visible, this power will effect its domination over the mind, the conscience and reason, by the most peremptory and rapid means possible." How do you

* See Beaufort's Letter to the Archbishop of Besançon.

like this picture? But you should read the whole passage,
and what comes immediately after. Will you still approve
of this project considered in this point of view?

Ulric. Those who formed it are at least very well-informed
persons.

Odilon. I neither can nor will examine how far Beaufort
deserves that qualification. I only know that Tabaraud says
of him : " This enthusiastic re-uniter, was formerly a priest,
a rector who married, was divorced, married again, and
sought in apostacy for a cloak to conceal his steps." As to
his project, it is said, that instead of being well received, it
only got the author a severe reprimand. It seems, moreover,
that this author had very little confidence himself in his intentions and his theological knowledge, since in his first work
he called himself a *lawyer*.

Ulric. But the Review which also extolled the project—

Odilon. I see you mean to speak of the *Jason*, the author
of which was Count-Benzel Sternau, formerly minister of
finance in the grand duchy of Frankfort.

Ulric. Yes, and if you have read it, you will allow it is
perfectly well written.

Odilon. We are not talking about style, but truth, in this
matter. Would you wish to hear what a writer, who seems
to have known that reviewer very well, says of him?

Ulric. It would give me great pleasure.

Odilon. I will pass over his expression relative to the political part of the Review, and only mention what he says of
the reviewer : " This writer has ridiculed, as far as was in
his power, all that is religious, holy, and true in human nature ; his insipid sophisms, that have not the merit of the
least wit, have defiled and poisoned every thing."

Ulric. You will admit, however, that the Review has
proved, with much erudition, not only the great influence
which the emperors always had over the church, but moreover the constant re-union of the imperial dignity with the
pontificate.

Odilon. I will not examine the degree of erudition of this
author; but I could not help being often struck with the
strange singularity of some of his remarks.

Ulric. Would you have the kindness to tell me some of them.

Odilon. He says a great deal, for example, of the great influence which the emperors had over the church, as protectors or executors of the decrees of the councils; and certainly it was not the power which they wanted in this respect. But had he wished to be impartial, he should not have passed over in silence, that the Emperor Constantius, irritated against Pope Martin, because he would not approve the *type*, which was the work of that prince, had him dragged out of Rome, thrown into a dungeon, and treated in the cruellest manner, and finally banished him into the Crimea, where that pontiff died, after an imprisonment of two years. But had the reviewer related this fact, he would merely have proved by it that there were formerly emperors who tyrannized both the church and its head, but nobody would have discovered in these outrages any union of the imperial dignity with the pontificate.

Ulric. Very true; but the reviewer proves, notwithstanding, that the emperors bore the title of *Pontifex Maximus*.

Odilon. There is nothing new or extraordinary in that. This so *learned* man should have known that this title did not concern the Christian church, which had already its pontiff, its head, acknowledged by all Christians, as you will find in Irenæus and Cyprian; but that it only concerned Paganism, from which it passed to the Christian emperors; that they preserved it as long as they had Pagan subjects, and renounced it when idolatry was generally destroyed. If Constantine the Great thought, that by this title he also obtained, at the same time, that of supreme pontiff of the Christian church, why, instead of deposing Pope Sylvester, who, on this supposition, would only have been a usurper of the imperial rights, did he honor, on the contrary, Hosius, bishop of Cordova, and legate of the Pope, during the Council of Nicæa, and so far as to give him precedence in that Assembly? Read Eusebius, and you will find that the emperor conducted himself, in general, on this occasion very differently from a sovereign pontiff.[*]

Edward. This is undoubtedly true.

[*] The fable of the re-union of the imperial dignity with the pontificate, since Constantine the Great, if it be not a dream of the German reviewer, belongs to Van Dale's ninth dissertation on *Antiquities and Marbles*. Though that emperor preserved, on account of his Pagan subjects, the title of *Pontifex Maximus*, borne by his predecessor, ne-

Odilon. But it is still more ridiculous to wish to maintain, like that reviewer, that for some centuries the church had two supreme pontiffs at the same time, that is to say, the Bishop of Rome and the emperor, and that one of them, namely, Constantine, had never been baptized. Is this ignorance or concealment? I could add other proofs against this singular reviewer, extremely remarkable, were it not losing one's time to employ it in refutation of such palpable errors.

Edward. Nevertheless, you will oblige me very much; for I must confess to you that such prodigality of erudition in the reviewer had prejudiced me very much in his favor.

Odilon. Know, then, when Constantine threw himself on the side of the Arians, Hosius, bishop of Cordova, wrote to him in the following manner: "God has committed the empire to you, to us he has confided the concerns of the church; and as he, who with an evil eye, should attack your authority, would act against the Divine order, so you likewise would be liable to a great crime by drawing to you the affairs of the church."[*] It is impossible to separate better these two powers. Constantine having declared in favor of the Arians, Athanasius wrote to him: "Nothing in Christianity can be considered more monstrous, than a king who arrogates to himself the right of judging ecclesiastical controversies." He calls it the horror of desolation, which Daniel had foretold, and says that Constantine did precisely what *the son of perdition* would do, whose precursor he was. When the Emperor Constantius attempted to violate the rights of the hierarchy, the abbot Maximus of Constantinople declared to him, in 653, as well as to the senate of that town, "that it was the business of the clergy to make researches, and pronounce opinions on the saving doctrines of the Catholic church." And he added, that the emperor could not be considered among the clergy. Ambrose wrote as follows to the Emperor Valentinian: "When did you ever hear, most clement emperor, that laymen judged bishops in matters of

vertheless he did not attribute to himself the pontifical authority in the affairs of the Christian church, much less did he ever consider himself as Pope. Theodoret, Sozomen, and Rufinus, show this to have been his conduct during the whole Council of Nicæa; and in his letter to Pope Sylvester he gives that pontiff all the titles that belong to the supreme head of the church. When the Donatists appealed to the emperor from the judgment of the bishops, he rejected their appeal, and called them *instruments of the devil*, who quitted the celestial tribunals for earthly ones. See Baronii Annales, a. c. 313, page 31.   [*] Athanas. op. tom. i. p. 480.

faith?" You will find in Cassiodorus, that Theodoric, king of the Goths, decided that ecclesiastical affairs were wholly out of the sphere of sovereigns: and in the Council of Frankfort, in 794, it was settled that the affair of the worship of images should be entirely left to the bishops.* I could quote a multitude of similar passages, which plainly refute the singular allegations of the reviewer, and which prove the truth of a maxim very applicable to him, namely, that before writing on any subject it is very proper to study it.

Edward. I admit that those passages are perfectly satisfactory.

Odilon. Considered in general, this project, according to my way of thinking, suggests many reflections.

Edward. What are they?

Odilon. For example, I think it very extraordinary that this project, originally proposed by Beaufort, and afterwards supported by the reviewer with a great show of erudition, should also have been recommended by other writers, just at the time when they were highly extolling the suppression of celibacy, which they represented as an excellent means of religious purification.

Edward. Who were these apologists?

Odilon. You will find them in the Munich newspaper, entitled *The Intelligencer.* They begin by declaring that celibacy is a thing as unjust as dangerous, and that its suppression, which is very desirable, is, at the same time, very probable, as it might take place without any injury to religion. At the same time the clergy are indulged with the fine prospect of the possibility of priests and bishops being married, or even the Pope; reciprocally, that priests and bishops, already married, may be chosen Pope.

Ulric. But what connexion do you find between those things and the re-union of the pontificate with the imperial dignity?

Odilon. You will discover it in the following passage: "The Emperor Napoleon might then place the papal crown on his own head; and in this way we should see an end all at once to that rivalry and those quarrels which, for so many

---

* Cassiod. lib. ii. cap. xxvii. Hardouin, conc. tom. iv. col. 904.

ages, have occasioned such fierce dissensions between the profane and spiritual power. The two confessions would be re-united, and all ecclesiastical intrigues would come to a most happy end."

Edward. But allow me to ask a secondary question : is not the author of the Munich paper justified in thinking that the execution of this project would terminate forever the old rivalships of the two powers in the state ? For if sovereigns, as you have just shown from the doctors of the church, have no right to meddle with her affairs, there would in reality exist *a state in a state.* With us, where the sovereign is at the same time *supreme bishop,* this inconvenience is not felt, and all quarrels are at an end.

Odilon. Yes, but the servility and degradation of the clergy has been the consequence of it, with a contempt of all that relates to them, together with the decline of religion, and sooner or later the inevitable fall of the throne itself. But as to the pretended *state in a state,* I can quote you on this subject the opinion of one of the most celebrated Protestant philosophers.

Edward. What is his name?

Odilon. Wolf, who says as follows : "Those who find an absurdity in the separation of the power over sacred things from the civil power, because they fear the result would be a state in a state, are too precipitate, and are unable to prove this absurdity. Certainly, in the Jewish state, the high priest enjoyed the right over sacred things, and the king over civil affairs, while each had his power fully and independently of the other. But who will be bold enough to assert that this was an absurd establishment, even abstracting from its divine institution ?* In reality, I do not find any reasonable answer to these expressions.

Edward. I agree with you.

Ulric. But what is it you find so alarming in this project?

Odilon. Are you ignorant that there has been a combination, for more than thirty years past, to overthrow the throne and altar ? More than one attempt towards this purpose has unfortunately succeeded, at least for a time, and when at length it was stopped, the remedy employed was almost as dangerous as the evil itself.

Ulric. I think I can guess your idea.

* Wolf, Jus Naturæ, cap. iv. p. 8.

Odilon. Well then, you know that to attain this frightful end they have only changed their plan. Yes, if ever this project of a re-union of the two powers in a single hand is entirely effected, religion and the church will fall; the earth will be desolated by the most dreadful religious wars, and the disorder will be as general as incalculable.

Edward. I agree with you completely on this point; and I am convinced that a religious re-union can never be effected in that way; it seems to me, on the contrary, that, exacted violently by that double power, it will present insurmountable obstacles. Minds are not to be forced: but, after all, I cannot conceive that there is any disposition on the part of Protestants to submit to the See of Rome.

Odilon. True, minds are not to be forced, and you know I said it myself yesterday. "As long as religion and faith," says a very learned writer, "are not dependant on human reason, (and that is impossible), so long a religious re-union can never be the work of human hands. All the power even of the most absolute monarch would split against it. All that he could produce would be a little troop of indifferentists, who would unite in an external religious worship politically arranged." And if an ecclesiastical and lay power combined employed its influence to unite the divided churches, it would only become still more impossible.

Edward. What, then, you are consequently quite of my opinion?

Odilon. No, indeed; you are of opinion that the Protestants would show no disposition to acknowledge the authority of the holy See; I, on the contrary, am firmly persuaded, that provided no power of the nature of that I mentioned before meddles with the business, nor renders it impossible, a re-union will not only become practicable, but will even be necessary, and the Protestants will not fail to return to the pale of the church.

Edward. How do you make this out?

Odilon. I proved to you yesterday that they will be forced to return of themselves, if they do not wish to perish entirely, and see naturalism succeed to Christianity, since it is excessively difficult, not to say absolutely impossible, for Protestantism ever to rise from the decline into which it has fallen, or ever form again a solid and regular Christian society; for I have demonstrated to you that without a supreme head to keep all the parts of the whole together, and without an authentic interpreter of the law, no human society, and consequently no Christian church can subsist. Two very learned and very judicious Protestants felt and publicly avowed the necessity of this.

Edward. Who were they?

Odilon. One is the celebrated Locke, whom nobody certainly will accuse of being a Papist. In his work, entitled "Reasonable Christianity," he has shown with great sagacity the necessity of a head of the church, and of ecclesiastical authority.

Edward. You astonish me exceedingly. But who is the other?

Odilon. A man, not only generally known as a great lawyer, but also as a very zealous Protestant—the Baron de Senkenberg. He speaks fairly out in the following manner: "There must be order in Christianity, and a head to maintain that order; but no one is more fit for that office than the representative of Jesus Christ, who occupies the place of St. Peter in an uninterrupted succession. He has at all times been ready to listen to the voice of his flock, and to relieve them in their distresses." And as if he had foreseen, that, like the editor of the Munich paper, the old debates between the temporal and ecclesiastical power would be brought forward, he adds, after having said a word about the discussions between the Popes and emperors—"One may assert with truth that there is not a single example of a Pope, who ever undertook any thing against those who confined themselves to the support of their rights, without an intention of transgressing the limits prescribed to them." To these two authorities allow me to add a third, which will surprise you much more.

Edward. Whom do you mean?

Odilon. Not only an Englishman, a Protestant, an Anabaptist, but a downright sceptic; in short, Hume. In his history of the House of Tudor, tom. ii, page 9, he presents the subject in a still more extensive point of view than Locke and Senkenberg, and expresses himself as follows: "The union of all the western churches under a sovereign Pontiff, facilitated the commerce of the nations, and tended to make Europe a vast republic. The pomp and splendor of worship, which belonged to such a rich establishment, contributed, in some sort, to the encouragement of the fine arts, and began to spread a general elegance of taste, by conciliating it with religion." Ah! gentlemen, truth is a wonderful thing. In vain are attempts made to obscure and oppress it; it rises unexpectedly all of a sudden, and appears where it was the least expected.

Edward. These quotations surprise me extremely, and I am greatly obliged to you, for having informed me of the opinions of such celebrated men. But, would you believe it, I still continue in my conviction, that notwithstanding the milder tone of opinion which exists in our days, the prejudices of Protestants against the Pope will not so easily be deracinated. These prejudices are too old; they are sucked, as it were, with their first education, and they find a daily aliment in modern writers, who are proud of showing that their heads have been warmed by the resplendent rays of the lights of the age.

Ulric. Notwithstanding these seducing expressions of Locke, Sendenberg, and Hume, it seems to me that those writers forgot, for a time, what men have filled the See of Rome, and how much mischief has been done to the world by the Popes. This circumstance alone would be sufficient to prevent our uniting with a church, of which the Pope is the head.

Odilon. What things could I quote from the history of emperors, kings, and princes! and yet I am certain you consider them as good and necessary. But, without recalling the sentence of Jesus Christ, who said, "Scribes and Pharisees are seated on the chair of Moses; observe and do what they shall tell you"—I will confine myself to the opinion of Leibnitz concerning those Popes, to whom so many bad actions have been attributed. You know, that besides his other qualities, that philosopher had a profound knowledge of history. In the volume called "L'Esprit de Leibnitz," you will find as follows: "It must be admitted, that the vigilance of the Popes, respecting the observation of the canons, and the maintenance of ecclesiastical discipline, produced, from time to time, very good effects, and acting seasonably or unseasonably with kings, either by remonstrances, which the authority of their office gave them a right to use, or by the fear of ecclesiastical censures, prevented many disorders; nothing was then more common than to see kings, in their treaties, submit to the censure or correction of the Popes, as in the treaty of Bretagny, in 1360; and in that of Etaples, in 1493."

Edward. This is undoubtedly a very remarkable avowal, and especially from such a man as Leibnitz.

Odilon. A little knowledge of history, with impartiality and equity, would suffice to form an opinion on this matter, and would soon remove the obstacles which prejudice has thrown in the way. However, it is another question to know, how far an external temporal power would be useful to unite all Christians into one body under one head. It is thus, that without Constantine the Great, the world might not have become entirely Christian. Even Protestantism would never have come to what we have seen it, if it had not been supported by some sovereigns.

Edward. This is all that is wanting to fill up the measure of our evils. But why have you this opinion?

Odilon. First, because indifferentism for all that regards God and religion, has already made such progress, that it is scarcely possible to remedy it oneself, to lay down one's prejudices, or form better opinions. Secondly, because human society cannot possibly subsist without a *positive* religion, in the midst of the daily increasing horrors of a destructive naturalism. Princes, therefore, as the heads of society, which they are bound to preserve, while they preserve themselves, must descend themselves into the arena; and as it is impossible that Protestantism can be formed into a religious body, united in all its parts, and presided by *one* supreme ecclesiastical head, they will finally be obliged to co-operate themselves towards a re-union with the Catholic church. As to the *manner*, it depends on God, on time, and circumstances.

Edward. I think with you as to the two latter points; but considering the indifferentism of our times, I see much greater difficulties than you appear to imagine.

Odilon. Have the goodness to explain your meaning.

Edward. This indifferentism having rendered men very unconcerned about all religious dogmas, it is certain they will never fight in an outrageous manner about them again, as formerly, and will be more flexible towards a re-union, when it pleases any external temporal power to recommend it. But, from the same motive of indifference, nobody has religion sufficiently at heart, to trouble himself much with

the nature and greatness of the danger in which Christianity
is plunged; nobody thinks of the future situation of his
family and friends, and still less do people think of such a
proposal as that of uniting with the Catholic church, in order to save Christianity.

Odilon. Do not adopt such an opinion as that; notwithstanding all the pains of your divines and preachers to destroy the principal truths of Christianity, there are still faithful souls, to whom those truths are any thing but indifferent.
It is but too true, that the tolerantism and indifferentism,
which now reign among Protestants, have inspired a great
coolness for all religious dogmas; but this indifference has at
least loosened that obstinacy which was peculiar to them.
If those, who are not entirely indifferent to religious feeling,
look at the same time on the Catholic church with a more
favorable eye than formerly; if they inform themselves better concerning the true nature of our religion and that of
modern Protestantism; it seems certain to me, that those who
wish to effect a union, from whatever motives, will undoubtedly find fewer difficulties than formerly.

Edward. But I could mention another great difficulty,
which I imagine would not easily be got over; only that I
am afraid the subject might displease you.

Odilon. Fear nothing and speak openly; truth is sometimes
bitter, but one must learn to submit to it, when one sincerely
wishes to do good.

Edward. You, Sir, are a person of a mild disposition and
full of benevolence, such as St. Paul (Galat. vi,) desires we
should be. But the spirit of your church is very different
from that of the religion of the sublime and supreme friend
of man, who detested all persecution. Can we forget so
many cruelties against pretended heretics, and feel any disposition to unite with a church, that will perhaps seize the
first opportunity to re-establish the tribunals of the inquisition?

Odilon. What, do you seriously dread that bugbear, in our
days?

Ulric. Yes, he is right; and allow me to tell you frankly
that nobody will think of uniting with a church, in which
an inquisition is still to be found, with all its horrors. What
scenes does not history present on this subject! Think of the
bloody executions that took place in Spain; of the cruelties

exercised against the *Barbets*, in Piedmont; think of the St.
Barthelemy; of the executions against the Hugonots, in
France; of the Dragonades; the banishment of those Hugo-
nots, and the persecution of the innocent Camisards!

Odilon. Allow me to interrupt you a moment. Speaking
of the Hugonots, you forgot that, in the 8th article of the
edict, which revokes that of Nantes, it was expressly forbidden to quit the kingdom, and that those who had already
quitted it, were summoned to return, with a promise *of re-
integration in their property, without being exposed to be
troubled, under pretext of their religion, till it should please
God to enlighten them.* But, as to the Camisards, I beg you
to read the history of them, which appeared at Weimar, in
1790; I am persuaded it will give you quite different ideas
of them.

Ulric. That may be; but do not forget however the executions that took place in England under Queen Mary, and
in the low countries under the Duke of Alba, &c. They
completely belie the maxim, which says that *the church has
a horror of blood.* Certainly no Protestants will unite with
one that authorizes such abominations.

Odilon. I might answer you, that when, at the instigation
of the bishops Ithacus and Idacus, different Priscillianists
were executed, Pope Siricus, and several distinguished members of the episcopal body, heard this event with horror, and
the sanguinary authors of it were even excommunicated
from most of the churches. More than a century before this
event, Lactantius said: "It is not by executions, but by dying
oneself that religion is to be defended; it is maintained by
patience and not by cruelty. If you should wish to defend
it by blood, torments, or any other evil, instead of doing it
good, it would only be polluted and violated." Thus, you
see that from the beginning the church was never inspired
by the spirit of persecution. Nevertheless. . .

Ulric. Nevertheless you mean to say, she acquired a taste
for it afterwards, and most certainly history will not con-
tradict you, for it contains innumerable examples of it.

Odilon. No, my dear Sir, no; I merely meant to say, that
when one has studied history carefully, and above all impar-
tially, one is soon convinced that a great deal must be struck
off from the great register that you have exhibited. The
church took no part, or very little, in all the persecutions
and cruelties you have mentioned, which were mostly owing

to political causes. But let us rather draw the curtain over all this; and I exhort you to do it as much for your church as for mine.

Ulric. Well :—but, alas! I know another very important, and even in my eyes an insurmountable difficulty: for it is founded in Scripture, in reason, in nature, and in all the sentiments of humanity.

Odilon. Announced in this way, it certainly merits all my attention.

Ulric. I will add, moreover, that in all the discussions that have taken place between the Catholics and us, and in all the attempts made towards a re-union, it has never been mentioned, as far as I can remember.

Odilon. Have the goodness to mention it; perhaps I may be fortunate enough to remove this impediment, at least in part.

Ulric. I am happy to declare, my dear abbot, that you have told us many true, solid, and edifying things; and what is more, I will frankly confess that they have cured me of many prejudices I had against your church. But supposing all that you have asserted respecting the doctrine, hierarchy, and worship of the Catholic church to be perfectly exact, still it is certain that every pious and feeling Protestant will act like that King of Saxony, who, when he was on the point of being baptized, having asked where all his ancestors were, and being told with the devil, suddenly withdrew and renounced the church.

Odilon. I declare, I do not understand a word of what you mean by this example of the King of Saxony.

Ulric. Nevertheless, it is very plain ; I mean to show that the principle of your church and of your divines, *no salvation out of the church,* will be an eternal wall of separation between you and all good and pious Protestants, however much they may otherwise be disposed in favor of Catholicity. An old libertine, tormented by the fear of hell, may be induced to throw himself into the bosom of this church, which calls itself the only harbor of salvation; but it will have no effect with a reasonable religious Protestant, of a pure and calm conscience; he will never be won by that famous sentence, *no salvation out of the church,* for it properly signifies—" Become a Catholic under pain of eternal damnation."

Odilon. I am much inclined to think you are going to verify again the reproach I have already made against you, of not being well acquainted with our maxims: for I think I am certain that in our day, now that a milder way of thinking has succeeded to the ancient rigor, not a single Catholic will use such a harsh expression towards you, however much he might wish to see you return into the bosom of that church, the common mother of all Christians.

Ulric. This principle, then, *out of the church no salvation,* is it not adopted by the Catholic church?

Odilon. Yes.

Ulric. If it be so, no Catholic, who is an obedient son of the church, has the liberty of thinking otherwise; and Rousseau was perfectly right, when, considering this principle as a cruel dogma, he exclaimed, in his *Emile*—"God forbid I should ever preach to men the cruel dogma of intolerance!"

Odilon. Believe me, we had better let Rousseau alone, with his variations and paradoxes: for you know, that notwithstanding this fine exclamation, that tolerant philosopher, speaking in his *Contract Social* of such as would not act conformably to his *civil religion,* declares "They must be put to death!"

Ulric. True; but still I do not find that sentence so hard as the one which deprives every man who is not a Catholic of eternal bliss. It is in vain that you, and a thousand other Catholics, as moderate as yourself, tell me you do not pronounce this condemnation; it is enough for me that it is decreed by your church, in consequence of the principle, *out of the church no salvation.* Yes, according to this maxim, we are heretics struck with anathema: and though our whole life had been a model of Christian behavior, we should nevertheless be deprived of eternal salvation!

Odilon. I would say of such a doctrine with St. Paul, "It is zeal without science."

Ulric. Do you not then damn Protestants, according to this principle, as cursed heretics?

Odilon. God forbid!

Ulric. But how then can you reconcile such a mild opinion with this principle of damnation?

Odilon. Without much difficulty. When some apply to Protestants with an exaggerated zeal this maxim, *out of the church no salvation*, they show either great ignorance, or an extravagant extension of the anathema pronounced by the church.

Edward. I am very curious to see the development of this point; for Ulric has here brought out a very important thing, which I confess I did not think of.

Odilon. The principle, *out of the church no salvation*, will be always invariable as well as that maxim of St. Paul—"If any one does not love our Lord Jesus Christ, let him be anathema." It is founded on the express explanation of Jesus Christ himself, when he says: "Nobody comes to the Father, unless through me." It is also conformable to the following decision of St. Peter: "There is no salvation in any other; and no other name is given to man by which we may be saved." But far from us the pretension to decide whether one is ignorant, by his fault or not, of the one true church established by our Lord; for St. Paul says: "Who art thou that judgest a foreign servant? He stands or falls for his master."

Edward. Ah, here is my belief! here is my faith! And if such be the opinion of Catholics, the maxim, *out of the church no salvation*, is conformable to Scripture, and the honor of the Catholic church is intact.

Ulric. Not yet. For as Protestants are struck with anathema as well as all other heretics, schismatics, and unbelievers, I still behold this maxim in all its odious rigor, and in perfect opposition with the decision of St. Paul just cited. I still persist in thinking you will continue to treat us as heretics and condemned by the church; and we shall be obliged to walk into hell all the same, unless we become Catholics, and shall still be considered by you as subject to this hard law.

Odilon. Let us choose the mildest expressions in this affair; and the more so as the church, while it condemns every *error*, contrary to the doctrine of the church, as is just and equitable, does not however condemn him who *errs*, unless he does it knowingly: she even prays for him, and we have generally adopted the principle "of only calling those heretics who maintain with obstinacy a known error."

Ulric. But what is the result of all this?

Odilon. It is that the church, while it entirely condemns errors, has still great mildness, for persons; and that, especially, she is very far from declaring those to be deprived of salvation who are in error through invincible ignorance. But before I go farther, in this respect, it is necessary I should give you two more very remarkable explanations, not at all foreign to our subject.

Edward. You will do us both great pleasure.

Odilon. The first is from St. Augustin, who thus expresses himself in his 43d, or, according to others, 162d epistle: "Those who do not defend a false and perverse opinion with violent animosity, especially if that opinion is not the work of their audacity and presumption, but the inheritance of parents who were seduced and fell into error themselves; those, in short, who freely seek the truth, and are ready to stand corrected, must by no means be reckoned among heretics."

Edward. This is certainly a very mild and remarkable expression.

Ulric. And what is the other?

Odilon. You will find it in the decrees of the Council of Trent, while it anathematizes the *doctrines* of Protestants, who separate from the faith of the church, nevertheless, in the 13th session, speaks of *persons* with real affection: "The holy synod, like a tender mother who groans and brings forth, wishes and labors that there may be no schism among those who bear the name of Christians; but that, as they all acknowledge the same God and the same Saviour, they may also have the same language, the same faith, and the same opinion: confiding in the mercy of God the synod hopes they will return in hope and charity to the holy and saving unity of the faith, and will most willingly give them all suitable facilities for this purpose." This is certainly not the language of a judge who *damns.*

Ulric. This is certainly language full of mildness.

Edward. I could not have expected all this.

Odilon. From all I have hitherto said of those who are properly heretics, and to whom alone the maxim, *out of the church no salvation,* applies, as well as of the sentiments and conduct of the church towards Protestants, whose errors indeed it condemns, but prays for them at the same time, you may judge yourself whether the reproach made and directed against us by some zealots, honest, perhaps, but indiscreet—you may judge, I say, whether this reproach can properly be brought against us.

Ulric. But if all this be as you have said, and I confess there is no longer reason to doubt it, why should we unite with the Catholic church? Why do many of your controvertists give themselves so much trouble to drive the Protestants into the fold of the Roman church?

Odilon. I imagine our preceding explanations will sufficiently account for this zeal that you complain of. Nevertheless, as every well informed Catholic acknowledges his church as the true one—as he knows, from facts avowed even by Luther and Melanchton, when in cool blood, that this church has great advantages over all other Christian societies, it is quite natural that he should desire and labor to make his separated brethren return to it. You know what St. Paul said to King Agrippa: "I wish in God that not only you, but all those who now hear me, might become what I am."

Ulric. But what then are these great advantages?

Odilon. It seems to me that they must be evident from the whole of the discourse we have had together. Nevertheless, I will draw your attention again to some very essential points: all our religious system is very far from being subject to the shocks and changes, and above all, to those entire revolutions, which yours has not ceased to undergo down to our days. All that our fathers believed eighteen centuries ago, we believe still: what consolations and what fine maxims of amendment of life are contained in all our doctrines on the sacrament of penance! what a soothing calm for the heart in the doctrine of the intercession of saints, who, by our prayers are placed in the most intimate and most delightful connection with us! Shall I mention again that intermediate or purifying state? the sacrifice for the living and the dead? the true and real presence of Jesus Christ in the sacrament? What a powerful effect all this must have on the heart and conduct of man! What charms, what life, what elevation, and what motives for edification, are found in all our worship! See how our hierarchy and all our ecclesiastical constitution have preserved us from that decline into which your church has already fallen! No, no; there is no more need of insisting on all these points.

Ulric. Very well; but—

Odilon. Consider also the state of Protestantism, a state into which it has been brought from the entire nature of its internal constitution, by various circumstances, and finally, by the efforts of its *enlighteners.* The state is such, that instead of the ancient doctrine, nothing hardly is to be found but an overwhelming naturalism, so that in a few years there will remain no trace of the sublime edifice of Christianity, nor of its fortunate influence on the morals and happiness of man. All our discourse has led us to be convinced, from the writings themselves of your modern divines, of the incurable state of decline, both internal and external, into which modern Protestantism has fallen. We have seen multiplied proofs of the loss you have made of your faith in revelation, and in the fundamental truths of Christianity. We have seen, in fine, that morality even has been shaken among you in the most terrible manner; that you are a prey to all the desolating doctrines of naturalism, and that it has even been projected to amalgamate you with the Jews and Pagans. Read, I beseech you, the work which Grégoire published in 1810, entitled "History of Religious Sects." Though that work contains many blameable things, it also exhibits many excellent truths. The chapter which treats of *the recent state of Protestantism,* paints, in a manner that equally inspires pity and horror, the lamentable situation in which your modern church is plunged, from a multitude of proofs drawn from its own new divines, and quoted by that author.

Edward. This, alas! is but too true!

Odilon. If this be the case, is it not as reasonable as urgent to cherish the desire of snatching every one from such an incessantly impending danger? "Is it not quite natural," as a worthy writer says, "to exhort the proprietors of a dilapidated hovel, which can hardly shelter them against the storm, to quit it, and to take refuge in a solid building, the foundations of which are untouched, and the possessor of which is constantly occupied in keeping it in a good state?" Grégoire also, in his history above quoted, says with much truth : "Protestantism will never be again what it has been, and it cannot remain as it is. An irresistible bias draws it towards its end, or it will undergo a new metamorphosis. Its very constitution is the corrosive canker of its existence." I now think I have given a satisfactory answer to your last last objection, and consequently hope, that when the two parties have placed all in a fair scale, attempts at a re-union will no longer experience any very great obstacles.

Edward. Ah! Sir, prejudices! prejudices!

Odilon. Yes, undoubtedly; but if, on one side, the dangerous situation of Protestantism be better examined, to which it has been brought in consequence of the great political revolutions that have taken place in our days, and by the efforts of its own *enlighteners;* if people take the trouble, moreover, to search for better instruction in pure sources and impartial writing, all these prejudices will grow weaker and disappear, especially under the protecting auspices of Him, who, as I observed to you yesterday, directs our hearts and all events by his almighty hand. Then, Sir, then, we shall all shake hands like brothers.

At these words, Odilon rose and held out his hand, which even the Calvinist Ulric of Stetten took at last kindly enough, though shaking his head all the time. Theodulus then showed us a very remarkable parchment, which, from its numerical indication, we concluded must have formed a part of a very extensive work. He had found it in a book that he had purchased at the sale of the library of a suppressed monastery. This parchment had on one of its pages a painting, with a double subject, but extremely well done in the antique manner. One subject represented a stormy sky, with thick clouds, and flashings of lightning; below was a dreadful precipice, out of which there appeared, through a black vapor, a woman's foot and the paws of an animal. In the other picture, on the contrary, the sky was pure and serene, with the sign of the cross, all shining with light, and at the foot of it a venerable old man, decorated with the tiara and other attributes of papacy, was giving his benediction to a multitude of people on their knees. Under this last image were the following Latin verses:

> Tu vero gaudebis, post tenebras lucem videbis:
> Namque ante ortum duodecimi, bestia et scortum
> Præcipites ruent in abyssum, nec inde resurgent;
> Et signum crucis splendebit in gloriâ lucis,
> Cum fide et lege, unus pastor, cum uno grege!*

Ulric began to shake his head again; and said, smiling: "It is thus that each party has its prognostics and hopes, which charm it as long as they can."

---

* "But thou shalt rejoice, thou shalt see light after the darkness; for, before the birth of the twelfth, the beast and the prostitute shall fall headlong into the abyss, and never rise again; and the sign of the cross shall shine in the glory of light, with faith and law, *one* pastor with one flock."

As the day was far advanced we separated, all delighted with the erudition of Odilon, and the mildness of his disposition. Edward asked me, significantly enough, what was become of my *extract* and *quintessence?* "'They are," said I, "with your alarms of yesterday." But, to conclude, as the Catholics will never acknowledge a church without a supreme head, without confession, without mass, nor with ceremonies entirely altered, with married priests, and every thing else which ignorant projectors have thought fit to propose: so, in like manner, if a change were to take place, judicious Protestants would never re-unite with a Catholicism thus constituted, and there would be just as little hope of gaining the naturalists to Christianity. Let us, therefore, determine to wait the event; being convinced in the mean while that things cannot remain as they now are, and that it is the duty of every one to seek and to adopt the *safest side* of the question.

THE END.

www.ingramcontent.com/pod-product-compliance
Lightning Source LLC
Chambersburg PA
CBHW020628030726
47497CB00007B/2459